A SULTAN IN
PALERMO

By the same author

Tariq Ali

A SULTAN IN PALERMO

VERSO

London • New York

This paperback edition published by Verso 2015
First published by Verso 2005
© Tariq Ali 2005, 2006, 2015

1 3 5 7 9 10 8 6 4 2

Verso
UK: 6 Meard Street, London W1F 0EG
US: 20 Jay Street, Suite 1010, Brooklyn, NY 11201
www.versobooks.com

Verso is the imprint of New Left Books

ISBN-13: 978-1-78168-930-1

British Library Cataloguing in Publication Data
A catalogue record for this book is available from the British Library

Library of Congress Cataloging-in-Publication Data
A catalog record for this book is available from the Library of Congress

Typeset in Fournier by M Rules
Printed in the US by Maple Press

For

Mary-Kay and Sam

Contents

Glossary

Al-Andalus	Islamic Spain
Amir	Commander
Amir *al-kitab*	Commander of the Book
Amir *al-bahr*	Commander of the Sea and from which 'Admiral' is derived
Allahu Akbar	God is Great
Atrabanashi	Trapani
Balansiya	Valencia
Djirdjent	Agrigento
Gharnata	Granada
Habibi	my love; from which 'hey, baby!' is not derived
hammam	public or private baths
Ifriqiya	North Africa
Ishbilia	Seville
Jiddu	granddad
Khutba	the Friday sermon at the mosque

Lanbadusha	Lampedusa
Malaka	Malaga
Marsa Ali	Marsala
mehfil	a meeting/assembly, often by invitation; from which 'mafia' is not derived
qadi/kadi	the Chief Law Officer of a Muslim city with extraordinary powers to preserve order
Qurlun	Corleone
Qurtuba	Cordoba
Shakka	Sciacca
Siqilliya	Sicily

SIQILLIYA

1153–4

ONE

*Idrisi's reflections on beginnings and chance encounters.
His first meeting with Rujari.*

The first sentence is crucial. He knew that from instinct and his study of old manuscripts. How well the ancients understood this, how carefully they chose their beginnings, how easily their work must have progressed after that decision had been made. Where to begin? How to begin? He envied them the choices their world had made possible, their ability to search for knowledge wherever it might be found.

His mother had taught him that the people of the Book, who insist that all knowledge before the time of their own Prophets is worthless, betray their own ignorance. She had told him of how, when the city had been taken by a special breed of the Prophet's warriors – men who feared knowledge more than death – her grandfather, a venerated mathematician of Qurtuba, had been publicly stripped of his dignity and put to the sword, together with eighty other scholars. The zealots who killed in the name of religion referred to the world of the ancients as 'the time of ignorance', a world in which people were unburdened by the need to worship a single god. How they must have blasphemed to their heart's content. A world without apostates. A smile lightened his face for a moment before the cloud returned.

Unlike us, he thought. We are fated to drown in the whirlpool of eternal repetition. In the Name of Allah the Merciful, and Muhammad his Prophet, his truest Messenger. The only consolation was that the blaspheming Nazarenes were much worse. How could Allah be the father only of Isa? How could the All-Powerful produce just one son? And why had the Nazarenes invented this untruth? It could only be because they were closer in time to the Roman world and its gods. To win converts they had to inject some magic into their creed. How he wished they had kept the old gods or, at least, the best of them. Zeus could have been Isa's father or Apollo, Ares or Poseidon … no, not Poseidon. He was very stupid. Mariam lived far away from the sea and Yusuf was not a fisherman. Perhaps the lame, lustful Hephaestus had entered … He came up on to the deck of the royal ship and took several deep breaths. Washing his lungs with sea air had become a ritual. He smiled. The sun was about to set. The sea was still calm. Poseidon willing, they would reach Palermo without another storm.

This was his last voyage before the completion of his book. The vessel had encircled the island twice and he had checked each detail in his map of Siqilliya against the actual coastline. Occasionally they had disembarked to collect fresh water and food and the fresh herbs he needed to test his medical formulas. Idrisi was both geographer and physician. Even though the journey had taken less than a month, he was tired. He slept more than usual and in most of his dreams he went back to his childhood – his mother looking at the stars, the cobbled streets of Noto, the tree trunks scarred by lightning, the women milking cows and goats, his father's pock-marked face – but when he rested in the afternoon he invariably dreamed of Mayya, usually the same dream with hardly a variation. They lay naked in each other's arms after making love. It was always in her bedchamber in the palace harem, outside which the eunuchs kept watch. Nothing else ever happened. The repetition annoyed him so much that he even thought of going to the dream-interpreter, but something always stopped him.

Last night, for the first time, he dreamt of something different. He was a warrior engaged in combat, but when he woke he had no memory of the enemy. He thought of that now as he stood on the deck, watching the sea change colour, and wondered whether he would have been of any use as a soldier. He was of medium height with delicate features and a soft, fair skin, as if his gender had been decided only at the last minute. The sun had darkened his face, exaggerating the whiteness of his beard. It was neatly trimmed, mimicking the style of a Qurtuban scholar. He was fifty-eight years of age, a time in life that compels most men to think of the past, not the future. And so it would have been with him were it not for the fact that he was possessed by a mighty anger, of which only his two closest friends were aware and even they could not understand its causes. To the Sultan and the courtiers in the palace at Palermo, he was a scholar of some importance and a man of calm temperament. They had no idea of what lay beneath the mask or that he inwardly raged about the oddest things. Once his closest friend Ibn Hamid, whose heart was heavy-laden, had looked at the sky and muttered, 'O the poetry of the stars', and Idrisi had responded in an angry tone, subjecting him to a lecture on astronomy and the movement of the Earth. Had he noted how each night a movement was repeated? The ancients had tried to penetrate the secrets of the heavens, but failed. If what he thought was true then al-Quran was mistaken and if al-Quran was mistaken, who had made the mistake? Allah or his Messenger? Ibn Hamid became fearful that his friend might be charged with blasphemy and advised him to leave such questions to the future.

Idrisi's reply had been a withering look and they had not spoken for the next few days. Now Ibn Hamid, too, had abandoned the island, leaving his friend more isolated than ever. Harsh words had been exchanged and Idrisi accused of providing succour to the foreigners who occupied the island.

Perhaps, thought Idrisi, he too should have gone and established a life in Ifriqiya or perhaps Baghdad where the Caliph was a patron of thinkers and poets. But his life was changed by a chance encounter that offered him more freedom than he had imagined possible.

His thoughts flew back to a late afternoon when he was working in the library of Sultan Rujari's palace at Palermo. He had obtained special permission to do so and was delighting like a child in every new discovery. He recalled the excitement that had gripped him almost twenty-seven years ago when he had first sighted the old Greek al-Homa's manuscript. Could this be the work of which his paternal great-grandfather had spoken all those years ago in Malaka? His grandfather had entrusted the memory to his father and he could still hear the loud, slightly agitated, voice of his old father punctuating the story by plucking the white hairs out of his still dark brown beard. He spoke of how the *qadis*, fearful of the power of poetry and its capacity to mislead Believers, had decreed that only three copies of the Arabic translation be permitted so that theologians could study the pagan religions that led to the period of Ignorance in Arabia at the time our Prophet was born.

Twelve men were entrusted with the task. The most skilled translators of ancient Greek, they had translated the works of Galen and Pythagoras, Hippocrates and Aristotle, Socrates and Plato, and even the plays of Aristophanes. All these works were in the Baghdad library. But translators, although carefully chosen, trusted employees of the palace, were not permitted to read the entire work. The calligraphers doing the transcribing were sworn to silence. If they were to divulge the nature of this work to any person – and this included their wives and lovers – the penalty would be swift and the executioner's scimitar, in a lightning flash, would detach head from body.

His father had smiled. 'Threats never work in our world. It is possible that if nothing had been said the calligraphers would have copied the work and moved on to their next assignment. The danger excited their curiosity, but while eleven of them accepted the inviolability of a *qadi*'s injunction, the twelfth managed to copy half of the first poem and most of the second part and sent it to his family in Damascus. His son, also a translator, came to work in the school in Toledo. He married a woman from Qurtuba. Her grandson discovered the incomplete manuscript hidden underneath al-Quran in an old chest and allowed my great-grandfather to read it in his house. This was how our ancestor discovered that the Greek book had been lodged in secret compartments in the library of Palermo. Special permission had to be obtained from the Caliph before any scholar was permitted access to the hidden section of the library.'

It was during his first year in the library of the old palace in Palermo, the longest voyage his mind had ever undertaken, that he stumbled on the secret section and informed the palace Chamberlain, who informed his master. Sultan Rujari had interrupted his meal and rushed to the library. Idrisi, meeting the Nazarene ruler for the first time, explained his excitement. The Sultan had not heard of al-Homa, but declared his immediate intention of studying the manuscript himself. His spoken Arabic was not perfect, but he read the language well. The Chamberlain took the manuscript and was about to leave the library, but was restrained by the Sultan who, noticing the disappointment on the face of the young scholar, instructed the Chamberlain to find the best calligraphers in Palermo and set them to work. He wanted a new copy waiting for him on his return from Noto. Then he turned to the turbaned youth who had assumed a modest posture.

'Your name?'

'Muhammad ibn Abdallah ibn Muhammad al-Idrisi, Your Majesty.'

'Master Idrisi, after we have both read this work carefully we shall discuss it together. Let us compare the knowledge we derive from it. If the Arabic used in translation is too complex I will summon Ahmed from Djirdjent.'

◖◗

Six weeks later, summoned to Rujari's presence, the young scholar had memorised some verses from al-Homa's work.

'I cannot understand why this work upset your theologians so much.'

'I think they could not tolerate the intermingling of gods and humans, Commander of the Wise. And gods created in the image of men and women were unacceptable to them. There could be no other reason.'

'But that is the most enjoyable part of the work. Their gods were part of everything that happened: wars, floods, mishaps, adventures in the sky and on the sea, family quarrels, births, marriages, deaths, re-births. Do you think the wife of the seafarer Odysseus, who resisted earthly suitors, might have succumbed to a god's charm? I'm surprised none of them tried. I must give instructions for it to be translated immediately into Latin, unless a manuscript already exists. Will you find out for me? If it's only in the Vatican, then we will need our own translation. The monks won't like it any more than the *qadi*. What aspect of the work most appealed to you? Was it the wiles of the women? Or the fear of the unknown? Or life as an unending journey, interrupted by tests of endurance?'

'All appealed to me, Your Majesty, but I was distracted by something else: al-Homa's sense of geography has amazed me. In the second part of the work he describes our sea and the islands and countries and trees. In ancient times people did not travel as much as we do. Most of them were buried in the village where they were born. Al-Homa told them there was another world outside their village and island. In the mouth of Menelaus he puts these words:

> *I wandered to Cyprus and Phoenicia, to the Egyptians,*
> *I reached the Ethiopians, Eremboi, Sidonians, and Libya.'*

'And one-eyed giants and the temptresses who wreck ships not far from these shores?'

'Transient mischief, Exalted Sultan, nothing more. It reveals the power of the poet's imaginings, but nothing more. For me, what is truly remarkable about this work is that the descriptions of real things are almost exact. He visited our island and called it Scylla. I am convinced al-Homa must have been a seafarer. And he fought in a war, but it was the map of his travels that distinguished his memory'

'The Chamberlain informs me that you, too, are a mapmaker.'

Idrisi bowed.

'When you have finished your work in this library, I wish to be informed of all your discoveries.'

For the next thirteen months Idrisi had abandoned all – lovers, friends, pupils – in search of the truth. The Sultan had given him the freedom of his library and apart from eating and the bodily functions that it necessarily entailed, he spent each day buried in a manuscript. The palace eunuchs often referred to him as Abu Kitab, the father of the book. Later, as a trusted confidant of the Sultan, his enhanced status required a superior title: he was now spoken of as Amir *al-kitab*.

Those months in the library had been pure joy. Al-Homa was only the beginning. He would visit Ithaci and the other islands in search of traces. He often wondered whether al-Homa alone had written such beautiful works or whether he had inherited the stories and covered them with his own divine mantle. And how amazing it was to discover that only a few generations after al-Homa's death, Xenophanes denounced him in language that echoed the theologians of today: 'Homer has attributed to the gods everything that is disgraceful and blameworthy among men – theft, adultery and deceit.' And did the story-tellers in Baghdad who compiled the stories of a thousand nights have Odysseus in mind when they created their own tales of Sinbad the sailor? These questions, and even al-Homa, were soon forgotten as other treasures, closer to his preoccupations, began to emerge.

Reading the Arabic translations of Herodotus, Aristotle, Galen, Strabo and Ptolemy was like discovering distant lands familiar from travellers' tales. His tutors had introduced him to the Greek venerables but he had been too young to really appreciate them. His knowledge remained incomplete till he began to study the texts for himself. Ptolemy's ideas still echoed in his mind like music from a distant flute.

One day he came across an anonymous manuscript which delighted him. Who was the author of 'The Library'? He could still remember the first sentence: *Sky was the first who ruled over the whole world.* Here was the story of the gods and how they populated the world and although not as stimulating as Ptolemy or even Strabo, much more exciting. It was here that he read of Hercules' short visit to Siqilliya. *Sky was the first who ruled over the whole world.* The sentence reverberated. Why should he start *In the name of Allah, the Beneficent* ... just like every other scholar in his world. Why?

During his first year in the library, the Sultan would often summon him to his chambers and question him closely on his reading. Rujari was not a big man, but he had strange swinging gestures and when he became excited his arms swayed like sails in a storm. His open-hearted welcome touched Idrisi.

'What will you do with all this information, Master Idrisi? You can teach your own children and mine, but will this be enough to satisfy you?'

Idrisi recalled his worried, self-deprecating smile as he confessed his ambition. 'If the Sultan permits I would like to write a universal geography. I will map the world we know and seek out the lands still unknown to us. This will be useful to our merchants and the commanders of our ships. This great city is the centre of the world. Merchants and travellers stop here before going West or East. They can provide us with much information.'

The Sultan's pleasure was visible. He sent for the Chamberlain, instructed him to make sure that henceforth the scholar and master

Muhammad al-Idrisi was paid the sum of ten *taris* each month by the Diwan and provided with lodgings close to the palace. As the Chamberlain bowed and prepared to leave Rujari had an afterthought.

'And he will need a ship, ready to sail anywhere at his command. Find him a reliable commander.'

Idrisi fell on his knees and kissed the hands of his benefactor. He was delighted by Rujari's generosity, but more than a little apprehensive at how it might be perceived outside the palace. His work would proceed without hindrance, but most of his friends might begin to regard him with suspicion. Every Friday night, after the city had gone to sleep, a small group of poets, philosophers and theologians – thirty men in all – met in a small room located at the heart of the Ayn al-Shifa mosque. Till the *mehfil* was disturbed by the morning call of the muezzin it would discuss matters pertaining to the needs of the community of Believers on the island. Till now, they had accepted his presence as one of them, but for how long?

Rujari's sympathies were not concealed. Like his father, he preferred to ignore the Pope and rely, instead, on the loyalty of his Muslim subjects. They knew that left to himself, Sultan Rujari would not harm them. It was his Barons and Bishops who filled his ears with poison. They were determined to either convert all Believers or drive them off the island. The talk in the bazaars of Palermo, Siracusa and Catania suggested that the English monks, on papal urging, were advising Rujari to clear the woods and valleys of Believers and join the holy crusade against the followers of the false Prophet. According to some, the most detailed plans had been made to burn Noto to the ground and bury the survivors alive. The rumours usually emanated from inside the palace. Any child in Palermo knew that there were no secrets in the palace that had not been penetrated by the eunuchs.

But there were other voices, too, for no single faction dominated the Court. If anything, Rujari was inclined to favour his Muslim advisers. Younis al-Shami, his old tutor from Noto, the scholar and sage who had taught him

Arabic, astronomy and algebra, was treated with reverence. He was still at the palace, supervising the tutors responsible for the education of the young princes. The three tutors were young men he had carefully selected, but he was never satisfied with them and often discharged them with a choice curse and took over himself. It made the boys giggle and they would report all this to their father, knowing full well that it would please him. According to palace gossip, Rujari took no major decision without consulting Younis, but gossip, as any eunuch can tell you, is only reliable if the source is pure.

The sun had become too strong for Idrisi. He descended the ladder and returned to his cabin. He sighed as he sat down on the soft cushions that had been specially put down to spare his behind the discomfort of the rough wooden bench nailed to the floor. Once again he stared at the voluminous manuscript lying on the table before him. Yes, the book was complete, except for the first sentence. For several weeks during this voyage – he felt instinctively it would be his last – he had agonised over the first few words. Indecision had numbed his brain. He was so convinced it was the beginning that was troubling him that he did not consider the possibility that it might be the end. He had, after all, been working on this manuscript for almost eleven years. It had become a substitute for everything. For his friend Ibn Hamid whose reproaches still echoed in his head; for his wife Zaynab, who had left him alone in Palermo and returned to her family home in Noto with their two daughters and, above all, for his younger and favourite son, Walid, who had boarded a merchant ship destined for China and, without a word of farewell, had disappeared from their world. If a customs guard had not seen him board the vessel they would not even have known where he had gone. That was fifteen years ago. Nothing had been heard of Walid since that day. Zaynab blamed her husband for having neglected the boy. Idrisi sent her away to his estate in the country.

'You spend more time with the Sultan in his palace than with your own family. Perhaps he could find you some rooms in the harem.'

As a result, the book had become the repository of all his emotions. But it, too, was about to leave him and, though he did not know it, this was the true reason for his melancholy. Not the opening lines. That was simply a pretext to prolong the parting. The sound of the water gently slapping the ship's hull was calming, but he knew he could delay no longer. They would soon sight the minarets. He took his finely sharpened pen and dipped it in the inkwell.

If he remained loyal to his intellect, he would break with the old style and suffer in silence the inevitable abuse that would follow. Many of his acquaintances, some of whom he liked, would regard such a choice as a confirmation of their suspicion that he was really a traitor, an apostate who had secretly abandoned the faith and sold himself to the Christian Sultan. He could reply by informing them that his father claimed direct descent from the family of the Prophet. But so did thousands of others, they would reply. Everyone knew the Prophet's family had not been that large.

Perhaps he should remain faithful to the old tradition and start in the time-honoured fashion by praising the generosity of Allah, the single-minded devotion of his Prophet, the impartiality and equity of the Sultan and so on. That would please all and free him to start work on another book. But why should he and others like him be condemned to eternal repetition? The answer continued to elude him and he began to pace his cabin, concentrating on his inner turmoil. Perhaps, just this once, he would surprise them all. He would start in the name of Satan, who challenged, defied and was punished. The thought made him smile. The waves below seemed to encourage the heresy. They were whispering, 'Do it. Do it. Do it' but when he put his ear to the partition to hear them better they became silent and he reverted to his state of indecision. He was angry with his world and with himself.

In the past, the simple act of observing the lines of the coast, reproducing them in his notebook and making sure that the map lying pinned to the table was accurate, was enough to distract him. This was his third complete journey around the island. If only he could have mapped the whole world like this instead of relying on merchants and seafarer tales, which often contradicted each other when describing the shape of China or the lower half of India. Strange how often they picked on different kinds of fruit to describe the same region. A tiny island off China became a lychee or an apple, the bottom half of India a mango or a pear.

There were times when, more than anything else, he wanted to fly, float above the sea like a hawk. Why had Allah not created giant birds that could drag a chariot through the sky? Then he would have gazed on the lands and seas below and refined his maps. It would have been so simple. Or ride a giant hawk as it flew over the continents. Only then could he ensure that his map was a true representation of the world. He knew the contours of this island as well as his own body. Sometimes his imagination bestowed human shapes to the landscape sighted from the sea: occasionally an ancient angry god, but often a woman. Sometimes she watched him, propped on her elbows, and he would smile at her Greek eyes, marvel at her light Damascene hair sparkling with stars and changing colour as it caught the sun. With the movement of the ship came the realisation that she was not really looking at him. Her gaze lay fixed in the direction of Ifriqiya.

He, too, looked away and wondered how long it would be before he encountered another favourite. If his estimates were correct they would reach the northern tip of the island in a day and a half. Last time the sea had become rough, delaying the journey. Three days later he saw her, a beautiful warrior-woman, erect, angry and threatening, unlike the famed sirens in al-Homa's poem. 'I'm not an enemy,' he would whisper as the ship passed by. 'I'm a maker of maps. I want to preserve, not to destroy.' She, too, disdained him and, disappointed, he would turn to the waves and complain. But on this latest journey he had not shown the slightest interest in these old friends. He did not even bother to look at the women as the winds pushed the ship beyond them. He was distracted.

The older members of the crew, including the cook with greying hair, had travelled with him many times. They knew his moods, understood his passions and respected his obsession to draw a map of the world. They had noticed his sad eyes and distant stare, as if time had lost all meaning. They talked about him to each other. What might be ailing him? Could it be an affair of the heart? The young man with the dark eyes from Noto? Surely he could not still be pining after the *houri* in Palermo? Not Mayya? They had convinced themselves that only Mayya, the merchant's daughter could explain the despair in the master's eyes. Mayya, whom the mapmaker had loved more than any other living creature in this world and wanted to make his wife; Mayya who had betrayed him luxuriously while he was journeying. The Sultan had beckoned and she had followed him willingly first to the royal bedchamber and subsequently to her own set of rooms in the harem of the palace. How the mapmaker had controlled and hidden his grief from the prying eyes of Palermo had become the talk in the coffee shops of the bazaar, but not for long. The bazaar has its own priorities and the broken heart of a young mapmaker did not detain their attention for more than a few hours.

It was the same Sultan Rujari for whom Muhammad al-Idrisi had written this book. His own title had been simple: 'Nuz'hat al-mushtaq' or 'The Universal Geography', but Rujari's old tutor Younis had advised him that since the book would never have been completed without Rujari's material assistance, a more appropriate title might be 'al-kitab al-Rujari' or 'The Book of Roger'. In the face of such a suggestion from the heart of the palace, what could he do but bow and accept. Idrisi repressed his anger, but the Court eunuchs ensured that every shop-keeper in the Palermo bazaar had news of the title alteration. The bazaar believed, wrongly, that Idrisi had offered the delights of his body to the Sultan. The new title appeared to confirm the slander. And each spiced the story before passing it on to the other and thus the vanity of a ruler became an epic with many layers in which a follower of the Prophet had been deeply humiliated and not for the first time.

The subject of all this attention began to ask himself whether the trouble he was having with an opening line had now been transcended by the new title. A recurring dream had disturbed his sleep for over a year. It was Sultan Rujari, always in the same multi-coloured satin robe, lying half-naked under a lemon tree weighted down with ripe fruits. Rujari would stand, discard the robe and attempt to seduce a tethered doe, but just at the point when the union between the human and animal worlds was about to be consummated, Muhammad would wake up in a state of complete unrest. He would get out of bed, pace up and down on the cold marble floor muttering, 'You shouldn't be in my dreams so often', and then drink some water slowly to calm his fractured nerves. It was always difficult to resume his sleep. Why did the dream only come when he was in Palermo? Never when he was on the sea or when he went to visit his family in Noto or in the house of his close friend, the physician, Ibrahim bin Hiyya of Djirdjent. Once he had tried to discuss the matter but Ibrahim had laughed, disclaiming any interest in the phenomena of dreams.

More than once, he thought of paying a visit to Ibn Hammud, the richest silk merchant in the *qasr*, who, in his spare time, interpreted dreams and calmed the fears of worried men. He was much in demand and once Muhammad got as far as the front of the shop, but he did not enter. His caution had become an insurmountable barrier. It was too dangerous. Ibn Hammud would not be able to keep the dream secret. Indeed, an exaggerated version would find its way back to the palace. The eunuchs would giggle as they regaled each other with it and each recounting would become more outrageous. Then these guardians of the harem would tell the concubines and one of them would goad a willing eunuch to whisper it in the Sultan's ear. The Sultan would be enraged and that could be the end of everything. Everything. Not just the book, but also its author. And if Rujari became really angry he would ensure that the eunuchs, too, came to grief. The risk was not worth the suffering.

🕮

The last ten years of Idrisi's life had been consumed by the book, but as the vessel approached Palermo, he knew the completion could not be delayed much longer. The Sultan would be angry. He wanted to read the book before he died and his illness had made him anxious. And Allah alone knew what would happen to a poor mapmaker after the death of his patron. Once again he heard the mocking farewell of his best friend the day Ibn Hamid had left the island for ever, boarding a boat destined for Malaka in al-Andalus.

'Come with me, Muhammad,' the poet had said. 'Here you will be nothing more than a melancholy beggar in a foreign capital.'

Why should he feign any longer? Why should he not write what he wanted? With a sense of determination, Muhammad al-Idrisi retired to his cabin, sat down at the table and wrote a single sentence on the first page of his universal geography:

The earth is round like a sphere, and the waters adhere to it and are maintained on it through natural equilibrium which suffers no variation.

It was done. This would be the opening of his personal edition of the work. As for the rest, he would praise Allah, the Prophet, the Sultan and anyone else who had to be flattered. A compromise, but it satisfied him.

He climbed to the deck again and took a deep breath of sea air. Palermo must be very close. He could sense that from the laden breeze, carrying the rich perfumes of herbs and flowers and lemons. He knew these well and had carefully catalogued the plants and trees that produced them. None of his friends accepted that they were different from those of other islands and the cavalier fashion in which these men flaunted their ignorance angered him greatly. He had made extensive notes on the herbs and flowers of the Mediterranean islands and after his years of work and travel he could identify an island in the dark just from its smells. He smiled as he recalled the summer night he had been lying on the deck – the only sounds the tender lapping of the sea against the hard brown wood of the ship – gazing at the stars. Suddenly a breeze arose and a soft aroma assailed his senses. It was a special variety of thyme and he knew immediately they were approaching Sardinia.

The fragrance of Palermo was like a whiplash. Bittersweet memories of his childhood and youth could still overpower him. His thoughts were interrupted by a boy – he could not have been more than seventeen or eighteen years of age, the colour of bronze, with long golden hair – who came to him with a glass of lemon *sherbet* and smiled, revealing snow white teeth. How did he keep them so clean? He was glad Simeon was happy again, but that was not enough to assuage his guilt. Hearing his screams one night, he had remained silent, failed to intervene, even though he knew full well his presence would have ended the boy's torture. The commander of the ship was engaged in a time-honoured rite. Indifferent to Simeon's pain and fragility, he had violated him mercilessly. *Droit ancien de marinier*. And then, without warning, tears poured down his face as he realised that he had been thinking of Walid. What if some brutish captain had abused him just like this boy? The absence of his son made him mindful of the agony of the young flautist.

For a week after the assault, the boy had neither eaten nor played the flute, nor dared look any sailor in the face, even though some had endured the same violent torture themselves, experienced the same insufferable grief and would have been sympathetic to his plight. Others had laughed and teased him and, in time, the boy recovered. The first sign of his return to the rhythms of everyday life came when the anguished sounds of a flute were heard at sundown, bidding farewell to the dying day. Few eyes remained dry. The man who made maps, consumed with guilt, pledged inwardly to find a better place for this boy. Muhammad drank the *sherbet*, handed back the glass and stroked the young head.

'Have you ever travelled to Baghdad, master? Have you seen the House of Wisdom which has large rooms to observe the sky and many more books than in our Sultan's library?' the boy asked. 'What does the city look like? Is it true what they say, that our city is larger than Baghdad? Could this be so? And Qurtuba? You know that city well, don't you, master? Will you return there one day?'

The mapmaker nodded, but before he could elaborate, the minarets of Palermo had been sighted. Suddenly, the deck was crowded with men shouting 'Allahu Akbar' and 'Siqilliya sana-hallahu' [Sicily, may Allah preserve her!] and preparing for their arrival. A group of tired young men, their burnt bodies and worn-out faces reflecting the exhaustion of a day's work, brought down the rust-coloured sails and were folding them on the deck. In the twilight the crew began to sing a soft, mournful chant, as they rowed the ship into port. The captain, in search of praise for the discipline of his men, came up to the scholar and bowed, but Idrisi ignored him, still wanting to punish him for abusing the boy. But chiefly the author of the universal geography was preoccupied with the sky, still clear blue, and with the moon, already out and competing for attention with the setting sun. It must be the seventh month of the year, he thought. He had been away for nearly four months. Too long. And then the city was before them.

As the sailors approached the minarets they chanted 'al-madina hama-hallahu' [Allah protect this City]. He smiled as the ship entered the harbour, an expressionless smile, a slight softening of the eyes, nothing more. He was pleased to be back. The gentle breeze stroked his face like the soft touch of Mayya and inadvertently his hand went to his face to savour the memory. Below a boat was waiting to transport him to dry land. Walking past the men, he thanked each of them in turn. He suppressed a sigh as he was gently tied with silken cords to a chair, which was then lowered on to the boat. He would have happily climbed down the rope ladder, but the captain forbade it. As the chair reached its destination the boatmen welcomed him with 'Wa Salaam ...'

Nearing the shore, he could see the familiar faces of the courtiers sent to receive him. He knew that underneath their smiles and the exaggerated noises of welcome, they hated him because of the easy access to the palace he enjoyed. And there was the white beard of one of the palace Chamberlains, Abd al-Karim, shouting as loudly as his years permitted.

'Prepare to receive the Master Ibn Muhammad ibn Sharif al-Idrisi returned home from a long journey in search of the roots of knowledge.'

As was the custom, the others responded to the safe return of the ship and its passenger.

'There is only one Allah and he is Allah and Muhammad is his Prophet. Welcome home.'

The irritation he felt on these occasions had, in the past, been countered by the presence of his friend Marwan, whose grinning face was the welcome he most enjoyed. But Marwan had left the island. He had abandoned his estates and his peasants in Catania and fled to al-Andalus, to the city of Ishbilia. Here the Sultan al-Mutammid had provided him with both protection and employment. Letters arrived irregularly, always carrying the same message. Muhammad, too, should leave Palermo and return to the House of Islam. He never replied and Marwan stopped writing.

Now he was alone.

'Will the master be carried or will he ride?' Abd al-Karim asked.

'Is my horse here?'

'It is.'

'Then I will ride.'

'The Sultan awaits you tonight. A banquet has been prepared to honour your return.'

'And if a storm had delayed us?'

Another voice replied. 'It never has. You always return on the designated day, Ibn Muhammad.'

The scholar smiled. The voice and the face pleased him. It was the Berber, Jauhar, who had married Marwan's sister.

'Any news from Marwan?'

The man shook his head.

'And you? Is your family well? Do you need anything? I have brought some silks for Marwan's sister. We exchanged them for some food. A merchant ship from Genoa was in some trouble.'

The man smiled.

'And now I have a favour to ask of you. Go to the palace and apologise to the Sultan on my behalf. Tell him the journey has exhausted me and I would only fall asleep at the banquet. Tomorrow I will attend on him and provide him with the new discoveries he requested. I wish to be alone tonight. I have something to tell the stars.'

Jauhar looked worried and whispered: 'It is an unwise decision. The Sultan is ill. It has made him irrational. He might misinterpret your refusal to go to the palace tonight. Monks surround him. Franks and Greeks. Vultures. They whisper lies in the Sultan's ear. We are being accused of fomenting rebellion.'

Idrisi shook his head. He would not change his mind. 'His Exalted Majesty knows I am the most loyal of his servants, but I have travelled for many days without a bath and will not present myself in such a state of unseemliness. I will call on the Sultan after the morning prayers. Make that clear to the Chamberlain.'

The courtiers had overheard most of this exchange and smiled. He had gone too far this time. He would be punished. They were determined to reach the Sultan before Jauhar to give Rujari their version of the story.

Idrisi, accompanied by a single groom, rode back to his house, which was situated outside the *qasr*, close to the sea. He could have lived in the precincts of the palace. The Sultan had offered him that on many occasions, but Idrisi had insisted that he needed solitude in order to think. He worked on his manuscript in rooms adjoining the palace library and often ate with the Sultan, but he had chosen to live in a modest house in the Kalisa, overlooking the sea.

It was a choice he had never regretted. The permanent view of the sea he found comforting. Becalmed or white-capped and rough, it never tired him, despite the long journeys on which he had embarked or the storms that had almost taken his life. It was a short ride but one he enjoyed. Gusts of that same wind that had brought the ship into the bay now carried scents of herbs and wild flowers and lemons. The scents brought some painful memories with them, but he repressed them.

As he neared the path at the bottom of the hill he caught the first glimpse of the house. The soft light of candles and oil lamps filled every window. Then he looked more closely. Light was shining even from the windows of the rooms above the courtyard, rooms that had been dark since the day of Walid's departure. His heart began to race and, almost involuntarily, he spurred his horse on.

TWO

Family life and domestic idiocies.
Idrisi foils a plan by his daughters to trap
and betray their husbands, but is determined
to educate his grandsons.

The retainers, as was their custom, awaited him outside the house, torches held high to light his path. He dismounted and shook hands with each in turn, but before he could question any of them he was distracted by the scent of grilled lamb and fresh herbs, an aroma of special significance. He hurried into the house to see if Walid had returned. But it was his daughters who greeted him, taking his hands and kissing them. Idrisi embraced each in turn and gently kissed their heads.

'Welcome home, Abu Walid,' said Samar, the younger of the two, her red hair shining under the oil lamps.

'What brings you here, Samar? And you, Sakina? I thought your mother had forbidden ...'

'You haven't seen your grandchildren for three years, Abu Walid. Our mother agreed we could make this journey.'

He chuckled. 'Old age must have softened her. Are the children asleep?'

His daughters nodded.

'And am I correct in assuming that you have prepared the lamb according to your mother's instructions?'

Samar laughed. 'We weren't sure you would return today, but a messenger from the palace arrived some hours ago to inform us that your ship had been sighted and you would be home tonight. The garlic and herbs travelled with us from Noto.'

He smiled appreciatively. 'I hope, like you, they retained their freshness.'

Before either of them could reply he clapped his hands, raised his voice slightly and summoned the steward of the household. 'Is my bath ready, Ibn Fityan?'

The eunuch bowed. 'Thawdor is waiting to rub oil on Your Excellency' and the bath attendants have their instructions. Will Your Honour eat inside or on the terrace?'

'Let my daughters decide.'

Usually, when he lay on the slab of marble, he let the Greek do his work in silence. Not today. 'Do you have any children, Thawdor?'

The masseur was shocked. In the six years he had served in the household, the master had barely spoken to him.

'Yes, my lord. I have three boys and a girl.'

'I suppose two of the boys have been pledged to the Church?'

'I believe in Allah and his Prophet, but my wife is a Nazarene and insisted on having one of them baptised.'

Now it was Idrisi's turn to be surprised. 'But your name is Greek and I thought …'

'My name is Thawdor ibn Ghafur, O Commander of the Pen. My mother was Greek and even though she converted to our faith, she insisted on the name of her grandfather Thawdorus for me. My poor father, who could deny her nothing, agreed.'

Idrisi's curiosity had been aroused. He would ask Rujari to organise a register of all the mixed marriages on the island.

'What about your boys?'

'They are young men now. The youngest was on your ship on this last voyage. His mother will be happy to see him again.'

On hearing this, the master of the house became agitated. He rose, draped a towel around his naked body and clapped his hands for the bath attendants. Two young men entered the room and bowed.

'Thawdor, describe your boy.'

Idrisi was now sure. 'Simeon? I spoke with him on the ship. Why did he not tell me that you were his father?'

'It probably did not occur to him. I'm amazed he had the effrontery to address you, master.'

'I spoke to him first. The boy is sensitive and intelligent. What he cannot speak is expressed through the flute. He is a gifted boy and must be educated. I will speak to old Younis at the palace and see whether we can find a tutor for him.'

Tears filled Thawdor's eyes. 'Your kindness is well known, sir. The boy's mother might even pray to Allah to reward your goodness.'

Idrisi nodded and the attendants escorted him to the bath next door. They soaped and scrubbed him with the most exquisitely soft sponges. Then he was ready to be dried and dressed. By the time he reached the terrace, the tiredness had been removed from his body. And the lamb was ready to be consumed. How odd it was, eating with his daughters. Why in Allah's name were they here at all? He did not believe they had come all this way in order for him to see his grandchildren. It was not in their character. Nor, now that he thought about it, was the trouble they must have taken to prepare the lamb. Their mother Zaynab must have whispered nonsense in their ears: 'Flatter the old man, make him feel you love him, make sure the lamb is cooked in the special way he likes, wait till he has tasted it and then ask what you need to ask.' The memory of her insinuating voice and the false flattery was not pleasant and he was irritated with himself for having thought of it. It was bound to give him indigestion.

And where were the girls' husbands? Suddenly he realised that they had come to plead on behalf of their men. Something must have happened. There was always unrest in Noto and in the countryside surrounding Siracusa. In the palace it was referred to as banditry, but he knew it was much more. Well, he would listen when the time came.

He enjoyed the food. The lamb was succulent and tasty, the vegetables fresh and the flask of wine sent by the palace, tasted by Ibn Fityan and pronounced free of poison, had revived his spirits. Noticing this, Samar and Sakina exchanged a knowing look, while Idrisi thought to himself how like their mother the two were.

Nature had not endowed them with his looks or physique. As he recalled Zaynab, whom his father had compelled him to marry and whom he had glimpsed for the first time on the day of his wedding, he shivered at the memory of that night. There had been no light-hearted pleasure for either of them and even now it was a mystery to him how they produced four children. His mother claimed the credit. She told the entire family of how, aware of the problem, she had insisted that Muhammad drink an unpleasant concoction of boiled coffee-plant leaves sweetened with date juice, whose aphrodisiacal effects had first been noticed by the medicine men of Ifriqiya. And, in those early years, on each occasion – not that there were too many of them – that he mounted his wife, he could smell the bitter taste of the leaves. His mother remained convinced that without it he would not have succeeded in producing four children.

If Zaynab's character had been different he would not have encouraged her departure from Palermo. But she possessed no redeeming qualities, none. Her loud voice heaping abuse on the household servants angered him greatly. And it was even worse when she praised him. He never thought of what it must have been like for her, growing up in a wealthy nobleman's household, frowned upon by everyone because of her looks, the result of too much inbreeding. He knew that and would sometimes remark to Marwan or Ibn Hamid how the Arabs paid more attention to ensuring thoroughbred horses than their own children. It was not Zaynab's fault but why had Allah not given her a few brains to compensate?

That Zaynab's features had been reproduced in both the daughters might have been a misfortune but for the position Idrisi occupied at Court. They had married men from the Arab nobility in Siracusa, whose forebears had arrived from Ifriqiya and laid siege to the city a few hundred years after the Prophet's death. The girls' dowries had been generous, their husbands not unkind and, more important, they had managed to perform their duties without the aid of coffee leaves. Children were produced, a son for Samar, and twins – a son and a daughter – for Sakina. The future was secure. The land was now safe, a fair portion already registered in the name of the two boys to avoid property disputes and, at the same time, to reassure the women and their father that whatever else happened the inheritance could not be challenged. Their sons were their official heirs. Having exerted themselves mightily in order to achieve this, the two husbands had moved on and, compatible with their religious beliefs, had begun to till other pastures. It did not take long for Samar and Sakina to realise that there would be no more children. As for the pleasures of the bedchamber, a luxury lost.

It was while they were sipping mint tea after the meal that their father decided to strike first. 'My children, you know me well enough to understand that I detest those who hide their real thoughts in the depth of their hearts and speak of something else. I know full well you have not come here out of the goodness of your hearts, but because you need something from me. I have no idea what it is, but I am your father and will help you. But in Allah's name I ask you to speak now and speak the truth.'

The women panicked, unsure as to whether this was the right moment to discuss their problems. They had thought it best to wait till the next morning when the presence of the children might make their father more receptive to their needs. Sakina made a brave, if feeble, attempt to create a diversion.

'But Abi you haven't told us whether you really enjoyed the lamb. We made it especially for you and …'

The sight of her father's anger-filled face brought her up short. Samar saw it was futile to conceal the purpose of their visit any longer.

'Abi, we have never asked anything important of you till now, but we are very unhappy. Our husbands have abandoned us and need to be punished and we thought you …'

He raised a hand to stop her. 'Before you proceed any further, I want to be clear on one matter. Have your husbands left your homes or have they asked you to leave and find shelter elsewhere?'

'No,' the women replied in unison.

'But …' Samar was about to continue when he interrupted her again.

'Listen to me very carefully. You began with an untruth. Your husbands have not abandoned you in the meaningful sense of the word. They may not share your beds, but that is a different matter. I want you to tell me as straightforwardly as you can why you are here, what you really want and how you think I can assist you. Start with that and then we might proceed to see how you arrived there. Am I making myself clear?'

Samar and Sakina looked at each other in despair, then sank into an uncharacteristic silence. He liked the silence. He could hear the sea again and the gentle breeze that made the palms sway gently. For a moment he forgot the presence of his daughters, but Samar's cold and now resigned voice interrupted once again.

'Very well, Abi. I shall do as you wish. We have come to plead with you to persuade the Sultan to disinherit our husbands, remove their names from the land register and put everything in the name of your grandchildren. That's all. If it will help we can produce witnesses who will swear on al-Quran that both Samir ibn Ali and Umar ibn Muhammad have been involved in conspiracies with the Amir against the Sultan. They are preparing for war.'

'Is that true?' he asked in a stern voice as he looked straight at them. It would be astonishing if the Amir of Siracusa were preparing a rebellion. They averted their eyes from his gaze and he knew then that they were lying. Why were they so intent on destroying the men who had married them? He knew the answer. They were both very stupid. They did not realise that when lands are seized from a disloyal family, the law does not discriminate between father and son. Everything is taken away.

'And will both of you be prepared to confirm what you have told me under oath and in the presence of the Sultan?'

They nodded their assent.

'Go to sleep now. I will reflect on your request and make a decision tomorrow.'

For the first time that evening, they thought that their plan would succeed. Foolishness has no limits. His wife had taken a violent dislike to both her sons-in-law and was bent upon doing away with them. She had convinced the girls of this and sent them to Palermo, loaded with false accusations.

Deep in thought, their father savoured the silence that followed their departure. The birds, too, had retired for the night. Only the sea was awake and the waves were growing noisy. He looked up at the sky. It was a clear, starry night. As he rose and walked to the edge of the terrace he saw the fireflies dancing in space. This always made him melancholy. They reminded him of the first evening, a dark winter's night, he had spent with Mayya after they had declared their love for each other, when he was twenty and she five years younger. The crescent moon had already disappeared. As they saw the fireflies, she had laughed and started dancing.

'Look, Muhammad,' she had shouted, 'look at me. I'm a firefly.'

He had sat and watched her until a sudden storm had erupted with thunder and freezing rain. He had taken her hand and they had run all the way back to the village. Before they parted he had held her close and kissed her lips.

He heard Ibn Fityan cough discreetly. 'Time for bed, master?'

'Yes. Come with me and press my feet.'

The eunuch followed Idrisi to the bedchamber where an attendant undressed him and gave him a robe for bed.

'Did you know Thawdor's youngest boy sailed on my ship?'

The eunuch did not reply.

'You did. Why was I not informed?'

'Thawdor felt it was best that way. He did not wish to trouble you.'

'It's your job to tell me everything. Is that understood? What are they saying in the *qasr*?'

'They are saying the Sultan is ill and might not survive the year. They are saying that his youngest son is a secret Believer and will restore our people to the positions we deserve. They are saying that you, master, have an important role to play. The Nazarenes are pressing the Sultan to teach us a lesson. They talk of conspiracies and are advising him to destroy all the mosques in Palermo because they are the breeding grounds of rebellion. That's what they're saying.'

He did not wait for a reply because he saw that Idrisi had fallen fast asleep. He covered his master's sleeping form with a sheet and tiptoed out of the room. But Idrisi was not asleep. He was thinking of the future. He knew the palace factions and their leaders, but he had always remained aloof from them. Now that his book was finished he would go to the Friday prayers and hear the *khutba*. Perhaps he should have gone to the palace after all.

When he woke at first light the next morning he looked out of the window to see if the fireflies had brought a storm with them, but there was no sign of wet earth and the sea appeared calm. He sent for his grandchildren and was surprised to learn that only the boys had been brought to see him. Samar's son Khalid was fourteen, his cousin, Ali, two years older.

'Wa Salaam, Jiddu.'

He hugged each of them in turn and asked them to sit on his bed. 'We shall have breakfast here and while you eat I will ask questions about your riding and your tutors.'

But what he really wanted to know was about the boys and their fathers. And what he heard pleased him. In each case the father took a great deal of interest and spent several hours a week with his son. Ali spoke of how Khalid's father had taught them to fire an arrow at a mark and hunt. Khalid recounted how they had been taught the poetry of Ibn Hamdis, which Ali's father could recite from memory.

'Do you like his poetry?'

Ali nodded vigorously, Khalid made a face. Their grandfather burst out laughing. 'I see that Ali is a sentimental man, much given to romance, while Khalid is more interested in weaponry.'

'Jiddu,' replied Khalid, 'Ali thinks we will be forced to leave Siqilliya one day, just like Ibn Hamdis. If that is so, what use is poetry? I think we must learn to fight so that we can defend ourselves. I will not see my family slaughtered like goats at festival time.'

Idrisi looked at them closely. He saw how carefully they ate the sheep's-milk yogurt and bread that had been placed before them. Allah had been kind. The boys were tall and resembled their fathers. Ali's ear lobes reminded Idrisi of his own father. He liked and approved of his grandsons. 'Jiddu,' asked Ali in a soft voice, 'in your book do you explain why the mountain in Catania breathes fire? Last month the villagers who live below it packed their belongings and ran away. But after a few fireballs, the mountain went to sleep again and the villagers returned looking somewhat foolish. Why does it happen? My father says it's because Allah is angry at the sins being committed by the Nazarenes against the Believers.'

'If that were the case, my sons, why would he be punishing us? It's our people who live in that region. I have not fully investigated this matter, but I am sure it has something to do with how this Earth came into being.'

'But it was Allah who ordered the Earth to come into being,' said Khalid with a trembling voice, which suddenly reminded Idrisi of Walid at that age, intense and questioning.

'When your uncle Walid, who I hope will return home one day so that he can see both of you ... when he was ten or eleven years of age we were in a large boat not far from Catania. And the fire-mountain became very active and the sea very rough and I thought we might not survive. But it did not last long and we came to shore safely. Walid asked the same question and I gave the same reply. And he then said what you just told me, young Khalid. So I told him a story that the Greeks used to tell in olden times about the fire-mountain. Are you interested?'

The shining eyes of his grandsons encouraged him to go on.

'A long, long time ago, the Greeks did not believe that there was only one Allah. They believed in many different gods. The Sultan of their gods was Zeus, who lived on Mount Olympus together with his fellow-gods and goddesses. The people on Earth resented the power of the gods. Why should only they be immortal? Why should they get the best things on earth and transport them to Mount Olympus? So it came about that Mother Earth decided that two giant twins, the Aloeids, who grew six feet taller each year, should steal the food that made the gods immortal, banish them from Olympus and rule the world themselves. Not a bad idea, eh? They captured Ares, the god of war, in Thrace and locked him in an iron chest.

'But they did not succeed. The wiles of Artemis defeated them and they killed each other by mistake. Mother Earth was really upset, but refused to give up. She decided to create a big, new monster called Typhon. This monster had the head of an ass, with ears that reached the stars and giant wings that could block the sun, and hundred of snakes instead of legs. He breathed fire and when he reached Olympus the gods were terrified and fled. Yes, they ran away to Egypt. Zeus went disguised as a ram, his wife Hera as a cow, Apollo became a crow and Ares a wild boar. But the most intelligent and wisest was the goddess Athena. She refused to leave and called her father Zeus a coward. This angered him. He returned and hurled one of his famous thunderbolts at Typhon who was burnt in the shoulder and screamed for help. Then Typhon, in a rage, seized Zeus, disarmed him and handed him to a big she-monster called Delphyne. The other gods decided to rescue Zeus. With the help of the Fates, they poisoned Typhon. Then Apollo killed Delphyne and rescued Zeus. But Typhon was not dead. He was in Catania, alive but weakened. Zeus took a giant rock and hurled it on top of Typhon and that became your fire-mountain. Typhon is still there and his fiery breath sometimes rushes up and frightens everyone. Isn't that a bit better than saying it's the will of Allah?'

The boys clapped their hands in excitement.

'Jiddu, did the Greeks really believe they could overthrow their gods?'

'Yes. And then the Romans came and took over the gods, but the Romans went one step further and their Sultans decided that they could become gods themselves. And they did.'

'How?'

'By informing their people that they were gods and having great statues built in their honour.'

'But we have only Allah,' said Khalid, 'and that's much better because he is all-powerful. Nobody can overthrow him.'

'That is true, my child,' replied their grandfather, 'but I think the Greeks had more fun with their gods.'

'But did they really exist?' asked Khalid.

'If people believe in them, they exist.'

'But Jiddu ...'

'Now listen to me. Go and have your baths and dress properly. I'm taking you to the palace today. You will meet the Sultan.'

As he went down the stairs, a retainer whispered that his two daughters wished to speak with him before he left the house. Samar and Sakina had heard the news about the trip to the palace from their sons and they assumed their father intended to ease the transfer of lands to the boys. So the brazen-faced women greeted their father cheerfully, showering him with honeyed words and asking his permission to return to their homes in Siracusa. A cold anger gripped him and made him unable to reply. Samar expressed concern. 'Are you well, Abi? We can speak after your return.'

'Sit down.'

They did as he asked.

'I have just broken bread with Khalid and Ali. They are intelligent and thoughtful boys and I would like them to stay a bit longer so I can get to know them better. I want to teach them something important. In this house we honour truth. That's what I wish to teach them.'

The women smiled appreciatively and nodded in agreement.

'For that reason,' he continued, 'I have decided to ignore the lies you have told me about your husbands. Each and every word you spoke was an untruth and you were prepared to testify falsely with your hands on al-Quran. I was aware that Allah had not blessed you with too much intelligence, but your stupidity is truly monumental. And behind this dishonourable attempt an even higher level of stupidity than yours appears to be at work. Was this foolishness your mother's idea? Answer me.'

Sakina began to weep tears as false as her earlier smiles.

Her father rose to dismiss them. 'I wish you to return to your homes and forget this whole business. Are you not aware that the boys love the men you wish to defame? If I hear another word from you I will make sure you are severely punished.'

Shaken by this display of anger, Samar and Sakina fell on their knees before him and kissed his feet. Samar spoke in a broken voice. 'Forgive us, Abi. You are correct. It was our mother's idea. We will not mention it to another person as long as we live.'

Then Sakina, desperate to restore herself to her father's favour, declared, 'We will never speak untruth again.'

Idrisi was unbending. 'You might as well say you'll never eat again.'

'Abi, a letter arrived from Walid.'

The shock almost felled him. He sat down again. 'If this is another falsehood ...'

'It is not, Abi,' Samar spoke to back up her sister. 'We saw the letter.'

'When did it arrive?'

'A year ago,' replied Sakina. 'It was delivered to us by a merchant who had met Walid.'

'Why was I not informed?'

The women bowed their heads and did not answer.

'Who was the letter addressed to? Do not fear. Tell me the truth.'

'To us,' replied Samar, 'but in it there was a sealed parchment for you. Our mother told us we should conceal it till you agreed to our plan.'

'I assume you have brought it with you?'

She nodded and rushed to her room, returning with a sealed roll of paper. Taking it from her, Idrisi asked them to leave him alone. He inspected the document closely to ascertain whether it might have been opened and re-sealed but, to his surprise, it had not been tampered with. As he stamped on the seal and watched it crumble, his eyes moistened. Walid was alive. The clumsy calligraphy was reassuring. There could be no doubt that Walid was the author of what lay on the table before him. On another piece of papyrus with the letter Idrisi saw the outlines of a map, but which coast could this be? For a moment the mapmaker took precedence over the father. He clapped his hands. It was the southern coast of India, but drawn with much greater skill than his own.

'Allah be praised,' he said to himself. 'The boy is more gifted than his father.'

Then he devoured the letter.

Most respected father, I hope this finds you in good health. I honour you and I love you. This is the third letter I am sending you. The first two were despatched through merchants who were on their way to Palermo. I asked them to deliver the letters to the palace, since I assumed they would reach you there. I have a feeling that they never reached you, because I know if they had you would have found a way of responding and I used to dream that your ship would enter this city of water and find me.

This letter I am sending with a seafarer who became a dear friend of mine on the first voyage and is now captain of his own ship. He is on his way to Siracusa. In my previous letters I asked you to forgive me for leaving without saying farewell. I did not want you to be worried or fearful on my behalf. I know how much you loved me and I did not want to let my absence become a permanent worry in your mind as yours is in mine.

I stopped travelling some years ago after I had endured some grim sorrows in my life. Now I am happy again and in the service of a very fine merchant, Master Soliman, who knows Palermo well from the stories of his grandfather who traded in silks and brought back many beautiful pieces of cloth from our city. Master Soliman does not travel any longer. He works mainly on curved clasps and silver necklaces for the ladies and, sometimes, gold cups for the palace. He is a very skilled craftsman and could make a silver planarian for your maps.

Father, I wish to see you, but I do not wish to return to Palermo. It will end badly for our people and I have no desire to witness more killings. As you know, it was the death of my mother's brother that was the cause of my leaving. I am aware that you had nothing but contempt for him, but he was an affectionate man, *always very kind to me and there was no real motive for his death, except robbery. The nobles who killed him knew he had no children and the land would revert to the Sultan, which it did and was handed over to the murderers. Here in the city of water there are not many Believers. Master Soliman, who is a Jew, thinks I might be the only follower of our Prophet who actually lives in this city. For that reason my presence is not threatening to anyone. I can't remember if you ever visited Venice on your travels, but if you ever decide to come here you can find me in the home of the silversmith Soliman who is known to all. The little map that I send with this letter was made by me when I was a seafarer and I travelled a great deal on the Eastern and Western coasts of India.*

Peace be upon you, Father.

Your obedient son,
Walid ibn Muhammad

A waterfall of emotions descended on him – relief, joy, love, anger, sadness all flowed together as he wiped the tears from his eyes. Unasked questions and unspoken bitternesses would continue to weigh down his heart unless ... He would ask the Sultan for permission to visit Venice.

THREE

Siqilliyan whispers. The Sultan in the palace informs Idrisi of the fate awaiting Philip al-Mahdia. Idrisi's encounter with Mayya and Elinore makes him forget all else.

After the formalities had been concluded and the two grandsons presented to Sultan Rujari, who gave each of them a little silk bag with freshly minted coins, the audience was over. The boys bowed and were escorted home by Ibn Fityan. The rest of those present were asked to leave the two men alone.

Idrisi was taken aback by how much weight the Sultan had lost over the last three months. His robust, vigorous, handsome friend had aged. The dark red hair of which he was so proud and which he had inherited from his mother, Adelaide of Savona, had now turned completely grey. The same fate must have befallen his beard, and was probably why he had had it removed. Appearances mattered to this Sultan. Idrisi looked at Rujari, who averted his eyes. Both men knew that death was not far away.

Just as Idrisi was about to speak, a young woman, not more than seventeen or eighteen years of age, ran into the room and embraced the Sultan, resting her head in his lap. As soon as she realised he was not alone, her face coloured and she muttered an apology. The moment Idrisi saw her he knew who she was and the beats of his heart increased. Her eyes and lips were an exact replica of her mother's at that age.

Rujari smiled. 'My daughter, Elinore, but then you recognised her, did you not? She is like her mother. Except for her thick, dark hair. That was my contribution. I think.'

She looked at him carefully now and whispered in her father's ear. 'How would he know my mother?'

'Master Idrisi, she wants to know how you knew her mother. You grew up in the same village, did you not? I think I first met her in your uncle's house in Palermo. You were there?'

Idrisi nodded.

'I must speak with your mother's friend, my child. He is the greatest scholar in our kingdom but he is rarely in Palermo. Tell your mother he's here. If she wishes, she may share our midday meal.'

Like a gazelle, Elinore ran out of the room, turning once to look back and smile.

'I hear you have news of your son.'

'Your spies are quick, Exalted One. And, on this occasion, they tell the truth. And your health?'

'See for yourself. I lie here in the palace of your Sultans, broken by cruel old age and the loss of my sons. You know how that can feel. Your boy disappeared on a vessel and I remember you could not eat for many days. Three of my boys have been taken away from me. Rujari I loved more than anyone else. He was learning fast. You taught him. Don't you remember? He was a healthy sapling, then shot up quickly like a young tree. I loved him, Idrisi. I tended him carefully. He was the pride of my orchard. God is cruel. Then Tancredi went, followed by Alfonso. Now there is Guillaume or "William the Conqueror", as his brothers used to tease him. He is a sweet boy, of even temperament, but ungifted and lacking in both wisdom and virtue. The crown will weigh heavily on his head and I fear he will rely too much on the sword. The sword, as you know better than most, is an essential defence against enemies at home and abroad, but must be used with care. If I had thought that all his brothers would die before him I would have ensured he was given the chance to govern or to work for the Diwan. His interests are limited to Arab poetry, discussions on love, consuming wine and fornicating. He has imbibed so much of your culture that I think he feels and thinks like an Arab. This is dangerous, Idrisi, and will anger the nobles. I want you to speak with him, teach him and help him. He could lose this kingdom as easily as my father won it. If he does, I hope your people will regain it, but I doubt their capacity to do so. There is a deep-seated weakness in your statecraft. You overestimate the power of the Word and the sword, but underestimate the necessity of law, especially in relation to property. Don't misunderstand me: the law is only an instrument to be used by the ruler as he wishes, but it creates the basis for stability. I would hate the Popes to take Sicily, or the English or the Crusaders. If they do, everything we have created will be destroyed. It will be the end. I was hoping that my young and beautiful wife might bear me a new son, but she has produced a girl and that is unhelpful.'

There were times when Idrisi had misgivings about himself and his position in the Court. He often imagined how, with his knowledge of Siqilliya and the world, he could guide his people to victory. But a lengthy conversation with Rujari usually dispelled his doubts. There was no other Sultan like him, either in Ifriqiya or al-Andalus, the two worlds that he understood so well. But the Sultan was too harsh in his judgements.

'I think you do William an injustice. It's because you have never been fond of him that he has retreated into his own world, but he is an intelligent boy. His knowledge of literature and philosophy is remarkable. It is true that he is too addicted to the pleasures of the salon and the cup, but I will do as you ask and give him some lessons in statecraft. Let us hope Your Highness lives for a long time. Have the physicians diagnosed your ailment?'

'The learned men from Salerno – and they have all been here – tell me there is no cure for my disease. They know I am dying. They recommend herbs and fruits and much else, but when I ask how long do I have they have no answer. They do not know. So let us speak today at length, my friend. There is much to discuss. I am glad you have news of your boy and am even happier that your book is completed. Your book will not make my English cousins happy. You describe England as a land of perpetual winter in the Ocean of Darkness. It's true. It's true. Even the priests the English send me to intrigue against your people and the Greeks know this well. Why else would so many of them come here to seek warmth in the arms of young men? It's not their fault, but yours. Why did an Arab army not arrive and build on what the Romans had left behind? Once you reached the Atlantic coast, you could easily have taken England as well and the island to its north. Those small Saxon churches we hear much talk of could then have been rebuilt as beautiful mosques and, later, the Banu Hauteville would have consecrated them as cathedrals. My cousins complained bitterly of having to build everything themselves. Castles, palaces and churches. I'm told that all their structures are perpetual winter.'

He smiled and looked at his friend. This was how their conversations had proceeded when both were young and became close friends. Their intimacy had led to a great deal of gossip in the streets, encouraged by the palace eunuchs. The Sultan waited for his response. Idrisi obliged.

'It was too cold to be conquered by us and even Allah has problems in changing the climate of a country. In al-Andalus and Siqilliya we could still smell the desert and grow our dates and lemons and pomegranates. But in England the cold would have killed the palms and those who carried the seeds. That island was meant for your people, not mine. Though what you say is true. We would have shone the light of learning on them. It would have spared Adelard of Bath the long journey here simply to learn Arabic. And we would have taught them the joys of food. They think and eat like barbarians. But I think your master-builders, too, like to work according to their own plans, not ours. The church you built in Cefalu could never have been built on the foundations of a mosque.'

They laughed. Much to the irritation of the English priests at Rujari's court, the bad luck of the cousins who conquered England was the target of much humour and ribaldry between these two old friends. Even that conquest had required the presence of Siqilliyan knights. And it was even claimed that a Siqilliyan arrow had felled the English king.

'Ah, Cefalu. That is where you must ensure that this weary body is allowed to rest after I am gone. The Bishops will want to inter my bones here, in Palermo. Don't let them do it. Some of my happiest moments were spent in the little palace in Cefalu where I lived and made sure the architects did exactly as I wanted. Why do you smile? Ah, I told you about the woman from Temim. She was helpful, certainly, but it was the church that preoccupied me much more than she. As for the design, I know you are making mischief. The influence of your architects is ever-present in that church. How could it not be when it is they who built it and it is how I wanted it to be? That is why I moved there to stop the Bishops from interfering. Come, Master Idrisi, how can you have forgotten those exquisite arches, slender like the curves of a beautiful woman?'

'A beautiful woman from Temim ...'

Rujari ignored the remark.

'What are those arches, but a tribute to the mosques of Palermo, which are still there as they were in my father's time. You were convinced I would not be able to protect them. Of course the church your people took and transformed into a mosque had to be re-consecrated. We are Christians, after all. But you will admit that all else is there. This is still the city of two hundred and ninety-nine mosques and I am still the Sultan Rujari of Siqilliya.'

'You certainly are Sultan Rujari in Palermo. And the Believers respect you for it, but how else could you run a city where the bulk of the population are of my faith? You could kill them, but who would run the Diwan, fight your wars, transport your goods, and pay your taxes? The Lombards your father encouraged to come here are barbarians. They know nothing except to rape and steal. And when you travel to Messina or Apulia you leave these beautiful long robes behind and dress in the armour of your forebears and your shield is painted with a cross and you become King Roger or Count Ruggiero depending on where you are and which of the competing Popes is coming to plead for your support.'

Rujari smiled. 'You know full well that my father refused to send our soldiers to fight in the First Crusade. Did I tell you that when an envoy of Pope Urban continued to insist we send soldiers, my father farted loudly and left the room? Even after they took Jerusalem he was convinced he had made the right decision. Urban never forgave my father and even threatened to excommunicate him. Now I hear that things are not going well for the Crusaders and they are fearful of losing everything. Only last week I received a message from Innocent, whose hatred for me is only exceeded by mine for him. He writes that there is pressure from the English and the Holy Emperor for a new crusade to relieve the pressure on the Crusader states and asks whether Siqilliya will participate. I will not send our soldiers to Jerusalem or Acre or to save my cousin's castles in Syria. But it would be foolish of me to reveal this too soon. So I listen and I play with the Pope and our English cousins. These are tiresome but sacred duties.'

'Some might say,' replied Idrisi, 'that it was not only concern for my people or our soldiers in your army that caused you not to help the Pope, but your fears and those of your father that the wheat trade might suffer and deplete the treasury. It is not for nothing that one of your names is Abu Tillis, father of the wheat-sack.'

Idrisi was about to continue when he noticed Rujari was having difficulty in breathing. He hurried to the door and asked the palace Chamberlain, who had been eavesdropping, to bring the physicians to the King.

Rujari had recovered but the effort to regain his breath had exhausted him. 'I will rest a while,' he whispered weakly. 'You must eat something, speak with Mayya and then return to my chamber. There is one important matter we have yet to discuss.'

The physicians had arrived and began to feel the royal pulse and head. Rujari drank the water he was offered and then, resting his arms on the shoulders of his two attendants, walked slowly to his bedchamber. Idrisi was saddened to see him in such a state. This Sultan would never leave Palermo alive. Of that he was sure.

A palace attendant entered the room and reproached him in an Arabic dialect spoken in Noto. 'You have forgotten me, master.'

Idrisi examined him closely and smiled. It was Abd al-Rahman, the steward responsible for the preparation and tasting of food in the palace kitchens.

'You have aged, just like the Sultan you serve. I'm glad you're still here, Commander of the Cooks. What delicacies have been prepared today?'

'I think you will be so pleased to see an old friend today that your mind will not dwell for too long on the quails or the nest of mashed eggplant and garlic on which they rest. And that is only to whet your appetite. The scent of the food alone could guide you to the eating chamber, but if you will follow me, Commander of the Maps, you will reach your destination much sooner.'

Idrisi was so used to the fact that few secrets survived in Palermo that Abd al-Rahman's casual reference to Mayya had not in the least surprised him. He knew the location only too well. It was Rujari's private trysting chamber where food was sometimes served and where only members of the family or lovers or privileged friends were permitted. Idrisi had eaten there on many occasions and, in fact, did not need the services of his guide. The chamber was set well apart from the large banqueting hall in the palace. The windows overlooked the sea, a perfect setting. And fate had willed that he would see Mayya without the presence of the Sultan. He knew that a eunuch's ear would be closely attached to the door and the entire conversation reported to the Chamberlain who would then decide how much of it should be revealed to the Sultan and how much retained for the purposes of blackmail. It had always been like that, but he was well prepared.

Mayya swept into the room like the princess that she wasn't and greeted him without looking in his direction. She, too, was aware that every palace wall had ears.

'Wa Salaam, Abu Walid. I heard you had returned safely and your great work is now complete, thanks to Allah's mercy. My daughter informed me she saw you with the Sultan.'

'Wa Salaam, mother of Elinore. I am sad the Sultan could not eat with us. I hope his health improves.'

Her only response was to stick her tongue out at him and suppress the laughter she felt rising inside her. Idrisi had not seen her for almost fifteen years. It pleased him that she had made no attempt to conceal her age by dyeing her hair with henna. She could have easily done so. Her hair had been a dark golden red, just like the faded depiction of the Greek goddess Demeter he remembered from the temple of Djirdjent. Her face, too, had changed, with lines on the neck and underneath her eyes and on the side of her mouth. He looked at her closely and was about to kiss her hands when the door opened and Abd al-Rahman led three attendants into the room, who carefully laid the food on the table.

'We will return when you call, Master Idrisi. I hope everything will be to your satisfaction.'

'Thank you, Abd al-Rahman, if it is not, be prepared to feel the scimitar on your sturdy neck.'

Mayya tried but failed to control a smile. The steward bowed and left the room, making sure to shut the doors with exaggerated courtesy.

Idrisi went on his knees, embraced her and kissed her hands. Then he whispered in her ear. 'She is a beautiful girl. Silver-footed and self-assured. You are sure?'

Mayya nodded and whispered in return.

'Thank Allah your hair, too, is dark. One day I will tell her everything.'

She stroked his hair and signalled that they should sit at the table. He followed her but could not restrain himself from touching her neck. She trembled slightly as they sat down to the tempting quails, serving him and then helping herself. She signalled that he should eat and said in a loud voice, 'When Abd al-Rahman goes to paradise, I'm sure the angel Jibril will appoint him to take charge of the heavenly kitchens. How was the food on your boat? As always?'

'It was unmentionable. Worse than usual. Let us not waste time on that. These quails are heavenly.'

And they managed to talk about the care that must have gone into each dish and the freshness of the vegetables for another half hour. Then Idrisi began to speak of his travels. And all this time while talking of food and maps and the sea, they were busy exploring each other's terrain. The incongruity of the words and actions was so pronounced that more than once he had to put his hand on her mouth to stop her laughing. While feeling her breasts beneath three layers of cloth he commented on the deliciousness of the melons upon which she laughed aloud. The noise frightened them and they rushed back to the table to sit at opposite ends. Then, from a safe distance their eyes continued to feast on each other. The risk of making physical contact became clear when, without warning, the doors burst open and the Sultan walked in with Elinore holding his arm. Idrisi rose to his feet in genuine surprise. Mayya smiled calmly, but underneath her multi-layered dress she could hear her own noisy heart which, faced with the quandary of pleasure or guilt, always chose the former. Idrisi, too, maintained his composure.

'Allah be praised. You are well again, Exalted One.'

Rujari did not waste time on formalities. 'Your laughter could be heard in every corner of the palace, Mayya. Won't you share the joke with us?'

She did not hesitate. 'It was the way Master Idrisi referred to the melons, my lord. He held them in each hand and spoke loudly, knowing full well that someone outside was listening and would report his comments to the kitchen. It was the look on his face more than the words.'

To back her up, Idrisi picked up the melons and took the pose of a Greek god.

Rujari smiled, while Elinore began to laugh, just like her mother. Strange, her father thought, how both of them have this brightly coloured laughter. Primitive, but pure. A real joy to the ear.

Idrisi began to study his daughter's features more closely. Her eyebrows reminded him of his mother. How she would have treasured this child. The Sultan was watching him intently.

'She is beautiful, is she not, Master Idrisi?'

Elinore's face flushed and she went to sit next to her mother.

'She bears a certain resemblance to your mother, or am I mistaken?'

'You are not mistaken. But I sometimes wonder whether the resemblance is in her features or her character. I can't decide. Either would make me happy. You may go, child.'

As she rose to leave, Idrisi addressed her directly. 'Are you happy with your tutor?'

'Yes, I am, master,' she replied with a confidence that pleased him enormously.

'He says my Arabic and Latin are now perfect and wants to teach me Greek.'

Idrisi surprised himself. 'If your father agrees, I will give you some lessons in geography. We think Palermo is the centre of the world and in some ways it is, but it is not the real centre.'

To the surprise of the girl and her parents, the Sultan was not inclined to agree. 'There are many other things a young woman needs to learn before we burden her with geography.'

Elinore was displeased. 'Name one other thing, father.'

The strength of innocence was remarkable and both men smiled in admiration.

'We shall continue this discussion on another occasion, my child, and perhaps I will relent on this question. After all, I helped Master Idrisi prepare the research for his book. That's why he has titled it 'al-kitab al-Rujari'. But now I must take him away from you. I need to consult him on a matter of great importance to the kingdom which may involve its future geography.'

Idrisi bowed to Mayya and smiled at Elinore. As the two men walked slowly to the private audience chamber, Idrisi commented on the speed of the Sultan's recovery and asked if these attacks were frequent. The Sultan nodded, but made it clear he knew that his time on this earth was limited and it was on another matter in preparation for the future that he needed advice. This was the third time that day that Rujari had indicated that something was worrying him. Idrisi wondered why he could not speak of it. They had been seated for some time and still the Sultan remained silent, his eyes refusing to make contact with those of his friend.

'Commander of the Powerful, for over twenty years now I have known you well. This is the first occasion I can recall that you have had some difficulty in entrusting me with something that is clearly worrying you.'

The Sultan looked at him. 'Something you said earlier continues to echo in my mind. You said I was Sultan Rujari in Palermo but King Roger on the mainland. Well, my friend, I have to become King Roger in Palermo as well. The Bishops have warned me that the Barons from Apulia and Messina and others who were not named have decided to act after my death. They aim to kill poor William and put one of themselves on the throne. The Bishops advise that in order to retain control of the future I must make my loyalty to the Church visible to all.'

Idrisi realised the gravity of the situation. 'A blood sacrifice?'

'I fear so.'

'If it's me you want, I would prefer the scimitar to the fire.'

'It is not a matter for frivolity. They want the head of Philip al-Mahdia.'

Shaken by the news, Idrisi rose to his feet, his face filled with anger. Philip was the most respected of the Sultan's counsellors in Siqilliya. He was a eunuch who had fled from slavery in Ifriqiya as a young man and found sanctuary in Palermo. Born a Muslim, after his father's death he had been sold into slavery to a Greek merchant. He was baptised and destined for the Church in Constantinople. But the merchant ship transporting him was raided by pirates and he was eventually sold to a merchant household in al-Mahdia. He converted voluntarily to Islam and soon escaped servitude by stowing aboard a vessel destined for Palermo. Equally fluent in Arabic, Greek and Latin, his facility with languages recommended him to the royal Diwan. His gifts were not confined to translation. Such were his capabilities as an administrator, he became the master of the household and, later, an effective Amir *al-bahr*, a sea-commander feared by the enemies of Siqilliya. He was often at the side of George of Antioch, the sea-commander who conquered the Ifriqiyan coastal city-states for the Siqilliyan king. After George's death, Philip was appointed as his successor. Within the palace, he came to occupy a position second only to the Sultan. A Grand Vizier, but without a grandiose title. And in Rujari's absence, Philip's authority was unquestioned. In the city itself he was seen as the generous protector of Jews and Believers.

Only a few weeks before his return to Palermo, when Idrisi's ship had docked in a small port in Calabria to replenish their supplies of drinking water, they had been told in glowing terms of Philip's triumph in Bone on the Ifriqiyan coast.

The Bishops undoubtedly found him a serious obstacle to their plans, most notably the slow forced conversion of all infidels. That could be the only reason for them to demand his removal. Philip also possessed a sharp tongue and made little effort to disguise his aversion to some of the priests, while maintaining a close friendship with others. Idrisi could understand why the clerics wanted blood. But what had happened to Rujari?

'What is the charge against Philip?'

'That he was too lenient to the prisoners taken at Bone.'

'Sultan, both you and your father in his time showed leniency in your dealings with defeated people. In itself what Philip did does not constitute a crime. Your Bishops and no doubt the Barons who feed them and protect the church estates are fearful of Philip's power and his closeness and loyalty to you. Send him away if you must, but do not burn him. It will not appease their hunger. You are ill and weak, I know, but your political strength remains. Burn Philip and those you appease today will destroy your heirs tomorrow. My advice as a friend is to resist the pressure. Turn their demands on them. You know better than me how the Barons have stolen lands and abducted young children for ugly purposes. Ask the bishops to try these men for their crimes before you touch Philip. Get something in return for the crime you are about to sanction. If they refuse, then you can return to being your old, compassionate self.'

Rujari did not reply.

'With your permission, I will take your leave now.'

A slight nod from Rujari was the only response.

The mapmaker was trembling with rage as he bowed and left the chamber. Outside he was escorted by one of the lesser Chamberlains and two slaves. As he walked through the outer courtyard, he saw a figure flying in his direction. He stopped till the apparition almost ran into him.

'Elinore, child,' he said, because the way she looked at him with a single raised eye reminded him of Walid. He bit his lip, but she did not appear in the least disconcerted.

'Master Idrisi, my mother and I are going to spend the day with her family next week. Since your sister will also be there it would be a pleasure if we could break bread together. You do not need the permission of the Sultan to visit your sister, or do you?'

'I will think about your suggestion, Princess.'

'If you are fearful of losing your way I will happily draw you a map.'

He burst out laughing. 'I will be there, provided you let me know the day.'

'Good. We will discuss Pythagaros of Samos and his ideas. I believe in the importance of numbers, but definitely not seven.'

On seeing the surprise on his face, she laughed and disappeared. Thank Allah that every day was not like this one. As to which of the two emotions he encountered in the palace that day affected him more, it was difficult to say. That he still loved Mayya was hardly a surprise. She was forever locked inside him. On his long voyages, she was always with him, a willing participant in dozens of imagined conversations that had become a balm to ease his mental exhaustion.

In the past when she had whispered in his ear that Elinore was his daughter, he had not completely believed her. He had thought this was her way of assuaging her guilt. He did not know that she had none; guilt played no part in her feelings. For her, the offer of a place in the Sultan's harem had not been a choice. It was a command. She had not had to be told that if she disobeyed, her entire family would suffer. In this respect all Sultans were the same: a belief in the prophecy of Muhammad or the miracles of Jesus made no difference. The satisfaction of their carnal needs transcended all spiritual beliefs.

Idrisi saw now that there was no way she could have conveyed this to him, but with his knowledge of the world he should have known. How they had managed to meet in secret and made love was something that still frightened and astonished him. She was sure they had not been seen, that not even the most hated eunuch of the harem knew what had happened, but could one be sure of anything in that cursed palace? Just as he should have known that for her, he, Muhammad al-Idrisi, would be the only man in her life. It upset her that the fever of love had left no mark on him, but here she was wrong. She looked for physical signs and wondered why he was not thin and distraught. That was how the poets described lovers who had been deprived of their beloved. If Qays could starve himself for his Laila, why not Muhammad for his Mayya? She did not know that she was ever present in his mind, that the book he had just completed was written for her, not the Sultan, that the main reason he stayed close to Rujari and, in consequence, angered many of his friends, was to be close to her. He had never told her that because he did not think she would believe him.

Of one thing Idrisi was now certain. Elinore was his child. All doubts had fled. And he feared that the Sultan suspected as much. The joy of holding Mayya in his arms and seeing his daughter had lifted his heart. But now, as he walked back to his house, acknowledging the greetings of passers-by as if in a dream, he could not get the thought of Philip out of his head. He knew him well, which did not make it easier to accept Rujari's decision. Philip had been helpful in regard to the book, on one occasion going so far as to capture and bring to Palermo a Chinese merchant for questioning on his country's coastal lines.

But it was a long-ago meeting that Idrisi now recalled. That day after patiently listening to him expand his ideas of the world for over an hour, Philip had smiled a sad smile and spoken words that Idrisi had never forgotten: 'I have never doubted that your work is of great importance for you, Master Idrisi. And for the Sultan, who waits impatiently for the completion of your book. I am also aware of how much it costs you in personal terms. I know of the men in the mosque, good people most of them, who are angry with you for not doing more to help their cause. For me – and you will forgive me for speaking plainly – geography has never been decisive for knowledge. If anything, true knowledge drowns all the maps you make. For this knowledge comes from those permanent storms that torture our minds, like the whiplash on the naked body of a sailor or prisoner. In both cases the scars left behind never heal. It is this experience of living that educates us, Master Idrisi. Not your maps. Don't misunderstand me. We need to know the size and extent of the world, but on its own the knowledge is useless. It is what we do with it that matters. Sometimes the followers of the Prophet become so distracted by new landscapes that they forget their origins. And one day, without warning, knights arrive. The cross that marks their shields is the colour of blood. Their fierce shouts resemble those of a hungry lion. It is this intrusion that reminds the Believers of who they once were and what they have become. But now it is too late. The damage has been done. They will not recover. Rujari is a wise and prudent ruler, but he will die. Then the knights will clamber over us like a lizard scaling a rock. They will decide that in order to preserve their own power they need to cleanse the court of people like you and me. Later they will wash Palermo with the blood of its people. I fear we have lost the war.'

These words reverberated in his mind as he thought of the consequences of Rujari's decision to sacrifice the most intelligent adviser in his kingdom. Could anything be done to help Philip? Why shouldn't he escape to Ifriqiya? It wouldn't be difficult to organise a vessel that would transport him across the water. Philip, who knew everything, must be aware of what was being planned.

An unexpected sea breeze took Idrisi by surprise. Instinctively, he clutched at his beard to prevent it from swaying, a sensation he disliked intensely, but he had forgotten that the beard had been severely trimmed only a few days ago. As he stood looking out to sea he knew that the eternal war between land and water was not over. Many battles lay ahead and perhaps even Allah was not sure who would win. Would this island still be there a thousand years from now?

FOUR

The mehfil *at the Ayn al-Shifa mosque in Palermo.*
Philip is convinced that the Barons and Bishops
are plotting a massacre or possibly two.

Idrisi breakfasted alone the next morning. He had been looking
forward to the presence of Khalid and Ali but it was not to be. His
daughters had departed, ignoring his request that his grandsons be left with
him. Ibn Fityan relayed his daughters' message to the effect that the boys
were desperate to return to their fathers. Even the servant smiled as he
delivered it. But Idrisi was angered by their disobedience. How those
wretched girls must dread his influence, fearing he might transfer his love of
books to Khalid and Ali. As he ate the freshly plucked figs he looked out to
sea. No breezes lifted the waves. Once this island was under water, of this
Idrisi was convinced: the congealed shells he had discovered on mountain
tops and the skeletal shapes of giant fish were enough proof of what once
was and might be again. It would be fitting punishment for the Bishops and
Barons.

The irksome thought of his daughters returned to him. Why had Allah
punished him with them? How could idiocy overpower all else? After today,
he no longer cared. He would try and ensure that he saw his grandsons

regularly. As for the fruit of his loins, it must have been rotten-ripe from birth. But the discovery of Elinore changed everything, like catching sight of a rich and fertile coast, with pure sandy beaches the colour of gold and a green mist rising from the rich forest of palms that lay behind. The barren rocks and dust-laden shrubs withering in the summer heat were soon forgotten.

Ibn Fityan, returning with his morning coffee, whispered close to his ear, 'The news from the palace is not good. They say that Philip has fallen out of favour and the Bishops are demanding his head. Could this be true, master? If Philip falls, who will protect us?'

Idrisi was not at all surprised that the worried palace eunuchs were spreading the news. He shook his head in despair.

'The Sultan is unwell. He thinks that offering Philip's head to the Nazarenes on a platter will ensure a safe succession. He thinks that William is a weak boy and will need much help from the Bishops and the Barons. That is why he is prepared to sacrifice Philip, a person whose loyalty to him cannot be challenged.'

The steward looked at him with hurt eyes. 'Treachery. And you have accepted it?'

Idrisi did not answer till he had finished eating the honey-flavoured sheep's milk curds. 'I will go to the mosque today and listen to the sermon, but after the Friday prayers are over. You may accompany me as long as you keep your dagger hidden. I don't want it said that Idrisi is frightened of the populace.'

Ibn Fityan smiled. It was what he wanted to hear. 'Not the populace, Commander of the Book, but a Nazarene stoked to fury by the monks who resent your closeness to the Sultan. The vile rumours they spread about you are truly unbearable and ...'

Idrisi interrupted him. 'If I can bear them you must try and do the same.' He understood the fear that the news had unleashed. He had known hunger, thirst, bodily weariness, and emotional anguish; sometimes, the thought of Mayya imprisoned in the harem induced a terrible misery. All this, but never fear. Now, he had to admit that the news of Philip's fall from favour had shaken even his self-confidence.

As they walked through the crowded streets to the mosque Idrisi noticed the silence of the multitude, straining to hear the words of the sermon, mutilated excerpts from *al-Quran*. Entering the mosque, the Believers made way for him so he could sit at the front, but he declined with a grateful gesture and sat in the open courtyard under the glare of the sun. He looked around to estimate the size of the gathering. There were at least three thousand people assembled, probably more. The *qadi* would speak for a long time today, overwhelming the faithful with a confusing mixture of dogmatic counsels and endless rhetoric, which flowed like a stream. When the crowd expressed appreciation of a particular phrase with cries of *wa-allah*, he would repeat it, enunciating each word carefully, his gaze directed towards heaven.

Idrisi stopped listening and recalled one of his earliest meetings with Philip in the palace. The Sultan was questioning his victorious Amir *al-bahr* on the pattern of a city built by Believers. Why the water? Why the gardens? Why the row of straight trees?

'Bountiful Sultan,' replied Philip, 'the garden is heaven on earth, the water must be kept pure and clear in canals, the trees must be planted in rows. The reason is simple. It helps us to develop pure and clear conceptions and guard against false illusions. The builders create cities like this everywhere to stress the universality of the Prophet's faith. And it is this that pushes the soldiers of the Prophet towards expansion and the enemies of this faith towards surrender.'

The Sultan smiled and nodded. 'When you speak like this I sense something. In your heart you remain a Believer in your Prophet. The conversion to my faith was a pretence. I do not blame you, but I would be happier if you admitted this and then you and Master Idrisi can pray together.'

Philip had paled, but apart from that his expression betrayed nothing. 'I am grateful to the Sultan. I pray in the large church built by your father.'

Suddenly Idrisi became aware that Philip's name had been spoken by the *qadi*. The other listeners had already succumbed to the preacher. Now Idrisi, too, strained to hear every word.

'It has been reported to us that Philip al-Mahdia, the great Amir *al-bahr* and a worthy successor to the late George, may Allah bless his memory, is the victim of falsehoods. The Nazarene monks charge Philip with treason because they say that when he conquered Mahdia he refused to torture and kill Believers or rape the women. Is this a crime? May the stars rain on the head of the Nazarenes and may they be forced to drink their own blood for making this charge. Sultan Rujari is our protector and we must not do anything to shake his throne. Hear me, O Believers. This Sultan has defended us against the madness of his monks. The Sultan and his family will guard us against all catastrophes and for that reason let us pray to Allah to guide the Sultan and urge him to spare the life of Philip.'

Idrisi joined in the prayer, cupped his hands and looked upwards. A collective 'Amen' rent the air and the sermon was over. As the faithful surrounded him, they shouted questions from every direction: Is what the *qadi* said true? Do you think Filib will die? Will our world end? Should we not resist now instead of waiting for the executioner's axe?

He smiled at them with sad eyes and allowed himself to be taken deep into the heart of the mosque, into a narrow room where the others had assembled. As his eyes became accustomed to the semi-darkness, he felt a lightning bolt. Philip, attired in long white robes, was seated on the floor with the rest of them. He rose to his feet and embraced Idrisi, kissing him three times. The others did the same. Apart from the *qadi*, Philip and himself, there was the Chief Eunuch from the palace and two young men who introduced themselves as Philip's captains in charge of their own ships of war. Philip had taught them all they knew and they would die for him. Once the introductions were over, a silence fell.

It was Philip who spoke first. 'What the *qadi* said today was true. There is a conspiracy being prepared against us. So much is certain. It is in its early stages, but our choices are limited. Any resistance at this moment would be easily crushed. The Barons and monks are hoping that when I am burnt at the stake, there will be an uprising.'

The two young sea captains shuddered in horror and the older of them spoke. 'Amir Philip, if they burn you, we will burn this city. The loyalty of the men on the ships is to you and no one else ...'

Philip raised his hand to stop him. 'It would be a tragedy if this were to happen. The Sultan is ill. He will die soon. He knows. The boy who succeeds him is even more sympathetic to us than his father. He has mastered our language and *al-Quran*. He has admitted to his tutors that he would like to convert to our faith. Is that not true, Master Idrisi?'

'It is true,' whispered Idrisi, 'but be careful. These are the wishes of an impressionable young man who is in love with our women and we should not assume that he will convert ...'

Philip smiled. 'Some men remain impressionable till the day they die. I am aware of this only too well. If the tide turns, William may float away. In a long war nothing can be taken for granted. That I know better than all of you. The fate of a battle is usually decided at the moment of victory or defeat. Who would have believed that a handful of Normans could have defeated our armies on this island? We outnumbered them, we had more weapons, more food and we controlled the towns and the sea. But they won. Till the last moment anything is possible. It is the quality of the men who fight, their mental capacity, that determines a great deal. It is the same in the situation that confronts us at this moment. But we must prepare carefully and give strength to Rujari by declaring our loyalty to his family.

For us the best conditions for the struggle that lies ahead would be if the Barons refused to accept William as their King. If that happens, you must resist them and defend him. Who knows, perhaps Siqilliya, with or without the Franks, will return to our faith.'

Then Idrisi spoke. 'There is a problem you have not taken into account. If they burn you, the charm will be broken and the beautiful illusion or hope – call it what you will – gone for ever. When our people see that Amir Philip, the most powerful man in the kingdom after the Sultan, can be burnt like a piece of wood and his ashes scattered in the sea, they will despair. They will think Allah has abandoned them. They will become embittered and desperate and in that state men can no longer think in a calm and rational way like you. Please do not underestimate the effects of your death.'

Philip smiled. 'Torture and death by fire is an abomination, but I think I will feel it more than you. I was sold into slavery and in that condition one is always prepared for death. It would worsen my misery if I thought you were all engaged in planning an action that was doomed to fail.'

Then the *qadi* spoke. At seventy-six years of age, the hair on his head had disappeared some time ago, but his long white beard, clutched tight during key moments of his sermons, had a touch of wild grandeur. Idrisi had heard him in this same mosque for many years and knew all his rhetorical ploys. They reminded him of the weather. When he began to speak it was like a hot moist squall that suddenly blows away and the air becomes stagnant and motionless. Then, suddenly, without warning, a dark cloud appears, followed by a thunderclap, exhorting the faithful to action. Sometimes there were variations, but nothing significant. And Believers, to their credit, learnt to display a stoicism worthy of their earliest forebears, applauding the same words week after week as if they heard them for the first time.

'Amir Philip,' he said, 'you are regarded as the wisest man on this island, wiser even than Master Idrisi. In the name of Allah I urge you to think again. Our Prophet, may he rest in peace, taught us to submit, but only to

Allah. No earthly ruler can take his place. For you to submit to the crime being prepared in the palace is unacceptable and will damage our community. I would urge you to board a ship and disappear. How did our Prophet win those early battles? Because in those early clashes with the armies of the Ignorant, the Prophet's soldiers were the only disciplined men of their day. It was not easy to elevate the mental state of the Ignorant to believe in one Allah, but finally we succeeded and they entered the stream of history. So Amir Philip, I plead with you to follow their example. There are many places where you will find refuge. Our Amirs in al-Andalus, threatened permanently by the Nazarenes, will reward your skills. And when stories of the battles you win, with Allah's help, reach Siqilliya, we will rejoice and, who knows, it might even encourage our poets to speak less of wine and more of our victories.'

In this vein the discussion continued for many hours, the young captains vigorously supporting the *qadi*'s suggestion that Philip take several ships and retreat to a friendly city. They described how, in the past, they had found a number of safe havens and marked them on their maps, not revealing the locations, even to Master Idrisi.

But they had all reckoned without the will and determination of Philip al-Mahdia. Once he had made a decision it was difficult to shake his resolve. With a simple gesture, he demanded and obtained total silence. Then he brought the *mehfil* to a close.

'Don't misunderstand me, friends, but I have thought about this very carefully. I have no desire to die, but none of your arguments has convinced me. How can my death have the effect you describe if so few are aware that I am a Believer? Most of our people think I am a Nazarene. They will not be affected by my departure. The *qadi* talks of the Prophet's disciplined soldiers. That is what we need, but it is the Franks who displayed that quality when they took this island. We were, as usual, busy fighting ourselves. If one of our Amirs had not invited the Franks to help him against other Believers, would they have come here in the first place? Allah alone knows. It is because we need discipline that I am prepared to die so that you have time to organise yourselves for the battles that lie ahead. The Nazarenes will not be satisfied till they have killed us all. That is the only language they understand. And, rest assured, I will not submit easily at my trial. I will defend myself against all their falsehoods. And I hope Master Idrisi will insist on being present so that he can convey what took place to all of you. To run away and hide is a sign of guilt and I will not afford them that satisfaction. If I were to leave they would revenge themselves on you. The monks find it difficult to conceal their hatred of Palermo. There are too many Believers and Jews here for their liking.

'So I say farewell to you my friends. Always think carefully before you act. Take everything into consideration. And one last thing for you Master Idrisi. Your hot-headed sons-in-law are preparing to take arms against the Sultan. That is what my men report from Siracusa and Noto. Naturally, I have stopped this information from being circulated, but urge them to be cautious. This is the wrong moment. And a last word of advice. The most dangerous man at the palace, because he is the cleverest, is Antonio, the monk from Canterbury, who was taught his trade by men cleverer than himself. He is not interested in wine, women or worldly goods. His only cause is to ensure the Nazarene triumph against Believers. Whenever I spoke with him, I felt I was being questioned by my executioner. He is a gentle fanatic, but don't be deceived. He never relaxes his faith, never doubts his God and will happily sacrifice himself to advance his cause. That is what makes him different from the corrupt and indolent monks native to this island. Master Idrisi smiles. Yes, my friend, he is not unlike me, except that my concern is to safeguard our people as best I can. Antonio is afflicted by a religious passion and that, I'm afraid, always verges on insanity, no matter what the religion. That is why I fear him the most and so should you. I think he will be present at my trial. I wonder whether the island you describe as being total darkness nonetheless produces men whose inner light makes their souls shine.'

And with these words Philip and the Chief Eunuch departed, leaving the rest of the company in a state of mute shock. Idrisi felt the *qadi*'s hand on his shoulder. 'Could you not intercede with the Sultan on his behalf?'

He nodded silently. As he left the room Ibn Fityan joined him and the two men walked in silence through the inner courtyard and out into the street. When he finally reached his house he was greeted by the soft sound of the flute. He paused before the door as Ibn Fityan asked his worried question: 'Amir Philip refused to leave the island?'

Idrisi's sad eyes turned towards his servant and the eunuch knew that it was too late to save Philip. The door opened. Thawdor had sighted them and the music had ceased.

'Bring your son to me, Thawdor,' instructed Idrisi.

The man did as he was asked. The boy fell on his knees and attempted to kiss Idrisi's feet, but he stepped aside, took the boy by the arm and raised him to his feet. 'Never do that again, Simeon ibn Thawdor. You are not a slave. Have you recovered from the journey?'

'Yes, master,' the boy replied with downcast eyes.

'I have spoken with your father. You will come with me to the palace where I have arranged for you to be taught how to read and write.'

The boy looked up and smiled. 'I am grateful, sir, but I am equally happy to go to the madresseh. I do not wish to trouble you any more.'

'Why should you trouble me?'

'The palace is for the children of the Sultan and I am not fit to learn with them.'

The men burst out laughing, before Ibn Fityan reassured him, 'Do not worry about that, young man. You will learn with children who are not so different from you. The palace contains the children of all those who work for the Sultan. That's where I was taught Arab grammar and Greek. What would you like to learn?'

'Music,' replied the boy without hesitation.

His father was incredulous. 'Music?'

'Yes, father. Music,' the boy replied.

Idrisi intervened. 'Listen to me, boy. I have heard you play the flute and I have no doubt that Allah has blessed you with the gift. You play well and you should also learn to play the lute, which will test your skills. There is a great master in Palermo, whose father, also a great musician, was known to my family. I will speak with him and he will teach you the art, but he will do so twice a week. For the remaining days you must learn grammar and logic. Believe me, it might even help with your music.'

The boy was overjoyed. 'Is the name of the master Abu Salim?'

Idrisi was surprised. The boy was more knowledgeable than he had imagined. 'It is the same. Have you heard him play the lute?'

The boy nodded. 'Once I was walking past the tavern, the one close to where the boats are tied, and I heard music which sounded as if it came from heaven. I sat outside and listened for nearly two hours. I asked a man who came out swaying from one side to the other who the musician was. He hit me on the head and said there was only one man who could bring the lute to life like that and it was Abu Salim. Never forget that name, the man said, because you might never hear him again. I never did, even though I often walk past that place, hoping he will be there.'

Thawdor and his son were dismissed with an affectionate touch on the head for the boy. 'I will keep an eye on you from afar. Ibn Fityan will keep me informed about your progress.'

After they had left, Idrisi signalled to Ibn Fityan that he should sit down. 'Tell me, who in the palace amongst the Nazarenes is closest to the Sultan?'

'None of them are close in the way Philip was or you are, master. But it is the pale monk, Antonio of Canterbury, who has the Sultan's ear. Because he is not from here, the Sultan believes his advice is disinterested. He does not ask for lands or money. He lives simply. They tell me that it was he who advised the Sultan to burn Amir Philip.'

Idrisi had seen Antonio moving around the palace, but had not properly registered his presence. Nor had the Sultan mentioned him, not even once. The Sultan was fearful. That could be the only explanation.

Ibn Fityan coughed discreetly. 'There is talk in the palace, master, of which you should be informed.'

'Speak, man. Speak.'

'There is a plan to kill Antonio.'

'Whose foolish idea is this? Philip will be enraged. It will not help him. Is the Chief Eunuch aware of this?'

'He is, but could not convince the others. They intend to kill him tonight or tomorrow and ...'

'And?'

'The plan is to blame Antonio's murder on the Greek monks who despise him even more than we do. The story that the eunuchs will circulate is that Antonio was caught in a delicate situation with a young monk and when his real lover realised this, he killed them both.'

'Is there any truth in this story?'

'None whatsoever, Amir *al-kitab*.'

'So there will be two murders.'

'If Allah wills.'

'Allah has not willed this any more than he has willed Philip's death. These are decisions taken by men on this earth and in Palermo. And both are wrong.'

'It is too late, master. There is nothing we can do. If you were to warn the Sultan, you would betray my confidence and that of the Chief Eunuch. We would all die together.'

Idrisi could see the logic of this only too well. He would have a bath and reflect on the crisis about to grip the island.

It was while he was soaking in the *hammam* that he realised the importance of what Philip had said earlier that afternoon. The best way to maintain the presence of Believers in Siqilliya was to support the Hauteville family who had seized the island through a combination of warrior-skills and luck – and the eternal fact: the followers of the Prophet were divided. This last was the real cause of defeat in Palermo and Jerusalem. Which city would fall next? Ishbilia or Gharnata? The sun would grow dark and the oceans boil before Believers would ever unite against an enemy of the faith and then it would be too late.

The attendants had begun to dry him when Ibn Fityan entered the outer chamber of the baths. 'A message from the palace has just arrived.'

'The Sultan?'

'No. It is from the young Princess Elinore. She truly is the Sultan's favourite and had he married the Lady Mayya, she might have become a Sultana. Allah's will. Allah's will. She and her mother will visit their relations on the Sabbath and wish you to join them in Siracusa. The messenger also whispered something else in my ear, master.'

Idrisi dismissed the attendants.

'Antonio left suddenly today. He boarded a ship for Marseilles. Nobody knows why. The Devil must have warned him.'

'Or his God. I am relieved by this news. Has the murder of the Greek monk been halted?'

'Of course, master. The assassins aren't foolish. What would be the point of breaking a branch while the tree survives?'

The news lightened his mood. Idrisi smiled inwardly. Perhaps with Antonio's departure, the decision about Philip might at least be delayed. He would write a letter to the Sultan pleading with him to rethink. It might be more effective than a meeting.

'Pack my clothes. I will leave for Siracusa early tomorrow. I have work of my own.'

'Will you travel by boat or horse and carriage?'

'Boat. If I leave early in the morning with the tide, we should be there by early evening. The moon is nearly full. It will be a pleasant journey.'

'Do you wish me to accompany you?'

'I need you to stay here and follow events in the palace. When the date for Philip's trial is agreed, inform me immediately. A single attendant will suffice for this journey.'

'Should we inform the Amir of Siracusa? You will be staying in the palace?'

'I would rather not stay with him. If we decide not to inform him, will he discover my presence?'

'I think he will and, given his temperament, will regard it as an unfriendly act. He might even think the Sultan has despatched you to look for a new Amir. The fragility of the situation should not be underestimated.'

Idrisi eyed his steward appreciatively. Ibn Fityan had been in his service for nearly twenty years, a gift from the Sultan. It was difficult to guess how old he was, but he was probably somewhere between fifty and sixty years of age. His hair had only just begun to turn grey and his dark-complexioned skin was smooth as satin. At first, Idrisi had assumed that he had been placed in his household to keep the Sultan informed of his favourite scholar's activities. But he had been wrong. The man was part of the Chief Eunuch's network and this was a group whose loyalty was to the faith into which they had been converted.

The Prophet had forbidden the castration of Believers, no matter what the circumstances. It was the Byzantine Court in Constantinople that had authorised a loosely regulated trade in castrated boys, supplied to the Pope and his Church for a variety of purposes, but mainly to serve in the choir. For the rest, they were sold in the open market in Palermo, the largest centre of trade between East and West, as well as Baghdad and Qurtuba. The Sultans and Amirs had special need of them. They were the trusted guards of the harem and, as such, acquired key positions in the palaces because of their unlimited access to their rulers. Often they worked closely with those who, like them, had been bought at a young age, but unlike them, had not been nipped in the bud. Philip al-Mahdia was one such person. And there soon developed between him and the circle of eunuchs a natural affinity, which meant that he always possessed alternative means of knowledge. He was not exclusively dependent on the information available to the Diwan. So close was he to the eunuchs that his enemies at Court spread the rumour that he was one himself.

Unlike others who had started life as young slaves in the palace, Ibn Fityan was not fair-skinned. Sold in Palermo at the age of two, his origins were a mystery even to himself. Despite the fact that he was not castrated, the eunuchs had adopted him. He had been circumcised and brought up as a Believer. He never talked about his wife or children. All attempts to extract information on this subject were politely, but firmly, repelled and had it not been for the indiscretion of the Chief Eunuch, Idrisi might never have known that Ibn Fityan's son had died in the recent war to re-take Mahdia.

Idrisi was no longer surprised by the intuitive political skills displayed by his retainer. His natural intelligence appeared limitless, and his experience and knowledge of the Diwan and the palace enabled him to be one step ahead of most of the courtiers. 'Tell me,' Idrisi asked him, 'how you will inform the Amir that I am on my way. To take him by surprise is surely inadvisable. That too might be misinterpreted.'

'It is not a problem, master. Tonight I will instruct the Keeper of the Watchtower in Palermo to send a message along the coast to Siracusa. You are aware, of course, that for secret messages we use a code that is known to only the most trusted of our people. The Amir will be informed of your arrival as he takes his breakfast tomorrow morning. That will give him enough time to prepare your reception.'

'Do you have a friend in that palace as well?'

'More than one.'

'Is there anything I need to know?'

Ibn Fityan sighed. 'The Amir is a devout ruler, but many in the city see him as someone who has sold himself to the Franks in order to stay in power. He knows that this is how he is perceived and it angers and upsets him.'

'In that case,' muttered Idrisi, 'we share a great deal in common.'

'With respect, master, that is not the case. You are a scholar. He is a ruler.'

'True, but we both serve Rujari. He with his sword and I with my pen.'

'The men who matter know full well that your heart is with us and when the time comes, so will the multitude. We are not sure of the Amir. He does not speak much. He has only one wife and no concubines, thus restricting our ability to find out what he is really thinking. Your visit will offer the first real opportunity. The question that we need answered is this: after Rujari's death, if we need to fight a war against the Nazarenes, will the Amir of Siracusa fight with or against us?'

Idrisi burst out laughing to conceal his anxiety. 'Why should he trust me?'

'That is a risk you will have to take. Was the master aware that the only wife of the Amir is the younger sister of the Lady Mayya?'

As Idrisi gasped in disbelief, he noticed the tiniest trace of a smile appear on Ibn Fityan's face as the man bowed and left the room.

FIVE

The Amir of Siracusa organises a dinner at which there is open talk of rebellion.

Just as the ship, taking advantage of an unexpected breeze, neared the bay of Siracusa, the light of the full moon fell on the darkness of the sea in the shape of a golden meadow. However many times he had seen this and in however many different waters, it was always breathtaking. As he watched, he saw the fishermen's candle-lit boats moving out to sea for a night's work.

As a child he had loved being woken at dawn to accompany the household servants to the fishing village closest to their home. The journey on horseback woke him up properly; half-excited and half-frightened by the thought of seeing a jaguar crossing their path, but he never did. The real delight was observing the fish being brought off the boats by the fishermen. Then the cook would ask him, 'Which one should we buy?' and he would point to the largest, which made the cook laugh. 'The big ones have too many bones. Let's take four of these …'

Since they had left Palermo, the most important person on board had ignored all attempts to flatter and please him. His manservant had tended to his needs and kept the other travellers, mainly traders, at a distance. This was the disadvantage of being known as an intimate of the Sultan. Throughout the journey he had avoided looking at the familiar coastline that he had mapped more than once. Instead his gaze remained directed at the sea, which had, thank Allah, remained calm as he reflected on the past and the future.

After having lived for countless years in the desert wildernesses of Arabia, he thought, my forebears were astonished by the unlooked-for prospects that greeted them in urban civilisations. They could not stay still and happily swallowed the best that the new civilisations had to offer them. The darkness of the desert was no longer visible, but they surprised the world with their learning and the opulence of their courts and bazaars. But the contrast between what they had once been and what they had become meant they could not build a lasting structure on these new foundations. Thus the waves of rebellion that arose from the deserts and the mountains ranges of the maghreb, rebels with long beards belonging to sects that preached the virtues of purity and abstinence, men who came on horseback with raised swords, screaming *'Allah Akbar'* destroyed the cities that had been so carefully built by the first wave of Believers. The puritans burnt books of learning, outlawed philosophical discourse, punished scholars and poets, thus beginning the process that would allow the enemy to enter through the pores of our weaknesses and destroy everything. They did all this for noble motives. They genuinely believed they were acting on behalf of Allah and his Prophet. Naturally, they did not see themselves as a monstrous aberration: that was how they regarded the heretics and softheaded Sultans they slaughtered together with the soldiers who defended them.

Idrisi was thinking of al-Andalus, fragmented, under permanent siege and possibly on the edge of extinction. Siqilliya was different. Here it was not yet over and like many of his co-religionists, he believed that the Hauteville clan, for reasons of self-preservation, might aid the restoration of the old order. The first serious doubt had been raised by the Sultan's decision to sacrifice Philip.

'Most respected sir, we have reached Siracusa.' The commander of the vessel was ready to lead him to the waiting boat sent by the Amir to row him to shore. Idrisi turned around and saw the row of lit torches on the shore. From the ship they appeared to be pallbearers, but he knew their presence signified that a person of importance had been sent to greet him.

As he disembarked, he was astounded to see the Amir waiting for him. The two men embraced. The Amir was dressed in a yellow silk tunic embroidered with gold thread, his trimmed hair and short beard dyed a darkish henna red went well with the tunic. He had a dour look. His eyes were dark, but deep-set, emphasising the corpse-like pallor of his countenance. The splendour of his garments could not conceal features that were not flawless and, even though he was some years younger than Idrisi, he had a stoop and walked with a slight limp. Nonetheless, the Amir had the air of a holy man, serious and penitent.

'Allah be praised for bringing you here safely, Ibn Muhammad. Welcome to Siracusa. I believe the last time you visited us was on your way to Noto, but I was in Palermo at the time. Our families are, of course, acquainted with each other. It is an honour to meet you in person.'

News of his arrival had spread through the town. As the two mounted men followed the winding street to the large square, a throng of onlookers made a path for them. The bystanders accompanied them with rapid steps to the palace gate and began to chant 'Wa Salaam, Ibn Muhammad al-Idrisi, Wa Salaam Amir al Siracusa,' '*Allah Akbar*'. A few young men bravely shouted 'Death to the infidels', before being silenced by their elders and hurried away from the square.

A lavish banquet had been prepared in his honour to which all the local notables had been invited. The Amir had left Idrisi to recover from his journey in the *hammam*. After a warm and a cold bath, followed by an invigorating massage carried out by two palace giants, Idrisi felt refreshed but still disliked the thought of a formal banquet. There was, of course, the novelty. He did not really know the city and he remembered Ibn Fityan's injunction. He would listen closely to what was said, but why should anything be said at a public meal? When would Mayya and Elinore arrive? Would they come here or go first to the family village, an hour away and not easily accessible? A knock on the door announced the palace steward who had arrived to escort him to the courtyard where the guests were assembled.

The Amir had discarded his listlessness and even the stoop seemed to have disappeared. With an unflinching gaze, he introduced Idrisi to the fifty or so men who, like carefully planted trees, stood in a straight line. Most of them were aged oaks, but towards the end of the row he observed two young men of chivalrous and attractive mien, who, defying convention, were deep in animated conversation, but fell silent at his approach. Each placed his right hand on his heart, bowed slightly and introduced himself in turn.

'Abu Khalid.'

'Abu Ali.'

Idrisi was stunned. They were his sons-in-law and must have been invited as a courtesy by the Amir. He embraced them warmly and whispered, 'I am happy to see you. We will speak on our own tomorrow.'

As they were being seated, Idrisi was struck by something odd: no Bishops or monks were present. As far as he could tell there was not a single Nazarene at the table. He could not recall having ever sat at an official banquet without the presence of a prince of the Church or a monk. True, the Amir was a Believer and the palace was without a chapel, but there was no shortage of Bishops or Barons in the region. Idrisi wondered whether this had been a wise decision. The answer came soon enough.

'I have noticed your inquiring looks, Ibn Muhammad,' began the Amir in a barely audible voice. 'This is an unusual gathering and not intended for many who are normally invited to the palace. I thought we would take advantage of your presence to invite a few chosen men who are filled with foreboding at the news that reaches us from Palermo. You appear surprised? Let me assure you that this is the first *mehfil* to meet at the palace. Usually some of us gather in the mosque after Friday prayers to discuss matters of common interest. But, as you know, some of our guests have travelled a long distance to be with us. You are amongst trusted friends. What you say will not be repeated.'

Idrisi felt trapped. He knew perfectly well that everything he said would be repeated in the tiniest villages in the region and by the time his words reached Noto, their meaning would be distorted beyond reason. He knew he must take great care.

'Friends, I am touched by your trust and honoured by your presence, but what I am about to say is no different from what I have said on many occasions to the Sultan himself. And I will be happy to answer your questions provided that I know the answers. I assume you have heard the news regarding Philip.'

All nodded sadly. Idrisi did not reveal the discussion that had taken place with Philip in the darkened room of the Ayn al-Shifa Mosque in Palermo, but he told them as much as he could without implicating anyone apart from himself. He talked of the loyalty that Philip had always demonstrated to the Sultan, of his administrative skills and how he had done his utmost to prevent injustices on the island. Even though he had not always succeeded, the Barons and other land-thieves saw him as an enemy, an obstacle that had to be removed if their cause was to triumph in the Two Kingdoms.

They heard him in silence.

It was the Amir who raised the first question. 'They will try him, find him guilty and burn him. And we are to watch this powerless and without making any attempt to save him.'

Idrisi responded: 'That is what he desires. He feels anything else would be regarded as a provocation and could unleash a bloodbath throughout the island, especially where we are still strong as in Siracusa and Noto.'

Next Abu Khalid spoke. 'Respected Abu Walid, not a single day passes without our land being transferred to their Church or the Barons. Even here, where you say we are strong, our people have become slaves. We are forced to work for them on the land and kill and die for them in the Sultan's armies. They don't trust us at all. That is why they bring the barbarians from the North to oppress us. Lombards they call them. These rude animals helped to destroy the great empire of the Romans. Now they adorn themselves with wooden crosses around their necks, but their heads remain empty. Anything the monks tell them is impure they kill. They dishonour our women and subject our men to unbearable tortures, leaving them to die slowly in the sun after they have been disembowelled. And all this to drive us off the lands they covet. If we delay too long, there will be nobody left to resist them. How long can we wait? Should we fight or leave while we are still alive? Perhaps Ibn Hamdis made the right choice seventy-five years ago, when he left this city and sought refuge with the Amir of Majorca.'

Idrisi was moved by his son-in-law's passion, but Philip had convinced him that timing was crucial. How many battles had been lost because the Amirs had chosen the wrong moment to confront the enemy or each other? He explained all this in a soft voice, while stressing that he was well aware of the cruelties that were being inflicted on the people.

'Never forget that it is sometimes possible to destroy the enemy, not by force of arms which we lack, but by the strength of the knowledge that we have accumulated over the last five hundred years. That is why my friend is still the Amir of Siracusa and Rujari converses with me in Arabic. At the moment our strength lies in this: the Franks have no other way of ruling this island. We must not run away from what lies ahead. You spoke of Ibn Hamdis, but his example is not a good one. The poet of Siracusa was never happy anywhere else. Siqilliya was the mother who fed him, Majorca the aunt whose breasts were milkless. Wherever he went he wrote of Siqilliya. Remember? *This is Allah's country/Abandon its spaces and/your aspirations to earth will be shattered.* And later in the same poem he writes: *Chain yourself to the beloved homeland/Die in your own abode/And as the mind refuses to try out poison /Reject the thought of exile.* He is not a good example. He was never happy anywhere else.'

But Khalid's father was not prepared to surrender so easily.

'Respected father, how would you respond to the words of Abd al-Halim? *I loved Siqilliya/In my first youth she seemed a garden of eternal felicity/Scarce had I reached maturity/Behold, the land became a burning gehenna.*'

Idrisi smiled. 'Good sentiments do not always make good poetry, my son. I agree with your poet, but to state the obvious is not a solution.'

Those within this small circle who spoke later merely repeated in different words what Idrisi had already stated. No decisions were made and nothing irrevocable said. If a Nazarene had been present, there was little he could have reported that had not been said before on many occasions. And yet underlying everything was a silent, formidable struggle between those who wanted to unleash an armed resistance now and those, like the mapmaker from Palermo, who argued that nothing should be attempted while Rujari still breathed. The Amir rose and said farewell to his guests.

Idrisi embraced the two young men and invited them to breakfast the following morning. They informed him that they had brought their sons along with them, which pleased him greatly. 'Bring them with you tomorrow. Your sons are a living proof of an old saying: they are the product of a combination in which the stronger element has, Allah be thanked, subordinated the weaker with which it was forced to be in contact.' A burst of spontaneous laughter from his sons-in-law pleased Idrisi. He had been thinking of composing a treatise on laughter. The role it played in everyday life. Laughter as a disguise, as a retreat, as an escape. Polite laughter to please the Sultan or the Amir or the Baron or the *qadi* or one's own father/grandfather/great-uncle. Malicious laughter to strike down an enemy.

The laughter of women, in particular, was severely curtailed. It was not permitted when outsiders or male elders from the family were present. Women could cover their mouths with a hand and smile, but not laugh. Idrisi recalled his childhood. The women of the household constantly regaled each other with the bawdiest of jokes, but fell silent when his father or uncle entered their space.

As he prepared for bed he thought about how he knew Mayya belonged to him when she had laughed in the most abandoned way during the months of their secret courtship, when she was sixteen and he had just marked his twenty-second year. She had never been formal with him, then or now. But why had the laughter been so decisive? Of course, the women in the harem ignored all conventions, often punishing eunuchs who could not make them laugh and insisted on everything being laid bare. But they were a special case. Idrisi was determined to find out whether the restriction on laughter was something confined to the towns or whether the same rules applied in the villages. The poets of the past had made no secret of the fact that in the desert encampments of the old tribes, the women laughed, sang, fought, fornicated and traded, just like the men.

The conquest of the towns had changed all that. Everything was carefully controlled. Including laughter? Possibly. The desire to control women obviously meant controlling their laughter as well. Nor was it just that of women. Slaves, retainers, peasants, soldiers, none of them laughed openly in front of their masters. Laughter was also an indication of equality and intimacy. Only equals could laugh together.

And yet some inner voice told him that it was still different in the desert or the mountain villages of Siqilliya. If only he had the time he could explore the interior of the island as thoroughly as he had studied its coasts. He was tired of plants and trees and the structures of rock formations and yes, even maps. More than anything else he wanted to speak with his people. To hear from their own lips how their lives had changed since the Franks had conquered the island. Ibn Hamdis was far too harsh on the Hauteville tribe that ruled over them. It could have been much, much worse and would be if they were replaced. Of that he was sure. Philip understood that better than anyone else. The thought that troubled him as he lay in bed trying to sleep was how long the Popes and Emperors of the Holy Roman Empire would permit this strange hybrid to exist. The irresistible expansion of the Church had been retarded, not extinguished, by the armies of the Prophet.

The muezzin woke him at dawn and try as he might, he could not go back to sleep. Instead he bathed, dressed and walked in the garden within the palace enclosure. The Amir, having completed the morning prayer, sighted him from the balcony of his bedchamber and came down to join him. Idrisi had taken an instinctive liking to the man and could not understand why Ibn Fityan had any doubts about him. True, a choice confronted those whose leadership was respected by Believers. The conquest had thrown them off balance, but it was the *qadi* of Palermo who had decided to surrender the city to Rujari's father on terms that were not as unfavourable as those imposed on Salerno. If the Believers had not surrendered, the Franks would have burnt the town and killed everyone. Would that have been better?

'Why did we lose Siqilliya?'

The Amir had not disturbed his thoughts, but entered them. Idrisi looked at him and smiled. 'Because we could not take Rome. Our ships were moored on the Tiber, but we were morally too weak to take advantage. They bought us off with sacks of gold. If we had taken Rome, our armies would have marched South and prevented the intrusion of the Franks.'

'And the Pope?'

'He would have worked with us till a more powerful force emerged.'

Both men laughed at the thought.

'Our faith,' Idrisi remarked, 'inspired devotion and conquests, but it is like a hurricane. Transient.'

'Let me ask you something, Ibn Muhammad. I appreciated your discretion last night. Everyone present was loyal, but it is better not to take risks. If they burn Philip it will be difficult to control the anger of our people.'

'But why? As far as they are concerned Philip is a Nazarene just like the Sultan. Might not some think it's good they're killing each other?'

'You underestimate the intelligence of our people. Few believe in Philip's conversion. I have noticed that those who do are themselves converts from our faith. What matters is what they say to each other at home or in the bazaar. And here as well as in Palermo and in the lesser cities, they whisper to each other that Philip remains a Believer. His punishment will only confirm this belief.'

'You are right, my friend. In fact, that is what they are going to charge him with.'

'There will be a response.'

'In Siracusa?'

'I will keep the city under control because anything that happens here has much graver implications. But your two sons-in-law will be able to give you much better information. And later today, my sister-in-law arrives with our niece Elinore. It would be a great honour if you ate with my family tonight.'

'The pleasure will be mine.'

As the Amir walked away, Idrisi wondered how much he knew. His wife must have told him about Mayya, but did he or his wife suspect that Elinore was not the Sultan's daughter? Before he could think about this further, his attendant came forward to inform him that his grandsons and their fathers awaited him for breakfast.

The boys ran to hug him and he kissed each of them tenderly. 'You little devils, why did you run away from me in Palermo? I was going to show you many things in the city and buy you gifts, but ...'

'It wasn't us, Jiddu,' said Khalid.

'Our mothers said you were angry with them and if we didn't rush home, you would put them in prison,' interjected Ali.

Idrisi threw back his head and laughed. 'Did you believe them?'

The boys shook their heads.

'Good. Now just look at this breakfast the Amir has had prepared for you. Eat all you want, but you must start with the fruit. What delicious figs and dates we have here. After that you can eat what you like. I need to discuss something urgent with your fathers. When you've finished, come outside and join us. There is a beautiful fountain and if it gets warmer you can take off your shoes and dip your feet in the water.'

Idrisi put his arms around the shoulders of his sons-in-law as he guided them out of the room. He wanted the boys to see he appreciated their fathers.

'We know why your daughters went to Palermo and we are grateful for your support,' said Abu Khalid. Of the two he tended to speak more openly. 'We do not know how to deal with the situation. If they were to speak like this to an enemy you can imagine the fate that would befall us.'

Idrisi's face became a rock and he spoke with a stern voice. 'Warn them both. Tell them we have spoken. If they behave like this again you must divorce them immediately and return them to their mother. If you feel that you need to do that anyway you will have my support. I will not see them while I am here, but I have already sent a message to their mother warning her against any repetition.'

'May you live long, Jiddu,' said Abu Ali. 'You have freed us from a highly painful task. For myself I will not divorce Ali's mother, but I will take another wife. I wish Ali to have brothers and sisters and that is no longer possible with his mother.'

With a despairing shake of his head, Idrisi indicated his agreement and then looked straight into the eyes of Khalid's father. His look did not waver.

'I will not wear a mask, Abu Walid. I can no longer live with Sakina. Our marriage has not been a happy one and was forced on me by my parents. The hurried union that produced Khalid was never repeated. I will abide by all the terms of the marriage and Sakina never need rely on anybody else while I am alive, but I can no longer live with her.'

'I understand you perfectly, Abu Khalid. You must do as you wish. I will make sure her mother understands this as well. We do not need more mischief. And Khalid? Is he close to his mother?'

There was a moment's hesitation.

'I thought you might receive us politely, but coldly. Your warmth has reached our hearts. What is the point of hiding anything from you? The answer to your question is no. Khalid is closer to my mother than his own. Children have a capacity to understand who is genuinely fond of them. They can sometimes see through pretence and falsehoods better than grown men.'

Idrisi was relieved. If he, as their father, felt little or no affection for his daughters why should their own children feel differently? When Samar and Sakina were young he had noticed the feebleness of their brains, but thought that in time they would attain their full development. Allah had willed otherwise.

'I am not surprised by what you say and I am glad you have spoken in a direct fashion. May Allah guide you both and protect your children. But there is a more important matter we need to discuss.'

The two men exchanged looks. How much did he know?

'Our faith,' Idrisi continued calmly, 'has produced brave warriors and brilliant minds, but we also possess a restless, impatient, unstable side that can flare up one moment and disappear the next. It produces a lack of discipline. I have no wish to know your exact plans. The fewer who do so the better, but I would urge caution in respect of timing. Nothing – I repeat nothing – must happen, while Rujari is alive.'

'Nothing at all?' asked Abu Ali.

'What do you have in mind?' inquired their father-in-law.

'We are not preparing a full-scale rebellion at the moment, but we are in touch with our people throughout this region. In each quarter of every city and in even the smallest hamlet there is a *mehfil* that meets every Friday to discuss the situation on the island. We will try and control the anger of the multitude after the martyrdom of Philip, but make no mistake. When the time comes Noto and Siracusa and the villages that lie in between will raise the banner of our faith and challenge the bishops.

'In the meantime, we have to maintain the spirit of our people and defend them against all tormentors. For that reason, we have decided to inflict a severe punishment on the monks and the Lombards who guard them in a village near Noto. The atrocities they committed have created a sense of fear. We need to teach these people a lesson. One Lombard will be left alive to spread the news.'

Idrisi did not reply, but from his eyes they could tell he was proud of them and this strengthed their confidence. 'Who is the preacher in your village, Abu Ali? I have heard talk of him. They tell me he sees visions of our armies fighting the infidels in the sky and recites poetry of his own making.'

'I'm truly astonished that you have heard of him, Jiddu.' Abu Ali spoke in such a soft voice that Idrisi cupped his ear. 'He is the son of our cook and has been prone to visions since he was a boy. He was born blind and that may have encouraged the visions. He is twenty years old but many people from neighbouring villages come to see and hear him. His verses burn with a religious passion and he sings them with a beautiful voice. If you have time, come and stay with us for a few days. Ali will be thrilled and you can meet the cook's son. I can't stress this enough, but there is something remarkable about him. As you can imagine, he sings a great deal of future battles, of victories and of the day we will occupy the palaces and Allah's vengeance against all those who collaborated with the enemy.'

The sound of children's laughter interrupted their conversation. Ali and Khalid, chased by attendants, ran towards the fountain.

Slowly, the three men began to head in the same direction.

'I will try and find the time to visit your village, Abu Ali.'

'It is more important you visit Abdu Khalid's estates,' replied his son-in-law. 'There you will meet the Trusted One.'

Idrisi was puzzled. 'I have not heard of him before.'

SIX

Love and a secret marriage in Siracusa.
The poetry of Ibn Quzman. Elinore asks many
questions, while Balkis listens.

Even though he had seen them only a few days ago, Idrisi could not conceal his delight at the sight of Elinore and her mother. And to see them now with Balkis, the only wife of the Amir and Mayya's younger sister who he had last seen as a three-year-old, was especially pleasurable. Balkis had long brown hair and a skin so fair that Mayya appeared swarthy by comparison. Her eyes and nose resembled the statue of a Greek goddess he had seen in Djirdjent. Or was it someone else? A thought entered his head and startled him. Perhaps Greek blood had flowed through this family. He must remember to ask Mayya.

At the palace in Palermo he and Mayya had been nervous. Here they relaxed and the Amir, aware that his retainers were all-seeing, dismissed them from the dining chamber with an imperious gesture. The food had been served. Large earthenware jugs containing fresh orange juice, lemonade and unfermented date wine were placed on the table. The Amir did not permit alcohol to be served in his palace except when the Sultan himself was visiting.

Now that they were on their own, Mayya lost any inhibition: 'Elinore, what do you think of your father?'

Elinore, who knew her mother better than anyone else, did not bother to reply.

'Mayya, please ...' her sister attempted to restrain her and the Amir, pleading matters of state, took his leave. He was, if truth be told, a little bit frightened. What if news of this reached the Sultan? Might he not be held responsible?

Idrisi burst out laughing. 'Mayya,' said Idrisi, looking straight into her eyes and then letting them travel all over her body. 'You will never change and I will never stop loving you.'

'Should the rest of us leave?' asked Elinore, as the black pupils of her deep-set eyes sparkled mischievously.

'No,' answered her mother. 'I will spend the night with your father. So you can stay till then.'

'Mayya,' her sister pleaded, 'nothing can be kept secret here. If news reaches Rujari that you and Ibn Muhammad were here together, he might ...'

'He might nothing. He simply does not care that much about women,' Mayya interrupted. 'We are there to produce children. Nothing more. Rujari's intimates are all men, including the great geographer who honours us with his presence tonight. There were times when I thought that Rujari wanted to raise his friendship with the great Master Idrisi to a higher level, from a spiritual to a physical union. After all, they spend a great deal of time together and it would only be natural, but the thought enraged me. I would have hated them spending a night together, but before I could ...'

Idrisi made an effort to control his temper, but the insinuation that he and Rujari were lovers was not confined to Mayya. During the early years of his friendship with Rujari, enemies at court enjoyed circulating the calumny. It used to drive him mad, but he always maintained an admirable self-control.

Now the suppressed, cumulative anger burst forth as he half-rose from the chair.

'It was never true, Mayya. You know that perfectly well. It was your inflamed imagination. That's all.'

She was delighted that she had managed to provoke him. 'Better my inflamed imagination than your inflamed arse.'

Balkis covered her mouth to hide a smile, but Idrisi rose from the table in anger. 'Mayya, this is unacceptable. My tolerance has its limits.'

'I'm happy that you're my father,' said Elinore, stepping in rapidly to mend the breach. 'It's not that I don't love the Sultan. But I think deep inside he knows perfectly well I am not his daughter. He talked of you and your work together on the book with so much intensity ...'

'How could he possibly know that, child? He chose your name, he insisted you were baptised, he supervised your education,' interjected her mother.

'I can tell by the way he sometimes looks at me that he is not at all sure I am his daughter. And even though I never told you, Mother, the number of times he mentioned his friend, the great scholar Ibn Muhammad al-Idrisi, was slightly strange. It was as if he was trying to interest me in my real father. Ever since you told me who my real father is, I've been thinking of many things the Sultan said to me. Now it's clear.'

'It was not at all strange,' replied her mother. 'The Sultan and your father spent a great deal of time together looking at the stars and questioning sailors from strange parts of the world. That's why he mentioned him a lot. Your imagination is far too strong, child. Try and curb it.'

'I think Elinore is right,' said Idrisi. 'The Sultan questioned me about you, Mayya. He knew we were from neighbouring villages, that our families knew each other well, and sometimes I got the feeling that he knew about us and wanted me to confess so he could forgive me and perhaps even hand you over to me as a gift.'

'Then why didn't you?' came the response from his lover.

Before he could reply, their daughter interrupted once again. 'Since you will have my father alone to yourself for the rest of the night, Mother, perhaps I could ask him three questions before you retire.'

'Ask,' said her father.

'When did you realise that I was your child?'

'A few days ago at the palace in Palermo. Your mother had told me long before – in fact soon after you were born – but I was not sure whether to believe her or not.'

Mayya screamed. 'Muhammad! You traitor. How dare you admit this?'

Idrisi ignored the outburst.

'And are you pleased with what you see, Father? I know you have four other children.'

'More than you could ever imagine, child. Of my other children the one closest to me is Walid. The rest? There is nothing to say.'

'We should retire,' Balkis muttered softly.

'One more question, please. Do you prefer Strabo to Ptolemy?'

Idrisi's surprise was visible. 'Who told you about them?'

'The Sultan. He said he preferred Ptolemy but that you modelled your work on Strabo.'

'Not completely true,' replied her father. 'Strabo was completely gripped by the location of places, their customs, crops, animals and the like. He wanted to compile the most accurate map of the known world. Ptolemy was more interested in the stars and the sky and the shape of the earth and the moon and how all this affected the change in seasons. They were both great masters and I have learnt much from them. In my heart I wished to pursue and develop the arguments advanced by Ptolemy, but I realised the dangers. It was a difficult path and in that direction lay trouble. Where others looked up and spoke of the poetry of the stars, I noted in great detail how close the ancients had come to solving the mysteries of the universe. Close, but they could not move further. I noticed that everything moved, how each night the movement was repeated and yet never the same till twelve months had passed. Yes, my child. Everything moved. If what I thought was true, the Book was wrong and if the Book was mistaken was it Allah or his Messenger who made the mistake? I did not let these thoughts settle in my mind. They were flashes of lightning that illuminated the future. I am sure that one day discoveries will be made that will challenge the teachings of all the Prophets, including our own. It will be a brave man who publishes such findings. It might cost him his life.'

'Isn't the search for knowledge always dangerous?'

'Perhaps, Elinore, I will return to the subject again before I die. Are you interested in the stars?'

'Yes, but not their poetry.'

'I'm tired,' said Balkis, yawning demonstratively and looking nervously in the direction of her older sister. 'And perhaps, Mayya, we should retire to our own chambers. Once the servants have left, Ibn Muhammad can explain the movement of the stars or the blemishes on the moon to you. I would suggest he does so from your balcony. The view is clearer.'

It was a warm night. Mayya had discarded her sleeping robe and opened the doors that led to the balcony. The full moon had begun to wane while they were drinking their fill of each other. Afterwards, as they lay silent on her bed, each buried in memories, a soft, refreshing sea breeze arose and brushed their naked bodies.

'Are there any blemishes on the moon?' she inquired.

'None,' he replied as he stroked her back gently, resting his hands on her softness. 'These two half-moons remain unchanged. They are exactly as they were ten years ago. You must bathe them in asses' milk.'

'They're softer bathed in your sweat. And I'm not satisfied with just once. Will not the young cock crow once more and hide in my nest again?'

'He is not as young as once he was, but why not ask him?'

She did and the response pleased them both.

They talked the night through and not just of the past they had not been able to share. That they had discussed many times as her refusal to leave the palace. He knew the reasons well and after a few years he stopped seeing her. They would exchange messages, but nothing more. His travels kept him away, but it was more than that: he did not wish to see her as long as she was a creature of the harem.

She knew the most intimate details about his life and had questioned him closely as to how he had managed to produce four children with his wife. It had made her angry: 'There is no difference between you and a donkey. You mount, ejaculate and plant your seed. Nothing more.' He agreed with her, but would she prefer him to take another wife, someone who might meet with her approval? That was usually enough to end the conversation.

He had written down the dates that Rujari had visited her bedchamber in the harem. There were not many, but it was a torment that he could not bear and after each of the royal visits he would not contact her for many months. She was astounded when he told her. She had not realised the efficiency with which information was conveyed out of the palace. He told her it caused him great pain, but she would shrug her shoulders and refuse to discuss the matter. It was not her fault that he had married someone else. Why had he not resisted? Was the joining of two estates more important than their love? And, of course, he had no reply. It had been deference to his dying father's wishes rather than cowardice that had decided the matter, but he had suffered enough. Was that not sufficient punishment?

Strange how these memories no longer pained them. The ten-year absence had been sufficient punishment and neither wished to prolong the agony. Nothing hurt any longer. Elinore was the balm. Elinore, who bore little resemblance to him in her features, but whose expressions and hand movements were extraordinarily similar. She was the product of their loins. If only …

'Muhammad?'

'Yes.'

'I was thinking. If we could have another child, a brother for Elinore ...'

He sat up in bed, startled by the symmetry of their thoughts. 'How strange. I was thinking the same. I was also thinking that after the Sultan dies, I should take you as my wife. We could live together.'

The suggestion irritated her. 'Everything must wait till he dies. The resistance of our people as well as our wedding. Was that Philip's recommendation as well?'

He held her close and kissed her lips and then her eyes. 'Why did you get angry?'

'Because I hate your plans. Why can't we just do as we wish? Why must everything be linked to death?'

'You know me better than anyone else. You know why I control myself.'

She calmed down and began to stroke his head. 'I know you rage inwardly, trying hard to repress your anger. You worry lest it damage those close to you. I know that, but I don't want to wait for anyone to die. Our love is not dependent on that, is it? Perhaps I will be with child after tonight. What then? This time Rujari will know it's definitely not his. Does the thought frighten you?'

He buried his head between her legs and muttered:

'What kind of musk is this? What scent?
From this magic others are created.'

Afterwards, she held him close and whispered, 'Who wrote the *zajal?* Not you. Not Rujari. Is it Ibn Quzman? Tell me now.'

'It is his verse. Poor Ibn Quzman. I hear he is in trouble with the new Sultan in Qurtuba.'

'Why can't he come here? Should I ask Rujari?'

'No. Ibn Quzman travels where he wishes. He has admirers in every city of al-Andalus. When he is in trouble in Qurtuba, he rushes to Gharnata. If his verse offends the Sultan in that city he flees to Ishbiliya or al-Marriya. Once he spent six months in Balansiya. That's where I met him.'

'You met him?'

'I did.'

'Why did you not tell me at the time?'

'I was away from Palermo for two years. When I returned the sight of you made me forget all else.'

'Did Ibn Quzman recite a *zajal* for you?'

'He did that too, but he had consumed a great deal of wine that day and was not sure whether it should be written down or even repeated.'

Mayya held his face in her hands. 'Recite it to me now. Now!'

He did as she asked.

> '*My failures in life so far you know,*
> *How will I spend the rest of it?*
> *Only among people who appreciate sodomy or adultery;*
> *Of this I am certain: I like both.*'

Mayya clapped her hands in delight. 'And you kept that from me all these years? Why? Could it be that you, too, prefer the company of sodomites and ...'

His hand covered her mouth.

She fell asleep just as the stars were beginning to fade. Admiring her sleeping form in the morning light, he covered her with a sheet. Then he put on his tunic and went to the balcony, the only one in the palace that was not overlooked. Thoughtful Balkis. Why can't it be like this always? The muezzin drowned all else. Idrisi left Mayya's bedchamber and hurried to his own, but he cursed as he saw his attendant in the corridor outside, his head touching the ground as he said his morning prayers. Idrisi slipped into his chamber and, soon after, clapped his hands to summon the man outside.

'The bath is prepared, sir.'

A few hours later a message from Elinore summoned him to a game of chess. He rarely took part in amusements and could not recall the last occasion he had played. His father had patiently taught him the rules and even though he became a competent player, he had never enjoyed the contest. Perhaps the avalanche of laughter from assembled relatives that had greeted his defeat when he was ten or eleven had discouraged him. Rujari was a keen player, but the scholar had declined to take part in palace tournaments. As he followed the attendant to the library where Elinore awaited him he wondered whether she had ever played with the Sultan. Who else could have taught her?

She greeted him noisily, abandoning the pose of a young lady.

'Wa Salaam, Abu.'

'Wa Salaam, daughter.'

'I told my mother I wanted to be alone with you. It was she who suggested a game of chess.'

'She doesn't play either,' replied her father and both began to laugh.

Elinore plied him with questions. Nothing could stop her onward rush. She did not wait for him to reply: it was her way of making him listen to her and understand her preoccupations. There was nothing false about her and he was filled with pride.

Her mode of speech, the way she emphasised some words and not others, her ever-alert eyes, the use of her hands and the way she touched her hair reminded him of Mayya. Suddenly she stopped. 'Well, what do you think? You haven't been listening?'

'On the contrary, I've been listening closely and carefully. Which part of your questioning requires a reply?'

'The Hauteville family. Were they as heroic as the Sultan told us each year?'

'Did the stories change at all with the years? Did you detect an increase in heroism as you grew older?'

'No, they were always the same. By the time I was ten I could recite them myself.'

'In that case, they were probably true. The men who left the northern part of the barbarian icelands in their sailing ships and came to burn and steal from the Franks were undoubtedly brave. They were masters of war and skilled in cruel combat. Finally the King of the Franks gave them a portion of the land and hoped they would live in peace with him. This they did, but as their settlements grew and families became larger, there was not enough food to feed them all and not enough land to share. So they began to travel again. One of their Barons, William, conquered a neighbouring island and Allah help them, Elinore, it is a cold and miserable land on which the sun never shines in the winter. Cold and dark, it rains and rains. For months it is impossible to see the sky or the stars.'

'Is that true?'

'Could I invent such a place?'

'And why did the Hauteville clan and its retainers come here?'

'They were warriors who fought for whoever paid them and like others in their position, they realised that the Amirs who needed them must be weak. And so they thought why fight for this man when we are stronger than him? We could rule in his place. They must have been blessed by Allah. Look what they found on this island. A great deal of wealth and cultivated land in plenty. Rich harvests of wheat and fresh fruits of every description. The papyrus from which we made paper they had never seen before. Nor had they imagined a city so rich and large as Palermo. Two hundred thousand people lived there when the Franks arrived. They came as conquerors and, at first, they were cruel. But once we decided it was impossible to resist them, they lived with us in peace and realised they needed us to teach them all we knew. And they liked our women.'

Elinore smiled.

'Do you know something, Abu? The story the Sultan told us each year was not so different. He talked of his father and uncle and the deeds of their family as well, but apart from that, it's the same story. Is that not strange?'

'It is rare for conqueror and the conquered to share the same story. The reason is obvious. The majority of those who live here follow our Prophet and to remove them all without anyone to replace them would make this island poor and forlorn. Roger and his father understood this well. Will their sons and grandsons?'

For a while they spoke of stars and ships and she wanted to know what he knew of Carthage, and of the Phoenicians who had built it. And was it true they had sailed to Ifriqiya simply by trusting the stars? He told her all that he knew and from the way her eyes attended he could see how she was absorbing the knowledge. Each knew it was not enough. They would return again to these matters and to the closeness they felt for each other.

After a silence she asked him about Walid. At first he did not reply. She pressed him again. 'I know you love him dearly. My mother has told me that, but she could never explain why he ran away or what happened to him.'

'He is alive and well. He works for a Jewish silver merchant in Venice. I will go and see him soon and bring him back, if I can. Sometimes children become gloomy and indolent if they are permanently in the shadow of their fathers. A period of separation can help. I was no different myself at that age.'

'Do you think that all these years in my mother's shadow have made me lazy and miserable?'

He took her hand and kissed it. 'No, my child. The stars have smiled on you and your mother. Also you are a woman. Men have different needs.'

Before Elinore could challenge this, her mother entered the library. 'Who won the chess?'

'We both did,' replied her daughter. 'As you can see neither of us has yet made a move. The table has not been touched.'

Then Mayya turned to him. 'Muhammad, last night we discussed something and your response made me angry.'

He frowned, indicating that the conversation she proposed was best held in private.

'Elinore and I have no secrets. It's best that way. It prevents us from eavesdropping on each other's conversations.'

'Very well,' he said in a resigned voice.

'I spoke to Balkis and Aziz a few minutes ago. He will marry us today if you agree.'

'But the Sultan...' Idrisi saw her expression and froze.

'I am not married to Rujari. I was his concubine, as you reminded me on many occasions. This is your daughter, not his, but if you wait till his death I will not marry you. You married your wife because you were a coward and you will not marry me today for the same reason.'

Idrisi rose and moved towards her, but she extended her arms to keep him away.

'Listen to me, Mayya, and listen carefully. This kingdom is on the verge of an explosion. Philip is going to be tried for treason and burnt. The Bishops would regard our marriage as an open provocation. Have you forgotten your conversion to their faith? I know it meant nothing to you and you were simply pleasing Rujari, but the monks do not take these matters lightly.'

Mayya was in no mood to listen to anything. 'The situation you describe will get worse after Rujari dies. Muhammad, we would have been crushed by sorrow had we not held on to each other all these years. I am not suggesting we endanger Elinore or ourselves. We will have to wait before we can live together, but the marriage must take place today. It can remain a secret for as long as you like, but it must happen. If you refuse I will never see you again. I will take Elinore and vanish.'

Elinore remained silent, waiting for him to speak.

'I know you would not do that because cruelty is absent in you, but if the marriage is to remain secret then I see no problem. Did you agree a time with the Amir?'

'After the evening prayer.'

'You realise that before I can marry you I will insist that you convert back to our faith.'

'It has already been done and in the presence of my sister and her husband. Anything else you require from me, husband?'

'Yes. Total obedience. Remember the *sura* in al-Quran, which …'

'Silence, Ibn Muhammad al-Idrisi. What I cannot bear is the thought of separation again.'

'Is there any reason for you to return to Palermo?'

'None, but where should I go?'

'You could stay here till we decide where you wish to live. Your sister provides a perfect excuse. And Rujari is far too preoccupied to notice your absence.'

'But all our clothes and everything else is in Palermo,' said Elinore.

'The clothes can be sent for, but what is the everything else that you speak of?' asked her father.

'Abu, it's Palermo I will miss. We cannot live in Siracusa. This is a city you visit.'

'Child, it's better you stay here for the next few months. The mood in Palermo will be ugly after Philip is burnt to death. We may not be able to control the multitude and they may attack the palace. Send for everything you need. When things have calmed down, you can return.'

Later that evening, the Amir summoned them to his private chamber, dismissed the retainers and performed a simple marriage ceremony.

A modest meal had been prepared so that there was not a hint of a celebration. Mayya and Balkis reminisced about their parents and their brothers, who had left the family home and moved away from the island to al-Andalus. Elinore and her father were happy to listen to the sisters so obviously enjoying themselves, but the Amir retired early, pleading a long journey the next day. After the table had been cleared they repaired to the moonlit terrace for mint tea, together with the sweet mixture of dates and hardened milk for which Siracusa was renowned. They could hear the sound of waves breaking gently against the rocks below.

'Elinore,' said her aunt, 'is this not the most beautiful sight? I will show you an even better view of the sea from my chamber and convince you to stay here for a few months. Come with me, child.' Elinore took her aunt's hand and the two women walked away.

'Why is your sister childless? Is it …'

'It is the Amir,' sighed Mayya. 'It is his bird that refuses to sing. Balkis is his second wife. He allowed the first one to depart when she did not have a child. It is clear the problem lies with him and nor does he pretend otherwise. He is a very kind man.'

'Ibn Quzman would not recognise that there is a problem.'

Mayya laughed loudly. 'Balkis is not unhappy. He is a kind and sensitive man and often, she says, the sight of her unrobed produces a pitched tent underneath his tunic. All that is lacking is the seed.'

'She is still young, so there is time, but she should consider a walk in a storm when the angels are in flight from earth to heaven. I'm sure the Amir would greet it as a gift from Allah and Balkis would be happy. She would not be cuckolding him in the usual way.'

'Really? Your knowledge never ceases to surprise me. So, she should accost a stranger and extract his seed. Interesting. I will pass on your advice. Though I always thought that conjugal treachery leaves a bitter aftertaste.'

Idrisi smiled. 'Only in cases where the couple is young and passion still strong. For older and more mature men, it is different.'

'All this talk is raising my temperature. It may be time to pitch your own tent once again and follow me. I will test your maturity with great pleasure. Or is it time for the prayer?'

'To know and sleep is better than to pray and be ignorant.'

SEVEN

*Idrisi is overpowered by memories of an
enchanted island. A first meeting with the Trusted One,
who preaches open rebellion against Palermo.*

It was not yet midsummer, the hour was still early, but he could tell that the day would be blazing hot and unpleasant. He sighed loudly, wishing he had not agreed to ride with his son-in-law to his estate. It was not a short journey and there would be no shade. The earth that, only a few months ago, was verdant and carpeted with wild flowers would be parched and barren, intensifying the rays of the sun. The thought of what lay ahead exhausted him. Perhaps it was not too late to change his mind. But when, a few minutes later, Abu Khalid's presence was announced and the young man entered the chamber, Idrisi's uncertainties vanished. The pleasure on the young man's face was visible. He could not control his excitement.

Abu Khalid had organised a covered cart for the older man, but Idrisi knew it would double the length of the journey and so he insisted on riding. 'My health is not delicate. I feel as robust as an ox.'

Abu Khalid and Idrisi rode side by side out of the city, each carrying skin flasks filled with water and followed by three retainers armed with weapons. It was as he had expected, the air dry, still and lifeless. The half-naked boughs of the stunted trees with their parched, withered leaves were all that remained of the spring. The sun glistened on the rocks.

After an hour on horseback it was difficult to tell whether the horse or the rider was sweating more. They stopped to drink some water and wet the cloths on their heads. When the journey resumed, Idrisi could not concentrate on the path or its abrupt elevations. Once he thought he saw a lake in the distance and was about to suggest that they stop and bathe when he realised his eyes were playing tricks, as they often did at sea. The glow shed by the small hills was deceptive and it was at that moment that a memory he kept firmly locked in the cellar, but that had been revived by the sight of Balkis, took hold of him. An image of an ancient Greek temple he had once seen on a mysterious island appeared.

He had just started work on his book and, with the eagerness of a novice, he would instruct the sailors to stop at each and every island. His curiosity was boundless. He would make detailed notes on the plants and the rocks and the shape of the coast. They had been at sea for some weeks when the island was first sighted. At first they thought it was uninhabited and the excitement of discovery cheered his spirits. It was when the sailors went in search of fresh water that they discovered the small lake and then saw the old Greek temple that decorated the shore. A sailor was despatched to inform the scholar.

The first thing that Idrisi noticed was that the temple was not a ruin. He wanted to study the building on his own and uninterrupted. The men were despatched to replenish their supplies of water and search for goats, usually in plentiful supply on uninhabited islands. He took the quills, ink and paper from his attendant and instructed him to return to the ship and find the old map of the region in the trunk that lay underneath the bed in the cabin.

He had seen many ruined temples in Djirdjent and Siracusa and had imagined what they must have been like when filled with worshippers, but this was different. In scale it was not as large as most of the wrecked temples he had seen in Siqilliya and the coastal cities of the great sea, but its structure was exactly the same. The pillars at the entrance led to a chamber and here he saw for the first time a giant statue of Aphrodite. To his astonishment it was not made of white marble. A light brown stone had been used. The sculptor had left little to the imagination. This Aphrodite had large red nipples and the same colour stone had been used to depict her mound. Could these be precious stones? If so, the men would insist on stealing them. He would not permit it, but it was best to avoid conflict. He would try and keep them distracted. And then he noticed that surrounding the goddess of love on each side were three graces. Just below the feet of the statue the sculptor had placed a high priestess. All were clothed in tunics and their throats, like white jewels, gleamed in the darkness. They appeared small in comparison to Aphrodite, but were in fact life size. He shivered as if an impetuous current had suddenly passed through him.

Everything appeared as if it was regularly washed, but there was still no trace of any person. Perhaps this was a secret temple where descendants of those who once worshipped the old gods gathered at special times of the year to preserve their traditions. The thought excited the scholar. If this were the case why had they chosen Aphrodite? Could this be the island where Homer's hero had found the enchantress Circe? And could that be the reason for this temple?

As he turned away and prepared to leave the temple, he heard what sounded like a gentle clearing of a throat behind him. He froze. It must be his imagination. He turned around and walked back to the statue. This time he looked closely at the smaller statues. There could be no mistake. He could actually hear the high priestess breathing. He went close and felt her face. Tears poured down her cheeks. He was dumbfounded and ecstatic. His hands felt the rest of her body. She was human.

'Who are you?' he whispered in the Siqilliyan Greek he had learnt at court.

'I am Eleni, the high priestess of this temple, and these are my priestesses.'

He was surrounded by seven women.

'Do you live here? Is this island inhabited?'

'Yes,' replied Eleni. 'Our families live behind the rocks where they are not visible from the sea. You are the first visitor for two years. The seafarers who came before you were not interested in the island. They just wanted some water, which as you can see is plentiful. Then they left. Will you leave soon?'

He nodded. 'But who are you?'

'We belong to families who started worshipping our old gods during the time of the Great Emperor. After he died the Nazarenes began to capture and kill us, so some families boarded a ship and sailed away from Byzantium, which the Nazarenes call Constantinople.'

Idrisi was bewitched. 'Which Great Emperor?'

'Julian. We named this island after him. This is Julian's island and Aphrodite is our goddess.'

He told them who he was and from where he came. They had heard of Palermo and knew the Arabs ruled there. As far as they were concerned the Nazarenes were the worst but the followers of Moses and Muhammad were no better. He was not in the mood for a philosophical debate on the virtues of one Allah against the stone gods of the ancients.

They told him of the rites they performed each spring, of the food they grew on the island, of how their numbers continued to decline. The men tended to leave and that is why they wished to entertain him and his men to a feast that night. They made no secret of their desires or intentions.

When the men returned, he told them of everything except the precious stones mounted on Aphrodite's breasts. But they were eager to participate in a feast and none showed an interest in even entering the temple. This surprised him and in other circumstances he would have questioned and reprimanded them on their lack of curiosity

After they had bathed in the freshwater lake and dried themselves in the sun and were lying unclothed enjoying the sea breeze, they were interrupted. The priestesses, who had been watching from the temple, emerged in the sunlight. The men were thunderstruck, just as he had been. They watched the women as a trapped animal sees a hunter. They felt in the presence of a fate they were powerless to avert and they covered their nakedness with their shirts and hurriedly put on their clothes. Once they were dressed, the women beckoned and, like men in a trance, they followed. They were in such a state, and this included Idrisi, that they did not notice the maze of winding paths through which they were led to the village. Here they were greeted by other women and of every age. Afterwards they were not sure whether a single male villager had been present. First, they were given love-pipes to smoke and then jugs of red wine were placed on the table underneath the tree. When the freshly roasted goat's meat, marinated in lemon juice and covered with thyme, was served, they ate like men who had been starved for months. They had, but not for the lack of food. It was the women serving them that they wanted. The food was simply a substitute.

It was not the wine but the dried leaves in the love-pipes that intoxicated them. They were ready to be led anywhere. They were. Idrisi remembered being taken by the high priestess. Later, they would boast that it was a night of uncontrolled passion, but when they woke next morning they were all lying on the shore. The only memory of the occasion was the earthenware love-pipe. None of the men were prepared to go back and search for the village where they had been treated so well. Idrisi sent them back to the ship and asked them to wait a few hours. They were frightened and believed they had been possessed by demons. It had been a test of their faith and they had failed. Allah and God would punish them. They pleaded with him not to go alone, but none offered to accompany him.

Idrisi thought he had found the track leading to the lake and the temple, but it was as if they had been led from the very beginning. There was no trace of the path. After several attempts he gave up, but all the time he was there he felt he was being watched. It was a challenge. He would have liked to stay and record the events, but the men were anxious to move on and, reluctantly, he agreed. The memory of the high priestess never left him. Balkis, the Amir's wife, had reminded him of her. He had made detailed notes on the location of Julian's island. It was a twenty-four-hour journey from … He mapped it from every direction, but he never could re-discover the island. When he described the incident to the Sultan he found Rujari at his most sceptical. Who could blame him? And as the years passed, Idrisi himself wondered whether any of this had really happened.

'My lord, we are stopping to rest and eat.'

He looked up and saw they were outside a large house. Two dogs barked furiously until a man emerged and walked towards them. He was thin and finely built, with brown hair and a fresh, if somewhat sallow, skin. What marked him was the fierce determination of his face as he warmly greeted Abu Khalid and bowed politely to Idrisi.

'Welcome to this humble house and treat it as your own, Abu Walid ibn Muhammad al-Idrisi. Who has not heard of your renown?'

'Too many people, I fear,' muttered the scholar as they were ushered into the cool of a darkened room.

'Baths have been prepared for you, but I hope you will forgive me. This is not Siracusa and we have no space for a *hammam*. But fresh water has been brought from the well and if you will accompany these men to the courtyard they will ensure you are well refreshed.'

'Who is your friend?' Idrisi asked Abu Khalid as they followed retainers to the courtyard.

'He is Tarik, my older brother. I think you must have seen him briefly at my wedding. You don't remember? He has had an interesting life. Now all that interests him are fruits and vegetables. He does not eat meat, even in the winter.'

'Does he have a family?'

'Not here. They live in Salerno.'

From Abu Khalid's tone it was clear that this was not a happy subject, but it provoked Idrisi's curiosity.

'Why?'

'Abu Walid, what can I say? When he was eighteen my brother wanted to be a physician, a healer. He would read al-Kindi's *Aqrabadhin* and Ibn Sina's *Kanun* from morning till night. My father, as you know well, was interested only in his estates and their well-being. He was not inclined to humour my brother. He wanted his oldest son to stay at home and help him run the estate and concentrate his mind on devising methods to accumulate yet more land. My brother refused. He ran off to the *maristan* in Salerno where the best physicians are to be found. It's a long story, Abu Walid.'

Water was being poured on their heads and both men shivered with delight.

'Where did he find the book of al-Kindi? I was not aware there was a copy in any library here.'

'You must ask him.'

Lunch was served in another darkened room. Root vegetables of different sorts cooked with the most exquisite herbs and spices were served with freshly baked wheat-bread moistened with olive oil. To drink there was cooled buttermilk, flavoured with mint leaves. And to sweeten their mouths, slices of melons and dates laid on a large platter.

Afterwards Tarik asked in a gentle voice, 'Perhaps you would like to rest?'

'If I rest, we shall never reach your brother's house today.'

'I insist,' said Tarik. 'You have had a long journey on horseback. I think a rest would be good for you. Two miles from here and you are already on the estate. This house was part of it, but he kindly gifted it to me. The family house is less than an hour away. Welcome, Ibn Muhammad.'

Idrisi was exhausted. The bath had helped, but the lunch had made him drowsy. A chamber had been prepared for him and he fell asleep immediately.

An hour later he was woken by a vivid dream. He sat up in bed and drank some water. Why was Julian's island so much in his thoughts today? That had happened twenty-five years ago and he barely recalled those days. Why now? Balkis. She did resemble the high priestess. Was she really Mayya's sister or had she been adopted as a child? And why had she married a barren man? A soft knock on the door interrupted him. It was Abu Khalid.

'We are ready to leave when you are.'

'I wanted to speak with your brother.'

'He will accompany us. He rarely visits the old house, but your presence has been beneficial. I am very happy. I never wished to inherit the estates. I thought I would travel and then settle down in Palermo. Once Umar disappeared my father would not permit me to leave.'

'So your house became a prison. And my daughter, I fear, did not provide stimulating company.'

His son-in-law did not reply.

They reached Umar's house just before sunset. The household had assembled to greet them. At their head stood young Khalid.

'Welcome to your house, grandfather.'

Idrisi embraced his grandson and kissed his cheeks with genuine emotion.

'My son. You have grown already and it's only a few weeks since I last saw you. Come show me your house. I was last here when your father was ten years old. Has it changed much?'

'No.'

It was Umar who replied.

'Nothing changes here. But it will soon. We are living in someone else's time.'

And then a strange-looking man, whom Idrisi had barely noticed, came forward and inspected the new arrivals. He had long grey hair, which almost touched his shoulders, a bedraggled beard, which covered most of his emaciated face, and a pair of fierce, piercing eyes that dominated his features. He wore a clean white tunic, which clashed with his appearance. In his right hand he held a battered old staff and it was this he now banged on the ground as he spoke.

'No!' shouted the man, whose age it was difficult to ascertain. 'Umar Ibn Ali speaks without thinking. It is the infidels who live in our time and we let them.'

Having made this pronouncement he walked away without acknowledging anyone else's presence. Idrisi smiled. He was not impressed. Talk of this sort was not uncommon in Palermo. He realised this was the man of whom Abu Khalid had spoken in Siracusa.

As they entered the house his daughter, Samar, greeted him in exaggerated tones. No longer capable of pretence, he touched her head in a perfunctory fashion. A set of rooms had been prepared for him and his grandson led him there.

'Jiddu,' asked Khalid, 'do you like my father?'

The question took him by surprise.

'Why do you ask such a question, my child. If I did not like your father would I have a spent an unbearably hot day journeying with him to his house?'

Khalid began to laugh. 'I only asked. I'm happy.'

'How many rooms are there in this palace?'

'Thirty-four,' Khalid replied. 'I have counted them many times.'

'Now tell me something else. What do you think of that strange man with long hair, who spoke so rudely to your uncle?'

The boy's face became serious. 'He frightens me sometimes, but when he sees I am scared he smiles and tries to make me laugh. His name is al-Farid, but everyone calls him the Trusted One. He is very poor and travels from village to village where they take turns to feed him. But he couldn't be eating too much. He's very thin. I think he prefers to drink goat's milk with a piece of bread. Abu says he is a great story-teller.'

A retainer entered with a basin and a large jug with water. Idrisi smiled and kissed the boy's head.

Khalid took his leave gracefully. 'I will see you later, Jiddu. There is a lot of meat being cooked for our feast tonight.'

Idrisi washed his hands and face and then allowed the retainer to wash the dust off his feet. The sun had almost disappeared and the muezzin in the village mosque was summoning Believers to the evening prayer. Idrisi covered his head and began to pray. At times of uncertainty, he thought, there is an inner comfort to be derived through prayer. He recalled that his father had described how, after Palermo was occupied by the Franks, many who had not prayed regularly began to attend the Friday prayers at the Great Mosque. For a long time, according to his father, the melancholy cadences of the call to prayer had affected every Believer in the city.

The very size of the midday gathering each Friday enables Believers to derive strength from each other. He had always understood that, but it was only recently that he had experienced the feeling himself. In fact, only two weeks ago when he was informed of the fate that awaited Philip.

The evening meal, as Khalid had warned, consisted of a great variety of meat cooked to honour the visitor. Had it not been for Umar's presence it is doubtful whether any vegetables would have been prepared at all. Idrisi tasted a morsel each from the grilled and stewed meats and exclaimed loudly and appreciatively how tasty they were, but he concentrated on eating the vegetables, raw and cooked, that had been placed before Umar.

'A word of advice for all of you,' Idrisi addressed the table as they waited for the sweet dishes. 'I have travelled to many hot countries and in the summer months very little meat is eaten. Any physician will tell you that meat in the summer produces a heaviness of the heart and slows the flow of blood to vital parts of the body.'

Umar smiled. 'And because Ibn Muhammad is saying this you might take it seriously.'

As platters of fresh fruits were being served there was a loud noise in the distance. The men exchanged uneasy glances as a retainer hurried in to whisper in Abu Khalid's ear. His face relaxed.

'I think the Trusted One is trying to attract our attention. He lit a small explosive to show his followers how the Franks can be defeated. If Ibn Muhammad is not too tired we could walk across to the village and hear his message.'

Idrisi rose from the table. 'A short walk after a meal improves the digestion. Is it too late for Khalid to accompany us?'

Both parents agreed that the best place for Khalid was bed, a decision he accepted with extreme reluctance.

The night was warm and still. As the men walked out of the house, Idrisi looked up at the sky and felt reassured. In front of them retainers carrying oil lamps lit the way to the village. As they neared they could hear chants from al-Quran, but the rhythm and style were different to anything heard in the mosques of Palermo and Siracusa or, for that matter, anywhere else. The Trusted One was reading the verses in short, staccato bursts and his listeners were responding in explosions.

When they reached the village square, Idrisi observed the makeshift mosque with its single minaret. There were at least two hundred men present and each of them had his face covered. The Trusted One had told them to be careful and not to trust anyone in the months that lay ahead. His eyes fell on Idrisi as he leapt to the small platform at the top of the square and began to preach.

'Look around you, Believers, and see who has come to join us tonight. Abu Khalid and Umar ibn Ali we know and respect. They have given me alms and provided me with shelter and they make sure that all of you and your families are fed when times are bad. But they have a special visitor with them. A great scholar from Palermo, he is a trusted counsellor of the Sultan Rujari. Muhammad ibn Muhammad al-Idrisi. Have you heard of him?'

They shook their heads to indicate their ignorance. Idrisi repressed a chuckle. He knew the influence that men like this preacher could wield over the poor and he understood why. Abu Khalid had given him an account of the man and how he lived.

Al-Farid's way of life excited admiration. He lived on alms but would never take more than he required for his daily needs, which were, in any case, modest. He refused all the gifts offered by the landed gentry of Catania, who were beginning to get worried. He did not sleep in a single place for long and when he needed a bed, he insisted on a wooden plank or a cloth placed on the ground. He spent most of his time with the poorest people in the village and it was they who sought him out and spoke to him of their problems. A few of them followed him from village to village and absorbed his message so completely that he sometimes sent one of them to distant regions to preach on his behalf. Despite the growing support for him, he remained remarkably detached and, unlike similar preachers in the past, he showed no signs of delirium or hallucinations. He subjected his body to terrible privations, often undertaking prolonged fasts to test his strength. This rude self-discipline had almost cost him his life. If a passer-by had not forced him to drink water and break bread he would have died. Umar had prepared special herbal mixtures and a careful diet of wild berries and vegetable broth to aid his recovery.

After every victory his body had achieved he would stand up, his face rigid and mask-like, and begin to dance, a strange ritual that nobody in the region had ever seen before, and all the while he would sing songs he had made up in praise of Allah. Legends sprang up about him and he was soon asked to resolve disputes between the peasants in various villages. For ten years or more his word was accepted as the final judgement and he had a huge following in every village. News of the arrival of the Trusted One would spread through the fields and that evening a *mehfil* would take place where the peasants would speak their bitternesses aloud.

It was said that several years ago a landlord raped a peasant woman and she became pregnant. Her husband wanted to kill her. The Trusted One had intervened and saved her life. He then organised the peasants to kill the offender but in such a way that it would appear as an accident. The peasants ambushed the landlord and pushed him and his horse off the edge of a mountain.

And now he was preaching rebellion. 'The news from al-medina is that the Sultan is sick and will soon die. May Allah send him to heaven for he has not been cruel to the Believers, but we cannot depend on the Franks to let us stay here after Rujari's death. They want our lands and they will take them unless we resist. I say this: after Rujari's death we surround Palermo from the outside. The effect will be that of a stone tossed into a beehive. Our people will rise and overthrow the infidel. Where will you be when we come, O great Master Idrisi? Hiding in the library with your books?'

Abu Khalid was angered, but Idrisi held his arm and whispered: 'This man is not at all stupid. The insults do not affect me.'

The preacher spoke for another two hours and the peasants listened to him spellbound. He spoke of the Prophet Muhammad's early life, he told them stories of how the armies and followers of the Prophet had reached the shores of three oceans within a hundred years, he made them laugh and he made them weep when he described how he had been wrongfully arrested and subjected to the vilest tortures. And then he would change his tone and explain how Believers still outnumbered the Franks in Siqilliya and how they could win a victory for their faith if they cast aside all petty rivalries and served in a united army.

'But there is a problem, my brothers. Who will lead us into battle? Whose banner will you follow?'

'You will lead us, Trusted One. It is your banner we will follow,' the multitude replied.

But he shook his head vigorously and raised his right hand to demand silence. 'I am not an Amir of the land or the sea. We can only win if our

Amirs who are today fighting for Rujari decide to fight for themselves and for the cause of Believers everywhere. It is them we have to convince and if we succeed we will have an army and ships at sea. I am a simple man, but I know how battles are won and lost. We will ensure that our faith gives us such strength that we lose the fear of death. That will give our Amirs a group of men who will rival the Franks and their Barons. We will drive them into a sea they should never have crossed. And I spit on the memory of Ibn Thumna who invited the infidels to cross the water and help him fight against other Believers. Let us spit on him together. Allah be praised.'

The multitude spat on the ground in unison.

'The man knows our history,' Idrisi muttered as they walked back home.

'Do you think there is even the slightest chance of success?' Abu Khalid asked him.

'There is a good chance if what al-Farid demanded could be achieved. He laid down three preconditions for success. The unity of Believers, the preparedness to die on the part of the new army and the defection of our leading nobles and military commanders from the Hauteville clan. If we could achieve all these things we could win. The preacher is far too modest. He could grow in stature. Men like him can be pushed forward into making history.'

'I agree,' said Umar, 'but if we are realistic none of this will happen. Our Amirs are far too selfish to even think of the needs of others. They are interested in their own survival and that of their families, and in order to keep their lands they will convert to the faith of the Nazarenes. My brother here will die for the cause, as you can see, and I will probably die with him. In Catania we will raise a large army, but those goat-fuckers in Qurlun and Lanbadusha will never leave their lands. Mark my words, Ibn Muhammad. They will convert.'

And a strange echo reverberated in the darkness. 'Mark his words, Ibn Muhammad. They will convert. They will convert.'

The Trusted One had followed them back and eavesdropped on the conversation.

'Trusted One,' Abu Khalid called out, 'come and join us.'

He came out of the darkness and walked with them till they reached the front of the house. He declined the invitation to share some mint tea with them inside, but fixed Idrisi with a stern gaze.

'I want you to know that even if the rest of the island fails us, Catania will fight. The Amir of Siracusa gave me his word that his men would be with us. The Amir of Catania has pledged his support. We will raise twenty thousand armed men and they will fight till victory or death. Do you think that is enough?'

Idrisi was greatly affected by the simplicity and determination of the preacher. The Trusted One, however, had yet to make up his mind regarding Idrisi. He was inclined to trust him, but he waited to hear his response.

'Trusted One, I will be honest with you. I'm not sure how many armed men will be required to recover this island. It was taken from us by less than a quarter of the number you propose. It is not numbers but strength of belief in our own cause that will determine the outcome. But the main question is as you posed it: will Believers in the hundred major towns of this island join the rebellion? If they do, we will win. The Barons have become lazy and greedy. They are unused to war. We could take them by surprise, but even if we take the island we will have to cross the water and take the fortresses in Salerno and elsewhere. Without them we will be vulnerable to another invasion. As for our people in Qurlun and Lanbadusha, perhaps what you say is correct, but being attached to the land and even conversions to the conqueror's faith are no guarantees that they will be spared if there is an earthquake. And are those people any worse than the communities in Marsa Ali and Shakka? They will blow with the wind. If the storm you are preparing in Catania is powerful enough you will unite many non-believers as well against the Barons. And before I forget, there was a question you posed directly to me. My answer is this: If there is a rebellion I will not act as an individual. If you need me I will be in the Great Mosque with the others, not hiding in the palace library. Does that satisfy you?'

The preacher extended his hand and touched Idrisi's head. 'I am satisfied, but Allah alone will reward you, Ibn Muhammad.'

'Then I am prepared to wait,' replied Idrisi with a half-smile.

They entered the house to the noise of wailing women and Khalid sitting in the hall, tears pouring down his cheeks. Idrisi hugged his grandson and asked what had happened.

'Umi has died.' Idrisi kissed the boy and held him close. And it was in his arms that the child fell asleep. A single tear wet Idrisi's cheek. He sat vacant-eyed until Tarik emerged.

'What happened Tarik? She showed no signs of illness. Where is Abu Khalid?'

'Umar is in his room. She took poison, Ibn Muhammad. A large dose and it must have been a painful death. She took it immediately after the meal. Even if I had been here I would not have had an antidote to that poison.'

'But why?'

'My brother had not been happy with her and scolded her for the treachery she and Sakina had planned. He had not divorced or threatened her. But he found it difficult to speak to her. I think she found the silence unbearable.'

Idrisi began to weep. 'Poor girl. It was their mother's fault, her stupidity and greed ... Tell your brother not to blame himself. It's Samar's mother who should have taken the poison. Has a messenger been despatched to inform her and Sakina?'

Tarik nodded.

'He left for Noto before we returned.'

EIGHT

Siqilliyan sisters. Mayya and Balkis discuss the merits of life with and without men. Secrets are revealed. A plan is agreed to extract Idrisi's seed.

The three women were alone. Elinore was busy packing her clothes and jewellery in preparation for their departure early next morning. Even though she had never met Samar, the news of her half-sister's suicide had disturbed her more than she had thought possible. The incident continued to reverberate in her mind and she was barely listening to her mother and aunt who had been in a strange mood since yesterday.

'If my life were to begin again, I think I would repeat it.'

Mayya was in a philosophical mood and even though Balkis was used to her sister's habit of reflecting aloud she was surprised by the remark.

'I thought you hated the palace-prison. Your description.'

'What I wanted to say was that if my Amir *al-kitab*, the great Master Idrisi, led the same life if I were married to him when he was never at home, the palace-prison was better. I had friends and was never lonely. It's much better than being married to a demanding but absent husband who insisted on being the centre of my life. It's different now that his travels are over.'

'My Amir leaves me alone. He never forces his presence on me.'

'But when he does, is it pleasant?'

'No, but nor is it unpleasant.'

Both of them burst out laughing.

'I know how happy you are these days, Mayya. And seeing you like this makes me both happy and sad.'

'When you said that I thought I heard our mother.'

They fell silent. Their mother had died when they were young. Balkis was only two and could barely recall her. Mayya, ten years older, had retained a few vivid memories. Aunts and their maternal grandmother had brought them up, the aunts out of duty and their grandmother because she loved them almost as much as she had loved her daughter.

'Is it true what they say?'

'Who?'

'They.'

'What do they say?'

'That our mother did not die a natural death.'

Mayya hugged her sister. 'I asked our grandmother and she said it was not true.'

'She would. If she had told you the truth our father would have pushed her out of the house. She had nowhere to go.'

'She could have gone back to Shakka where her sons lived.'

'Mayya, I can always tell when you're trying to hide things from me. What's wrong with you?'

'I think I'm pregnant.'

'Allah protect us!'

'He will. He did last time.'

'Are you sure?'

'I think so. The scholar's seed is as fertile as this island.'

'Not just this one, if the story you told me years ago was true.'

Mayya gave a gentle, noiseless laugh.

'I'm not sure he knows whether it actually happened or was a dream after they had smoked a strong hashish. But how could all the men have had the same dream? Funny you remembered.'

Balkis rose and walked behind her sister's chair. She began to plait Mayya's hair.

'You still haven't answered my question about our mother.'

Mayya sighed. 'I heard the same stories as you and probably from the same source. How do I know if it's true?'

'But Mayya,' pleaded her sister, 'if our mother was killed by her husband there must have been a reason. Our father could barely bring himself to look at me. I cannot remember a single affectionate gesture from him.'

'He wanted a son.'

'Why are you concealing the truth. Why? Will you never tell me? Mayya?'

Mayya had always known the truth but she had wanted to protect Balkis. They were all dead now. But something held Mayya back. An intuition, perhaps, that no good would come out of this story. It had already cost their mother's life. The sight of Balkis sitting on the floor with her hands cupping her face and waiting anxiously decided Mayya. There was no real reason to keep the truth from her.

'We had different fathers.'

The expression on Balkis's face did not change. 'That was obvious even to me. When I was five years old, your father had my head shaved because he couldn't stand the colour of my hair. They pretended I had a fever and grandmother said it would grow thicker than ever before. But I cried every night and you would comfort me till I fell asleep. Remember? As I grew older I realised he hated the sight of me. Sometimes he would leave the room when I entered. And then I realised why he hated me, but there was nobody to ask and you would always deny it. Who was my father?'

'He was a Greek merchant from Djirdjent who bought olive oil from my father. I remember him well. He was not only much better looking than my father but also more intelligent. Our mother must have thought the same. He would visit our house regularly. I suppose one day he found her alone and the gentle breeze of mutual attraction turned into a storm. You were the result. The surprise is that it took father two years to realise that this creature with blonde hair and blue eyes could not possibly be his child. I took after my mother. You were the image of your father.'

'What happened to him?'

'When I became one of Rujari's concubines I sent for him. This was several years ago. He came to the palace and I told him our mother had been poisoned. He had no idea that she was pregnant till after you were born and she sent him a message telling him never to return to Noto. He wept a great deal. He was desperate to see you but our grandmother was still alive and I thought it was unwise.'

'You were wrong.'

'You may be right. He was still young and I thought you could see him some other time.'

'He's dead?'

'Yes.'

'How?'

'An infection of some sort. One of the eunuchs in the palace kept an eye on him. We sent a physician to try and heal him, but it was too late. The disease had spread.'

'He had no family of his own?'

'No.'

Balkis began to weep. Mayya cradled her head and stroked her gently till she recovered.

'Mayya, I have made up my mind. I want a child.'

'Good. The only problem is finding a father.'

'You kept my real father from me. Swear on all you hold dear that you will let me decide who should father my child.'

'Of course I will. I swear on the head of Elinore I will support your choice and do everything in my power to help you trap the beast and extract his seed. I swear it. I swear it. I swear it.'

'Remember how when we were young and I had only to mention that I loved a particular dish for it to reappear the next day?'

'No, but what of it?'

'Who decided?'

'I have no idea. Probably grandmother. She was always complaining about how we never really appreciated her cooking and so when you said you liked something she would cook it three times a week. You are a funny creature, Balkis. We were discussing the father of your child and you turn to food. Do you have a man in mind?'

'We should keep it in the family.'

'Meaning?'

'Ibn Muhammad al-Idrisi.'

The very thought panicked her. At first she thought Balkis was teasing but the look on her sister's face suggested otherwise.

'No! No! Why him. There are enough men in Siracusa who would like nothing better. He's fifty-eight years of age, you know. Did you know that? Fifty-eight! Too old for you. His seed is not strong and ...'

'Mayya, you mustn't be selfish. You swore an oath.'

Her sister's stern tone added to the discomfiture.

'Oaths can be broken. Are you tormenting me? Is this a punishment because I did not let your father see you?'

'No. I just think he would be a good match and there is no risk involved. He is not likely to blackmail me, or is he?'

'But why him?'

'The real reason?'

'Yes!'

'There is something childlike and very attractive about his laughter.'

'Well he won't laugh when he sees you naked.'

It was such a ridiculous remark that both of them began to laugh. It was good-hearted, infectious laughter and it cleared the atmosphere. The over-powering tension that had gripped them suddenly disappeared. Once Mayya realised that her sister was in earnest she began to think seriously. Balkis watched her in silence for several minutes and then raised an inquiring eyebrow, only to be answered with a finger on the lips. Finally she could contain herself no longer.

'Well?'

Mayya was feeling light-hearted again. As long as she organised and controlled the whole affair it might be good fun. If possible she would find a hiding place from where she could watch the whole scene, unbeknown to the two principal performers. She still did not think it was a good idea, but if it had to be done, it should be done properly. Left to herself, Balkis might wreck everything. She would then look at Mayya in her unforgiving way and blame her for the disaster. And why shouldn't Muhammad al-Idrisi help Balkis in her hour of need?

She knew that people often preserve a memory of something, half-imagined, half-real that has happened to them in their youth. Later in life they think back on it as something exceptional or magical, outside the common order of things.

'I have thought of a plan, but for it to succeed a number of conditions need to be met. First, he must never know that I know. Second, he must not believe that the woman entering his bedchamber is you ...'

'But ...' interrupted Balkis.

'Please, let me finish. And lastly, when you see him again in the morning you must pretend nothing happened.'

'What if nothing did happen? I mean, what if we didn't succeed the first time?'

'You can try again, but in exactly the same way.'

'I accept the conditions. Now reveal each and every detail of your plan.'
She did, but before the rough edges could be refined, Elinore burst into the
room.

'Are we definitely leaving for Palermo tomorrow?'

Her mother nodded assent.

'Why do you want to go back so soon Elinore? Why not wait for your
father. He will be back in a few days and then both of you can return on his
boat. Much nicer than going on a cart.'

'I find Siracusa so dull, my aunt. All my friends are in Palermo.
Everything happens there. I have heard of interesting happenings near
Noto. They say there is a long-haired preacher with rapture in his soul who
is spreading disaffection throughout Catania. Is this true? Have you heard
of him?'

Balkis waved her hand in a dismissive gesture.

'My husband knows him and says the man is half-mad.'

Elinore was not going to accept this. 'That means he is also half-sane.'

Her mother glared at her.

'Well,' responded her aunt, 'if you're interested in the Trusted One –
that's what they call him – you had better wait for your father. He must have
met him on his son-in-law's estate.'

Elinore was torn. She was desperate to return home to see if any of the
eunuchs had succeeded in finding the flute-player who had entranced her
with his music. But the thought of waiting for her father was also attractive.
She debated the merits of each case in her head and decided in favour of the
boy who played the flute. They would return early tomorrow morning.

Her mother accepted the decision for her own reasons. She did not really
wish to be in Siracusa when Idrisi returned. Balkis making eyes at him would
be intolerable. Despite her show of support for her sister, Mayya was
nervous about the cruel and monstrous pact they had sealed. Her brain was
in a whirl. It was better if she was not present when Idrisi returned to the

palace. If he even suspected her involvement she would be covered in disgrace. Elinore's free-and-easy manner appeared to have convinced her aunt that they had to leave and unwittingly provided a neat solution to her mother's dilemma.

'Balkis, I do not wish you to wake up early on our account. We will leave before the sun is up, while Believers are being woken for the morning prayer. We will not disturb you. Let us say our farewells now.'

Elinore kissed her aunt warmly and left the room.

Balkis took hold of her sister's hands and held them tight. 'You are afraid of my impulsiveness. You're beginning to regret our agreement. I love you, Mayya. You were a mother and a father to me. If I have hurt you I am prepared to withdraw my suggestion and declare our agreement dead. I want nothing to come between us. Nothing.'

Mayya, touched by the offer, did not speak immediately, but embraced Balkis and kissed her. 'We have made a deal. Let us stay with it. It will not affect anything between us. That much I can promise you. I hope it works the first time, that's all. I don't want you to make it a habit.'

And on that note of warning the sisters parted.

NINE

Idrisi reflects on rebellion and is surprised in his sleep.
His seed is extracted more than once.

The resplendent morning cheered Idrisi. He had an early breakfast and left for Siracusa accompanied only by armed retainers. He had permitted neither Abu Khalid nor his brother Umar to accompany him. They had more important tasks at home.

The death of his daughter had led to much soul-searching on his part and Idrisi wondered if matters might have been different had he spent more time with his daughters and educated them. Then he would, once again, return to the root of the problem: his marriage. Even though he was only eighteen at the time he should have resisted his father.

Last night he had composed a short letter to Walid.

My dearest son:

I write with sad news. Your sister, Samar, died ten days ago. I was present in the house the day she decided to take her life. It took us all by surprise as there had been no indication that she was on the edge of despair. Young Khalid walks around in a bewildered state and it is difficult to console him. His father blames himself, but unfairly. He is a kind and considerate man and is not to blame for what happened. If anyone is to blame it is me. I should have been less harsh with her after uncovering a foolish and treacherous plan to bear false witness against her husband was exposed. It was her mother's idea. She and Sakina became willing tools through stupidity more than malice. It would be foolish to provide more details in a letter that might not even reach you.

Your mother and Sakina arrived for the funeral, but stayed only a few days. I spoke with them briefly, spending more time with my grandchildren whose intelligence you would appreciate more than most.

I have been thinking a great deal of the past and will come to Venice before too long so we can sit and talk. You can't imagine how much I miss your presence. The ripple of laughter and the babble of voices when your friends would come to see you at our house remains a cherished memory.

I embrace you,

Abu

He rode at a furious pace, anxious to reach Siracusa before sunset and set sail for Palermo early next morning. He had left the city in despair, searching for possible escape routes from the disaster that lay ahead. Rujari had not replied to his letter pleading for mercy. Perhaps he should have stayed and pleaded with the Sultan every day. Now he wanted to make one last effort to persuade the Sultan to spare Philip's life. Rujari had treated Philip as his own son. He knew that the human sacrifice demanded by the Church and the Barons – a sacrifice to which Rujari had agreed – must nonetheless be tormenting the Sultan.

When Idrisi had discussed Philip's imprisonment with the Trusted One, the preacher had mocked the community of Believers in Palermo. If they let Philip die without resistance, they would perish themselves.

Despite himself, Idrisi had begun to fall under the preacher's spell. At times his superstitious beliefs irritated him, but the fierceness and fervour with which he spoke against the land-grabbing Church and the mercenaries it employed as its hangmen were admirable. And the multitudes he aroused were far from credulous. They knew he spoke the truth and they compared him to their Amirs and landowners who vied with each other to appease and please their enemies, especially the monks, who were constantly preaching sermons advocating terror and violence to rid the island of Believers and Jews.

From where did this religious passion come? It was a response to the fires that had been lit to destroy what he had long regarded as indestructible. The early victories of the Prophet and the resulting triumphs had created a civilisation so proud and conscious of its superiority that, like the ancients of Greece and Rome, it became infected with the idea that this superiority made it invulnerable. A fatal error.

But the Trusted One had been right to draw attention to the treachery that had led to the invitation despatched by Ibn Thumna, the Amir of Siracusa, to the Franks. Events that had taken place a hundred years ago were still fresh in the imagination of most Believers. How many times had Idrisi heard the story of the evil and promiscuous Amir, Ibn Thumna, who had killed the pious and noble Ibn Maklati, the Amir of Catania, for reasons of sheer greed. He wanted more land. The murder was avenged by Ibn al-Hawwas, who inflicted a crushing defeat on the Siracusan Amir. It was then and simply to save his own skin that Ibn Thumna had invited the infidels to cross the water. He was killed in battle alongside them, so gained nothing in the end. He was probably roasting in the fires of hell at this very moment. It suited Idrisi to think of somewhere hotter than Siqilliya.

(@

He looked up at the sky. Not a cloud in sight, even though the shepherds had predicted rain last night. Sweat poured down his face and neck and he yearned for a moist sea breeze as they galloped on. He would not rest till the men pleaded on behalf of their horses. Coming to a grove of trees, the trunks and boughs twisted by the wind and wounded by lightning and the leaves parched and withered, he relented. As he strolled among the trees he could hear the men talk of the Trusted One. When he joined them they fell silent, but he asked if they had attended the *mehfil* at the village. They nodded without volunteering any information.

'Would all of you join the army of which the Trusted One spoke?'

Again they nodded.

'You are prepared to die, but for what?'

'So that the prayers can be said in the name of the Caliph once again.'

'Is that all?'

Another voice replied. 'Many of our people work as slaves for the Church. When we defeat the infidels we can free all our people.'

Then the youngest of them, who had not spoken, said, 'We are poor people and you are a great scholar. How can we tell you anything you don't already know. But you can teach us a great deal. Do you think we can win?'

Idrisi thought before replying. 'I don't know. There is a tendency amongst our people to boast loudly of our capacities. We became too selfish and vainglorious. If extravagant language could defeat the enemy, we would never lose a single battle. And then there is this island, which has a magical effect on all who come here, regardless of their faith. Geography and local conditions isolate us from other lands and, Nazarene or Believer, we begin to adjust to the conditions here. The geography of this island shapes our character and in fifty years or more – Believer or Jew or Nazarene – you will not be able to tell the difference between us. We become Siqilliyani facing the same problems.'

The men did not know what to make of this, and smiled but remained silent. Ready to move on again, they covered their heads and mounted their horses.

A gentle wind arose and clouds had already darkened the sky as they reached Siracusa.

Idrisi was greeted by the palace steward, who informed him that the Amir was expected back later that night. A bath had been prepared for him and the Lady Balkis would join him for the evening meal.

'Are the Lady Mayya and Elinore here?'

'They returned to Palermo a few days ago.'

He had been hoping to find his daughter on her own and take her back with him. Why had Mayya gone back so soon? Balkis would have the answers.

He went to the *hammam* where a warm aromatic bath had been prepared for him. Camomile, wild thyme, marjoram and yes, mountain-mint. Was that a bundle of black nightshade he saw floating in the water? It was. He lifted it out of the bath and handed it to the attendant.

'Who chose the herbs?'

'The Lady Balkis.'

He made a mental note to tell his sister-in-law that nightshade should only be used to cure insomnia. As he slipped into the bath he felt the soothing powers of the herbs extracting the tiredness out of him. He lay back and enjoyed an infusion that was poured on his head, after which the attendant massaged it for what appeared to be a very long time. He insisted on a cold bath to get rid of the slight drowsiness and soon emerged feeling completely refreshed.

A different bedchamber had been prepared for him, but since the view of the sea was even better, he did not complain. It was raining and the sea was rough. He could see the boats along the quay bobbing up and down like a row of horses before a race. An attendant knocked on the door to tell him that the meal was about to be served. He followed her to a set of rooms where he found Balkis awaiting him, dressed in a gaudy red tunic, her golden curls tied in a knot. The colour did not suit her.

'Welcome back, Muhammad ibn Muhammad. I am only sorry my husband is not here to greet you. As you can see, the weather is really bad and I think he will not arrive till tomorrow. The messenger who brought the news said that the Amir insisted you not leave for Palermo without seeing him.'

Idrisi bowed politely. 'I'm touched by your hospitality. If the storm carries on like this I doubt I will be able to leave in the morning. I will wait till the Amir returns. I, too, have things I wish to discuss with him.'

'I'm sorry to hear of your daughter's death. Were you close to her?'

'No and that makes me feel guilty. But let us not talk about sad things this evening. I was looking forward to seeing Mayya and Elinore. Why did you let them depart?'

'It was Elinore who insisted.'

For a while they ate in silence.

'Balkis, I have been wondering. You and Mayya don't look like sisters. Did you have different mothers?'

Balkis smiled and said as if it were the most normal thing in the world, 'No. Different fathers.'

'I'm sorry. I did not mean to pry.'

'Should I tell you the whole story?'

'Please do.'

While he was listening, a serving woman cleared the table, and another placed little bowls of herb infusions in front of them. So enraptured by Balkis was Idrisi that he sipped his without noticing the *shahdanaj al-barr** and honey. Its effects were not immediate, but even as he listened he felt a light-headedness emboldening him in the way he looked at her.

Abruptly he asked, 'Why did you decide to wear this unbearable red dress? The colour does not suit your complexion. Was it deliberate?'

'What would you like me to do?'

---

* Wild hemp.

'Take it off and ...'

Her laughter interrupted him. He was relieved it was not a stupid or a malicious laugh, but delicate and careful without being precious. There was no movement of the hand to conceal her lips, a gesture he disliked in women.

He returned to her story. 'Did Mayya know?'

'She knew for a long time but only told me the entire truth a few weeks ago. Ibn Muhammad, would you ever kill a woman who betrayed you?'

The reply was instantaneous. 'No.'

'And now it's your turn for a story. Mayya told me about the strange island of Julian, but she was not sure if it was real or imagined.'

Another bowl of the potent brew was placed before him. He accepted it eagerly. Then shut his eyes in silent appreciation. He told the story of Julian's island, not sparing her a single detail. He recounted the night of passion and the different ruses the high priestess had used to excite and revive him after they had made love the first time. Idrisi was so engrossed in his story that he did not notice her blushes. He had succeeded in physically exciting her without a single touch. She rose from the table and suggested they retire for the night.

｡

When he returned to his room, Idrisi opened the shutters to watch the storm. No stars were visible in the pitch black sky, only flashes of lightning and hard rain. He undressed and fell on the bed. A little later an apparition – or so he thought – floated into the room, dressed in white. It was ... no it couldn't be ... yes it was ... he was sure ... it must be the high priestess from Julian's island.

'Is it you?' he whispered in Greek.

'Yes.'

Idrisi fell on his knees before the keeper of Aphrodite's flame and slowly worked his way upwards till she, like him, was naked.

'The storm outside, it frightens me.'

She went to the window and closed the shutters.

He took her by the hand and led her to his bed. 'It is the storm inside that frightens me.'

What followed was a night of pure passion. Balkis had heard his story well and she mimicked each and every incident that he had described. Idrisi barely opened his eyes. He felt he was being washed in waves of bliss as he explored the mounds and crevices of her body.

She wanted to whisper in his ear: 'I'm Balkis, I'm not your stupid high priestess. It's my body you're pleasuring. Mine. And I want your child.' But her part of the bargain could not be broken. She had promised her sister that she would not reveal her identity. If Idrisi recognised her, she had another carefully prepared story. After they had made love for the third time her exhausted lover fell into a deep sleep. As he turned over to make himself comfortable, he broke wind noisily, like a thunder-clap. It was the only time that night she was reminded of her husband.

She left the chamber. Safe in her own rooms, Balkis could smell him on her and her body tingled with delight. I hope it didn't work tonight, she thought. Anyway, how could one tell? We will have to do it again just to make sure. Thank Allah she had not refused to learn Greek when she was a child. What if he decides to leave before nightfall? I will stop him. I will send a secret message from the priestess. I will do anything I have to in order to keep him here for just one more night. Just one more. And if necessary I will accompany him to Palermo to see Mayya. She'll kill me, I know, but I refuse to let him go. She shared Rujari with Allah knows how many other women. Why couldn't she share Muhammad with only me, a sister who loves her? What if Mayya and I are both pregnant? With this thought in mind she finally fell asleep.

And Idrisi? Perhaps it was the herbs. Perhaps the passion. Perhaps both. He had not slept as comfortably as this for a long time. He did not wake till he heard the muezzin early next morning.

He shivered slightly as he remembered the erotic dream of last night. *Ishq khumari*. Bacchic love. Then he smelt her perfume and her body on his. Had it been real after all? He sniffed his arms like a dog. Then he went on all fours and sniffed the sheets. Delicious scents invaded his nostrils. He lay back perplexed, but happy. There was no mistake. A woman had been here last night. They had made love. It was no dream, but how could it be the high priestess exactly as she had been all those years ago? Was that possible? And then he remembered the herbal infusion he had drunk. It was not dissimilar to what he and his men were given on Julian's island all those years ago.

The more he thought, the more agitated he became. Only one person could have wanted to test him. Mayya. But who played the part of the high priestess? The moment he posed the question he knew the answer. Balkis. The vulgar red dress was designed to distract him from what she would wear later on that evening. Ibn Hazm had argued that it was permitted to look at a woman once, but not the second time. He had looked at Balkis the whole evening and she had drugged him as well. And the reason now became obvious. It was he who had suggested to Mayya that in a storm many seeds begin to fly.

Three courses of action were open to him. The storm had died and the sea appeared calm again: he could leave for Palermo without saying a word. He could confront her, demand an explanation, and then leave. Or he could spend another night here. The thought of seeing her again – but this time as herself – began to excite him. His breakfast had been laid on the terrace and as he sat down he saw her on the neighbouring terrace, looking in the direction of the sea.

'Allah be praised, the sea is calm this morning, sister Balkis.'

She was startled, but only for a moment. She had been waiting over an hour for him to come out.

'Did you sleep well, Ibn Muhammad?'

'Better than I have done for many years. I can't imagine why.'

Her tranquillity shaken, she turned away from him. He stepped over the wall separating them.

'This is the Amir's terrace,' she said nervously. 'He has been delayed in Palermo and asks you to join him as soon as you can.'

'In that case I should leave immediately.'

'No,' she replied, her voice stifled with passion.

He took her by the arm and gently guided her into the room. He extended his arms and felt both her breasts. She flinched.

'Strange, these friends seem familiar.'

'You knew?'

'Not last night, but this morning when my head was clear.'

She fell into his arms as a devouring passion gripped them. Blind to all else, they made love in the Amir's large bed below a canopy embroidered with gold thread. After the storm had passed, he looked at her closely. 'Balkis, my dear, I think the seed will flower now. And for that reason it was appropriate that you chose your husband's bed. Have I your permission to return to Palermo?'

'No!' she shouted and slapped his face. 'No. No. No. No.'

'But I must go. Your husband and my wife await me.'

'It's not just your seed, it's you I want.'

'But you barely know me.'

'I do now.'

'First, you must answer me truthfully and avoid any further deception. And keep looking straight into my eyes. If your gaze falters I shall know you're trying to avoid the truth.'

'I will not deceive you. Ask your question.'

'I thought I detected the hand of Mayya behind this delicious plot, especially the opening scene last night. She knows everything?'

'It was my idea to extract your seed. She was not happy, but later when I insisted that this was what I wanted, she laid down a condition. If it had to happen, she would prepare everything. She did, Muhammad.'

'Including the *shahdanaj al-barr*?'

'Especially that ... the rest I learned from you when you described in such wonderful detail the love rites of Aphrodite's high priestess. It's as if you were describing a landscape or the flowers, herbs and trees that grow here. Now I understand why they say you are a many-sided scholar and if you will permit me I would ...'

Idrisi interrupted her: 'I will not deny that my eyes found themselves following you more than is permitted. And I confess that images of you entered my head during the long ride to Abu Khalid's village. And if you were not married to such an honourable and decent soul, it would not matter, but you are, and for that reason alone we must not repeat this. Ever.'

'He's such a decent and honourable soul that you dragged me into his bed and kept me there till your passion flowed. Now you talk as if nothing had happened. If you really want us never to repeat this then we won't, but I don't believe you. I've held you in my arms and I know you felt exactly the same as me. The situation is difficult, but solutions can always be found.'

'And what about your sister?'

'We'll agree to share you. She can have you for the first two days and me for the next three.'

'I thought there were seven days in a week.'

'After I've had my way, you'll have earned two days' rest.'

He began to laugh. 'You are impossible.'

Her eyes filled with longing. 'Why. It's quite normal, except that Mayya and I are half-sisters.'

'Balkis, you are married to someone else.'

'He will divorce me if I ask him. We can discuss this on the journey to Palermo.'

'You're coming with me? This is foolish.'

'Why? My sister and husband are already there. I will stay in the palace, not with you. There are no children to keep me here.'

'Balkis, listen carefully. You can travel with me, if you insist, but the ship is a public place and decorum must be preserved. If our weakness triumphs the whole of Palermo will know that the Amir is a cuckold even before you reach the palace.'

'Muhammad ibn Muhammad al-Idrisi, my Sultan of love, I will do as you say. Balkis will be the most modest and demure passenger your vessel ever carried.'

'I had a presentiment that it would end like this.'

'Surely you mean begin like this.'

A few hours later they were on the sea for Palermo. The veiled lady was sitting in a cabin sipping tea while the scholar-lover was pretending to make notes.

'I know they can see us, but surely we can talk.'

'Of course we can talk.'

'Then tell me about Abu Nuwas.'

'Balkis!'

'What? Just talk about him. If you don't I'll walk up to you in full view of the men and kiss your lips.'

'You promised ...'

'Yes, but only if you behave normally as well, agree to speak with me and answer my questions. Surely we're not going to make this journey in total silence. It's not often that a humble woman like me has the chance to travel with a great scholar. So perhaps we could start with the poetry of Abu Nuwas.'

Despite himself, Idrisi was amused and impressed by her.

'Abu Nuwas was born in Basra, a hundred years after the death of our Prophet. He moved from there to Kufa to study, Basra and Kufa being the cities where even well-educated scholars enhance their learning. Kufa was famous at that time for its grammarians and Abu Nuwas arrived to perfect his knowledge of our language. Later he moved to Baghdad, but this was largely for employment and pleasure.

'He was a poet much favoured by the Caliph and became the subject of story-tellers in the bazaar. According to one story, Shahrazad is late one evening and enters the Caliph's bedchamber to find him sprawled on his front with Abu Nuwas riding him like a horse. Shahrazad feigns horror. Abu Nuwas withdraws and stands up naked. She slaps his face. He replies: "We're just proud and penetrating men, Princess." She threatens to inform the *qadi* unless the Caliph releases her from her side of the bargain. He agrees, but pleads with her not to stop telling her stories. From that day onwards he pays her ten gold dirhams for each of her stories, which get better.'

A discreet giggle interrupted his flow. 'Muhammad, is that true?'

'It's a story they tell in the bazaar of Baghdad. It fulfils two functions. It informs us that Abu Nuwas and the Caliph liked men even though al-Quran forbids such acts on pain of death. Secondly, the story is designed to appeal to an important section of the audience, the street-traders. For Shahrazad to be paid for her daily labour would seem natural to them. And the fact that the stories improve is a hint that voluntary labour is better than slavery. The Zanj would have liked that.'

'I'm more interested in his poetry.'

'I have read it, of course, but can't recall it. I'm more familiar with the work of Ibn Quzman, my friend in al-Andalus. He is a disciple of Abu Nuwas and his verses are sung in many cities, especially after a few flasks of wine.'

'Is it true that Abu Nuwas has written of a perfect religion in which it is obligatory to make love five times a day instead of praying?'

'It's true but impractical.'

'Not for you.'

'Balkis!'

'I'm sorry.'

'What I meant was that the older men get the more difficult it becomes. Abu Nuwas was unaware of this problem, but old men would have to be pardoned their inability to perform five times. What would they do instead?'

'Dissemble as so many do now when they pray.'

'Let me finish the story of Abu Nuwas. The real subject of his poetry was the joys of wine. He was the link between the world that existed before our Prophet received the message and what was created afterwards. Wine was the substance that linked all worlds. It was timeless and universal. And many a time did Abu Nuwas inquire politely why, if wine and young boys were permitted in paradise as written in al-Quran, were they forbidden this enjoyment on earth. So he made fun and he had fun.

'Another time he developed an unusual interpretation of jihad. He wrote that the main obligation of jihad should be to permit the drinking of an amber-coloured wine that sprays fire when lit and, more importantly, have sex with young boys who had not yet sprouted beards as well as with old men. There was only one reward for victory in this jihad. Paradise.'

Balkis clapped her hands in delight. 'That also explains why the five obligatory fornications could work with old men. Once young boys are *hilal*, old men would have few problems in meeting their obligations. They could do so in a passive mode. Am I upsetting you?'

Before he could reply the agitated commander of the boat entered the cabin and bowed. 'Forgive the intrusion, Amir *al-kitab*, but an armed vessel has signalled us to stop. Their commander wishes to speak with you.'

'Who are they?'

'It is one of the Sultan's ships. It was once the favourite vessel of Amir Philip.'

Idrisi looked at Balkis who failed to hide her concern.

'There is no need to worry, Lady Balkis. I know the men on that ship well. They are completely trustworthy. While I'm away, think carefully of your five obligations and how you will fulfil them in Palermo.'

Idrisi followed the commander to the deck. The moment the men from the armed ship saw him they fired a cannon in his honour. Long years ago he had travelled with them to Ifriqiya. Now he waited as the elaborate ritual of transferring a distinguished personage from one vessel to another took place. A boat was lowered with Idrisi and two armed sailors, who rowed him to the adjacent vessel. A giant catapult was then lowered with a man casually clinging to it. He secured the scholar and then both were rapidly lifted to the deck at great speed.

Ahmad Ibn Rumi, the Amir *al-bahr*, had replaced Philip as commander of the fleet. He was a haughty man with an independent air about him. He often conveyed the impression of being impenetrable, to ward off syco-phants and time-servers, but Idrisi, who knew him reasonably well, knew it was a mask often worn by Amirs with real power. Philip had been the same. The two men embraced and Ahmad conducted his guest to his cabin. The first thing Idrisi noticed on the table was one of his maps. After admiring his handiwork, he turned to face Ahmad. The man was sitting weeping silently. In a world where many would have viewed the removal of an Amir with eager and greedy eyes, Ahmad Ibn Rumi was deeply wounded by Philip's fall from favour. Idrisi spoke softly. 'Ahmad, dear friend, I too am upset, but there is nothing we can do. Philip insists we let him die. He says we are not yet ready to win and we should wait till Sultan Rujari passes away.'

'May Allah roast that serpent Rujari in hell for this crime.'

'The monks pray that God will raise him to heaven for defending his faith.'

'It has nothing to do with faith. It's a blood sacrifice to save the throne for his family. The whole of Siqilliya is aware of this fact. Ibn Muhammad, I asked you here to discuss a plan.'

Idrisi knew what to expect.

'With four big vessels already in port in Palermo we have the capacity to take them by surprise and rescue Amir Philip.'

'We discussed all these possibilities with him in the Great Mosque. You know him better than me. He will not be moved.'

'He is wrong.'

'I agree.'

'He is the only leader we have capable of uniting the Believers after Rujari's death and leading us to victory. Do you agree?'

Idrisi fell silent. He knew where this sort of argument would end. He also knew that Ahmad spoke the truth. Without Philip, the community of Believers would be orphaned. It was Philip's military and political skills that had prevented a bloodbath on the island. He thought by sacrificing himself he would provide time and space for his people to organise, but he did not ask who would lead them. Rebellions without a plan were common on the island. Each and every one had been defeated.

'Why do you not answer?'

'Because kind friend, Ibn Rumi, to reply in the affirmative would encourage your adventure, to reply in the negative would be an untruth. Best to remain silent.'

'Ibn Muhammad, I was in Catania as well. I, too, met the Trusted One.'

Idrisi's heart sank. The preacher would have incited rebellion.

'He promised us an army of ten thousand armed men could reach Palermo quicker if I transported them in my vessels.'

'I hope you didn't agree.'

'No. I said I would think before taking any measures.'

'Allah be praised, Ahmad. Allah be praised. If you had agreed and let him down, word would have spread far and wide. The Barons and monks would have demanded that you be burnt with Philip.'

'I asked only for your advice. I will decide on my own.'

'Of course. But when you make the decision, ask yourself the consequences of rescuing Philip and hiding him in Ifriqiya. That is your plan, is it not? I thought so. But while your ships sail away, who will defend the Believers in Palermo? It will become impossible to restrain the Barons. They will want blood in the rivers on either side of the *qasr*. Our blood.'

'The alternative is to let Philip burn? Will not many of our people curse us for not even making a single attempt?'

'But if you make an attempt which fails you will die as well. Who will that help? If you succeed, all of us in Palermo, including your wife and children, could be killed. Rujari is no longer strong enough to prevent a massacre. I have a better plan.'

'Speak.'

'The day after Philip burns, the Trusted One should organise raiding parties to Catania and Noto to punish the Bishops and monks and the Lombards they have hired to protect them. They have stolen our lands and treat the peasants who once worked on those estates as slaves. The Bishops are hated and for good reason. They demand the right to deflower our women on their wedding nights. The Lombards flog the men at the slightest pretext. A carefully organised rebellion in this region where we are still strong would have an impact in every corner of the island. The Trusted One could make it clear that this is our response to the crime committed against Philip al-Mahdia. What do you think?'

Ibn Rumi reflected before he spoke again, 'You are determined to sacrifice the life of the only man capable of leading us to victory.'

'It is *he* who is determined, not me.'

'The path you recommend is not without merit. I will think about this carefully. If you see my ship heading back to Siracusa you will know I have accepted your plan. Otherwise we shall meet in Palermo.'

The two men embraced, but just as Idrisi was about to leave, Ahmad took his arm and whispered fiercely in his ear, 'Philip means more to me than my own father.'

Idrisi gripped Ahmad's hand. 'I know how you feel and how difficult this decision will be for you. Whatever you decide, remember I am always there as your friend and will help in any way I can.'

An hour later the two ships had still not lifted anchor. Idrisi anxiously paced the deck, waiting to see the direction in which the Amir of the Sultan's fleet would decide to sail. Balkis was walking with him. Hearing what had happened her first response had been to wonder where her child would be born. He became angry with her, then controlled himself and explained patiently why there were some things in this world that transcended love, passion or the production of children. At a time when the fate of the entire community of Believers was dependent on the decision of Amir Ahmad it was selfish and thoughtless to contemplate one's personal future. She had never heard him speak so harshly and angry tears filled her eyes.

She returned to the cabin and waited. How dare he assume she didn't care about anything else except her own life and that of her unborn child? She was determined to punish him. For a start, she would not speak to him for the rest of the journey. Before she could think of more severe punishments the men on the deck started cheering and, her dignity evaporating, she rushed to join them. Idrisi was laughing and waving like the others. Ahmad had set course for Siracusa. As the two ships passed each other, loud cries of 'Allah Akbar' rent the skies. Ahmad stood on the deck and raised a hand in farewell. Idrisi responded with the same gesture. Both men wondered whether they would see each other again.

'Hoist the sails,' shouted the Commander. 'With this breeze we may reach Palermo within the hour.'

Balkis walked back to the cabin in as aloof a fashion as she could invent. Her lover followed her but each attempt he made to speak with her was rebuffed. She looked away from him. He sat down at the table with a manuscript he had removed from the palace library at Siracusa and pretended to be deeply engrossed. After a quarter of an hour had elapsed he decided to break the silence.

'It is time for the afternoon prayer, but I am not in the mood. If you have no objection I will recite a verse for you.'

She did not reply. Idrisi rose from his chair, climbed on top of the rough wooden table that separated them and sat cross-legged on the table before her. She succeeded – just – in keeping a straight face. He then adopted a posture typical of a person preparing to read al-Quran.

> '*Say O disbelievers, I do not worship what you*
> *worship and you do not worship what I worship;*
> *My mores are not those mores,*
> *That's not my school or style*
> *Bacchic love, stand and rise!*'

She could no longer restrain her laughter, at which point he slid neatly off the table and placed himself on the bench next to her. He kissed her hands and then drew back.

'Where did the great scholar find this verse? Abu Nuwas?'

'No. Ibn Quzman.'

'I though you said we had to be careful on this journey.'

'The men are all busy preparing the ship for arrival and you dispensed with caution when you paced the deck with me, then quarrelled and abandoned my side. All that implies familiarity.'

'I am your sister-in-law.'

'Nobody knows that apart from us.'

'I hadn't thought of that, I confess.'

He held her close and kissed her mouth. Her hand moved down his tunic.

'You've pitched your tent early today Master Idrisi. I think the pole needs to be dismantled.'

'Enough, enough, Balkis. Your hands are on fire. When we arrive, you will be taken to the palace, where your husband has been lodged. I will go to my home, bathe, dress and visit all of you later. Perhaps we can all eat together.'

'With Rujari.'

'If necessary.'

'There are times when I cannot understand you at all. This man is about to despatch Amir Philip, burn him alive in public. Amir Philip, according to you, is the most intelligent and gifted political leader on the island. Perhaps you can't save his life, but to sit at the table with his killer? Is that not taking your sense of duty a bit far?'

'Listen to me, my dearest Balkis. One thing many of us had to learn, Philip included, was how to dissemble most effectively. If I refuse to eat with the Sultan he will know that I am angry and, given his state of mind, he could punish everyone associated with me. We must behave as normally as possible at a most difficult time. I hope Rujari does not invite me to the palace. In that case I suggest we break bread at my house.'

'That would be a delight.'

'And Balkis, remember what we discussed earlier. Not even a hint of what has transpired between us must reach your husband.'

'And Mayya?'

'Leave that to me.'

And then the sailor on lookout waved excitedly and the familiar cry was heard: *'Al-madina hama-hallahu.'*

Balkis recovered her composure, tightened the scarf that covered her head, veiled her face and the two of them went out on deck. As they were rowed to the shore he could see the unmistakable portly figure of the Amir of Siracusa in the distance. He gently nudged the Amir's wife.

When they docked, the two men embraced.

'Allah be praised, both of you have arrived safely, Ibn Muhammad,' said the Amir. 'The situation here is more tense than you could imagine. We need

to speak urgently about many things. The Sultan's health continues to dete-
riorate and the atmosphere in the palace reflects that of the city. Only the
Barons and the monks appear happy these days. They say the Sultan asks
each day when you will return.'

'I will see him today.'

'There's not much time, Ibn Muhammad. The trial of Philip is due to
start tomorrow afternoon.'

'Sooner than I had thought.'

'They want to make sure Rujari is still alive when Philip is burnt. A Baron
from the mainland who is here as a judge confided to me that if Rujari died
they feared a rebellion.'

Idrisi took his leave of them and joined Ibn Fityan who had been waiting
for him. The two men rode home together.

'In answer to the question you posed before I left I can say with confidence that the Amirs of Siracusa and Catania are with us.'

'Friends in the palace had already given me the good news. The Sultan
expects you for the evening meal.'

'I feared as much.'

Ibn Fityan told him that the city was like a mountain of fire. It could
explode at any time and the Barons had placed their own men at key points
of the city for the duration of the trial.

'Remember what Philip said at our *mehfil* in the mosque before I left: any
premature uprising will be defeated. So every quarter of the city must be
told that the trial of Philip is designed as a provocation to draw us out before
we are ready and kill us.'

'The *qadi* has already sent out this message, but people are angry. There
could be trouble despite the *qadi*'s best efforts.'

'Send out the word that the Trusted One has organised an army in
Catania that will take back a number of monasteries and inflict public
punishments on the Bishops. Tell people that we should wait for the news

from Catania before anything rash is done here. Why did the Amir of Siracusa prolong his stay in the city?'

'The Sultan asked him to attend the trial. He will ask you as well.'

'He will get a rough answer.'

'Master, there is a more delicate matter.'

'Speak your mind.'

'A report has reached friends in the palace about you and the Lady Mayya.'

'What do the idle minds say on this occasion?'

'They say that Elinore is your daughter and that you and her mother were married in Siracusa.'

'How did the news reach here?'

'The palace in Siracusa is filled with our friends. They hear everything.'

'What if what they said was true?'

'If the news reaches the Sultan he will react badly. He will compare his generosity to you with this betrayal.'

'Silence, man. Philip's trial starts tomorrow and I have neither the time nor the desire to discuss whether or not I succeeded in gaining the good graces of one lady or another.'

Three armed retainers accompanied him as he walked towards the palace. He could not recollect how often he had made this journey at all hours of the day and night. But this phase of his life was coming to an end. The steward who greeted him was an old and familiar face. He spoke in a voice weakened by old age. 'Welcome once again, Ibn Muhammad al-Idrisi. You come at a sad time.'

'Peace be upon you, friend,' Idrisi replied as he followed the old man through the usual set of rooms with wooden architraves and mosaics that recalled an earlier past.

The Sultan was in his private audience chamber, a room Idrisi knew well. But he had to wait in the antechamber until the Sultan's visitors had left. He wondered who they were and why they had been summoned at this hour.

Rujari usually conducted business during the first half of the day. The old steward sat next to him and, looking in the direction of the Sultan's chamber, whispered in a broken voice, 'A *mehfil* of killers is taking place. Last minute preparations for tomorrow's trial. Everything is already decided. He has been found guilty. Tomorrow they will burn him.'

Before Idrisi could reply several Barons and three Bishops came through the door looking pleased with themselves. The steward bowed and escorted them out of the antechamber. In contrast to previous occasions, none of them bothered to acknowledge Idrisi's presence. He strode into Rujari's chamber without waiting for the steward to return. The Sultan seemed genuinely pleased to see him. How could he be so remote from reality?

'I'm glad you're back. I need you by my side.'

'I just saw the men who are on your side. Barons bloated with too much food and Bishops living off the fat of lands they have stolen.'

'From your tone, Idrisi, I detect that you will not be present at the trial tomorrow.'

'The Sultan will forgive me, I hope. The sight of your foster-son being falsely accused, found guilty and burnt is something I do not wish to witness. It is bad enough living with my conscience, powerless to prevent Philip's death and too weak and cowardly to do anything myself. It would appear that we have returned to a primitive state of conflict between our two communities.'

'It's not easy for me, Muhammad. You know full well I have not long to live.'

'Philip al-Mahdia was your best chance of keeping your family on the throne. The Barons will not leave the Hauteville clan alone for too long. Who will defend them once you have gone?'

'I have made my choice, Master Idrisi. And I fully understand your repugnance at what I have done. It's best if you stay away from the palace for a few weeks till this storm blows itself out. And you have my permission to take Mayya and Elinore with you. She has inherited your intelligence. You should be proud of her.'

Idrisi, caught by surprise, asked in a low voice: 'You knew?'

'From the beginning.'

'Then why ...'

'Because to have acknowledged that I was aware of what had taken place could have established an unhealthy precedent. It was Philip who advised total secrecy. Your own Sultans would have ordered the executioner and made your neck taste the scimitar. For that reason Philip was against letting you know. But in my heart I was happy for you.'

'As always, Philip offered you sage advice. I thank you for your friendship and generosity. It has always meant a great deal to me.'

'I wish I did not have to do what I am going to do. I hope you believe me.'

Idrisi did not reply, but bowed out of the room. The steward was waiting for him.

'The Sultan suggested I take the Lady Mayya and Elinore home with me.'

'It was time,' said the steward in a soft voice. 'Follow me Master Idrisi.'

They walked to the harem, guarded by two eunuchs who rose on seeing the men approach.

'This is the harem of Sultan Rujari,' the shorter of the two men spoke. 'What business do you have here?'

The steward whispered something in the man's ear. The door was opened and the Chief Eunuch alerted the women.

'On the orders of our exalted Sultan Rujari, a male guest is entering to visit the Lady Mayya.'

A flurry of doors being shut and from behind exquisitely latticed windows curious eyes observed his entry. Idrisi followed the two eunuchs into the women's quarter and to Mayya's rooms. Answering the knock on her door, she was shocked to see him. 'Why are you here? This was not agreed.'

'I have the Sultan's permission to take you and Elinore home now.'

Mayya was astounded. Stepping aside, she invited him into her chamber. He had last come here eighteen years ago and the result had been Elinore. How different it had been on that occasion. He had been disguised as a woman and a small purse of silver coins was the price demanded by the eunuch on duty, who had subsequently disappeared. Had Philip ordered his execution?

They embraced each other as she wept.

'I never thought it would happen so soon. Do we have to leave now?'

'That was the Sultan's instruction.'

'But my ... our clothes ... our ... Elinore.'

'All that can be sent to my house tomorrow. The Sultan has asked me to keep away from the palace for some time.'

'I can't believe I'm free, Muhammad.'

'Let us not waste any more time. Where is Elinore?'

'She is with Balkis and the Amir in the guest chambers. I think I should break the news to her alone. Let me go and bring her. Should we meet you at the palace gates or would you like some time on your own to explore the harem? And we will have to pack some clothes just for tomorrow.'

'I will wait for you in the steward's chamber near the gates. Try and avoid too much excitement and invite your sister and her husband to join us for the midday meal tomorrow.'

'Muhammad, tomorrow is Philip's trial. The Amir of Siracusa has been asked to attend and there are notables from Qurlun and other cities here as well. And you?'

'I have told the Sultan I will not be present. In that case Balkis could come with you now. Why should she be present here tomorrow? And ask the Amir to come and join us after the trial. I doubt it will take a long time.'

'I will ask Balkis to come with us. The whole palace is upset. I had no idea that Philip had so many followers. The eunuchs can barely speak. Most of the old retainers walk about with sad eyes. As for those who work in the Diwan, they feel it's the end.'

She looked around her rooms for the last time, finding it hard to believe she would never live here again.

TEN

A twenty-six-year-old conversation on theology
in which Rujari and Idrisi compare the merits and
demerits of their respective religions.

The meeting with Rujari angered Idrisi. The Sultan appeared distant and unconcerned. Idrisi wished he were dead. How could Rujari have forgotten the past so soon and accepted the demands of corrupt Barons, hypocritical and grovelling Bishops and empty-headed courtiers? Then he controlled his thoughts. He did not wish to feel only hatred and resentment for his old friend. He recalled one of their many conversations.

It happened when they were still young. It was a stifling midsummer's day. There were no breezes on land and no waves on the sea, whose smooth surface shone like glass.

Rujari sent a message to his friend in the library, suggesting they board his ship and cool themselves in the sea. Idrisi remembered how shocked the Greek sailors were when, on his first voyage, he admitted he did not know how to swim. An islander who could not swim! With great patience they taught him how to use his hands and legs and breathe in the water, how to stay afloat, and gradually he acquired the skills.

They found a beautiful cove not far from Palermo. After their swim, they had mainly talked geography and astronomy and Idrisi had praised the accuracy of Ptolemy's maps, commenting that the Alexandrian must have had a fine eye and skills that had so far eluded him. Time had passed quickly. On the way home they sat on deck and savoured what was left of the day, enjoying the sea breeze that rose as the sun began to disappear. Each had won a game of chess before Rujari asked an attendant to take the pieces away and bring a flask of wine. Turning to Idrisi, he asked whether differences between their two peoples were rocks that could not be shifted, or might their faiths become intertwined in the years ahead. Idrisi hesitated before replying.

'There is no such thing as a rock that cannot be moved. When the gods are angry, as the ancients used to say, they shake the earth and whole cities are destroyed. It would need something on that scale to unite the armies of the Prophet and the Pope.'

Rujari laughed. 'I wasn't thinking about the world. I was thinking of Siqilliya. I meant that my people had learnt so much from yours that it seems to me natural for us to work together and share the same faith.'

Again Idrisi hesitated. 'Sultan, this island has changed a great deal since the Prophet's soldiers set foot here. My people have a natural tendency to exaggerate and boast, even when we are defeated. When we win, our pride reaches the heavens. The Greeks came here first, then the Romans. The Greeks built their temples, tended to the grape and the olive tree and philosophers from differing schools disputed in public in the Forum in Siracusa. The Romans cultivated the land for the wheat, needed to supply the imperial legions. My people have brought fruits of every description and cotton and the silkworm and the papyrus and made Palermo a city that cannot be surpassed. You inherited all this, but you too have contributed to the riches of the island. Your presence is proof that it is possible to buy gladiators and use them against the enemy. Your people were fighters and sailors.'

'I speak of now, Idrisi, now.'

'But honoured Sultan, with your permission I would like to finish. We do have much in common. Your people mastered the sea, my people the desert. You became great boat-builders, we learnt how to ride the camel and the horse. You burnt your way into the lands of the Franks and they bought you off with land and your own space. We defeated two Empires and created our own. Our ship was the camel, but much more reliable than yours. It could travel sixty Roman miles a day and go for twenty days without water. A few dates and camel's milk was a nourishing diet. The people in Makkah still enjoy cooking in the fat taken from the camel's hump. Which ship could ever be as reliable as that? In both our cases it was nature that determined what we did and how we moved. In the end our needs were greater and we were more successful.'

Rujari was slightly irritated. 'Our women were easier, accepting their place in our lives with dignity and calm. Yours were barbarians. Your Saracen women – and many Romans whose writings are in the palace library have testified to this – were too forward, too passionate, too demanding. Often they discarded their husbands.'

'Sultan, you speak of the desert people during the time of Ignorance, before our Prophet heard the voice of Allah. The women were brought under control by our faith.'

'Perhaps in public, Master Idrisi, but in the confines of the palace or the home nothing much changed. Why, your own Prophet needed a Revelation to silence the scandalmongers who alleged that his young wife, Aisha, had committed adultery.'

Both men fell silent. It was Idrisi who spoke first. 'You asked if on this island we might one day share a common faith. How can we ever believe that Mariam was impregnated by Allah to produce Isa? Your faith was too close to pagan times and you had to make compromises. You needed a virgin goddess who slept with your God. Was this not Zeus in another form? And we find it difficult to believe that Isa was resurrected.'

'Why? Your book talks of the Day of Judgement where every man will face his creator. Some will go to Heaven and others to Hell. If they can be resurrected at Allah's will, why couldn't God recall Jesus? As you know, Idrisi, these are unsettled questions in our Church. There are many Christians who do not accept the divinity of Jesus. Are there any in your faith who question the Revelation?'

'Too many, alas, and from the earliest times. The Prophet's own wife, Aisha, according to traditions, commented many times on the ease with which her husband obtained sanction from Allah to satisfy his personal desires. And the Prophet's successor Caliph Omar was heard to say that he was often surprised when the advice he had given the Prophet in private turned out to be exactly the same as a later Revelation. And a whole group of theologians in Baghdad argued that al-Quran was a man-made document, thus questioning its divinity ...'

'Enough for one evening, Master Idrisi. I readily admit that your religion permits far greater pleasures in this world and the next than does mine. For that reason alone, leaving aside the knowledge spread by your learned scholars, if it was up to me alone and nothing else was involved I would convert to your faith this very moment.'

'Perhaps, if the ships bringing Your Majesty's forebears to the land of the Gauls and Franks had been diverted by sudden squalls and had instead reached the ports of al-Andalus, all might have been different.'

'Why did that not occur to me?'

'Because geography and history are ever present in my thoughts.'

'One thing I promise you, Master Idrisi. As long as I am alive the Church will not be allowed to kill or burn a single person simply because he believes in your Prophet and not mine.'

And that is how the conversation ended or so Idrisi had thought. But later that night, Philip al-Mahdia had visited him in his rooms.

'I heard of the conversation you had with the Sultan today.'

Idrisi was stunned. How did he know?

'It is legitimate for you to question, but it would be unwise of me to reply. All I will say is that you made a great mistake.'

'In Allah's name, what mistake? Why do you talk in this fashion?'

There was an undercurrent of anger in Philip's voice. 'When the Sultan declared that if it was up to him he would convert to your faith, why did you not suggest that he should do so, but not make it public? For the Church and the Barons he would be a Christian, but in private say the five obligatory prayers. Why did you not suggest that, Master Idrisi? Do you realise what an opportunity has been missed because of your thoughtlessness? You are so concerned with your own work that you have lost sight of the larger world.'

Idrisi was so astonished by this outburst that for a few moments he stared at Philip in silence. 'I did not ask what you suggest for the simple reason that the thought did not enter my head. Rujari is a friend, but he is also the Sultan. It was not my place to suggest anything to him.'

'One day,' said Philip calmly, 'our people might suffer because of your mistake.'

'Why are you so concerned? You are not even a Believer.'

Philip smiled and left the room.

ELEVEN

The trial of Philip.
The Amir of Catania farts loudly
during the prosecutor's speech.

The large hall where the Sultan met his subjects once a month had been transformed. The throne remained on the elevated wooden platform, but the empty space in front was now crowded with wooden chairs and benches laid as a semi-circle. In the centre a platform had been prepared for the prisoners: in addition to Philip a few of those who worked for him had also been arrested and charged to create the impression of a conspiracy.

The Barons entered first, dressed in their regalia, their swords dangling from their waists, and took their seats on both sides of the throne. They were followed by other sections of the nobility and then the judges entered, flanked by the Bishops with several monks in attendance. The prosecuting judge was seated just below the Sultan's throne. After they had all been seated, the Amirs of Catania and Siracusa, together with a handful of Muslim notables from Qurlun, Djirdjent, Shakka and Marsa Ali as well as the *qadi* of Palermo, were permitted to enter and seated on the benches at the back, where it would not be easy for the Sultan to see them.

The hall fell silent when the Chamberlain entered and announced the Sultan. For the occasion Rujari had discarded his Arab robes and, like his Barons, was dressed as a Christian knight, the crown resting firmly on his head. Everybody present rose to greet the King in three different languages. Rujari nodded and the trial began. The prisoners, chained to each other with Philip at their head, were brought into the hall. He walked in with his head raised high, prepared to meet the eyes of the Sultan or his Barons. It was they who averted their gaze. Ten eunuchs known to be close to him were charged with exactly the same offences. They, too, conducted themselves with dignity.

The prosecuting judge, who had once worked for Philip, rose and listed the charges. 'Philip al-Mahdia, you and those creatures by your side are charged with having betrayed the trust placed in you by King Roger. You are accused of having aided our enemies in Mahdia and Bone in Ifriqiya. You are accused of having concealed your real faith from the King and his court. Beneath the cloak of a Christian you behaved like a child of Satan. In mind and deed you followed the doctrines of Muhammad and you instructed the State treasury to give unlimited amounts of money to maintain the mosques in good condition. You sent special emissaries with offerings to the tomb of Muhammad. When it was suggested that this money be registered in the records, you dismissed the suggestion with an arrogant wave of your hand.

'You frequently attended the synagogues of the Evil Ones and provided them with oil to fill their lamps. You offered them all the assistance they needed to practise their abominable faith. At the same time you rarely set foot and even then unwillingly in the churches of God. You ostentatiously ate meat on Fridays and during Lent.

'The King was alerted to your infidelity when it was reported to him how you had permitted Muslim scholars and pious men to flee to their villages after you had conquered Mahdia and Bone. It is reported that you punished some of your own soldiers when you saw them taking a few women prisoners for their personal enjoyment.

'And lastly, Philip al-Mahdia, we will produce witnesses who will swear on al-Quran that you have been a secret Muslim all your life. Your conversion was false. What trust can the King put in you after all these events? You were brought up in this palace and the King loved you like a son. You rose to the highest position in the land after the King. And you have brought disgrace on him. What do you say to all this?'

While the indictment was read the Amirs and the other Believers were restless. Their discontent was reflected in excessive shuffling, a regular clearing of throats, occasional sighs and at least two loud farts, all of which combined to produce a distinctly uncongenial atmosphere. As Philip prepared to address the court there was total silence. Whereas the prosecutor had addressed the court in stilted Latin, Philip spoke in fluent Arabic. 'I did not betray the Sultan's trust. This Sultan has, till now, been kind to me and regardless of what happens today I wish to state that Sultan Rujari Ibn Rujari has been a just ruler. He has treated all the people of this island well, regardless of their faith. He has never insisted, till now, that prisoners be brutalised and their women violated. So I reject the principal charge you bring against me, to the effect that I betrayed the trust of our ruler.

'Nothing I did was in secret. Yes, I provided oil for the synagogues. The Sultan knew and approved. Yes, I did not permit the decline of the eighty remaining mosques in Palermo. The Sultan accompanied me once to see for himself the improvements in the Ayn al-Shifa mosque of this city. When you say I was hardly in church you speak a deliberate untruth and may God forgive you. The Sultan knows how many times I attended his own chapel. He knows how often I went to the church he has built in Cefalu at every stage of its construction.

'Let us proceed to the next charge. I was too lenient to prisoners in Ifriqiya. I plead guilty. I treated them as I would treat any human being. The fighting was over. We had won an important victory. The Zirid dynasty crumbled to dust before my eyes. Had I been soft-hearted in the course of the battle you would have had cause to bring me before you. But on behalf of this Sultan, I took al-Mahdia, the city of my youth. I will not hide from you the inner pain I felt. That I was instrumental in taking this city gave me no pleasure, but my loyalty to Siqilliya was never in doubt. The Bedouin whom I paid to fight on our side wanted to loot the city indiscriminately and take their pleasure of any woman, young or old, who was not already in hiding. War arouses the lust for loot and human flesh. I gave firm instructions that this should not happen. When these were disobeyed I had three Bedouin and six of our own soldiers flogged in public for rape. Yes, I stood there and watched them bleed. Do I regret that? No. And I would do it again. I think in better times the Sultan would have defended all these actions.

'I have nothing more to say. I know that the fires that will consume me have already been lit and I am prepared to meet my Maker. I have done nothing of which I am ashamed. My only regret is that I had no opportunity to live among our people because whenever I asked myself how the earth procured the food we eat in order to survive the answer was never in doubt. It was the ordinary peasants on the land who produced the food and from the comfort of this palace, I sometimes envied them their closeness to the earth. I remember mentioning this to many people.

'To the Sultan I will say this: if I have offended you in any way I beg your mercy and I apologise. I have always been loyal to you and your family. Those who have poisoned your ears with regard to me are the same people who will try and get rid of your sons and the system of administration that your father and you helped to create. Think of that when you watch me in the flames.'

The Barons rose to protest and shouts of 'Cut off his tongue' were heard from the mouth of more than one monk. The prosecutor had worked himself into a confected rage.

'We have a witness who will testify that this man concealed his real faith behind a Christian mask. Bring him in.'

The guards brought in a venerable merchant, Ali ibn Uthman al-Tamimi. He was one of the most respected traders in the city and had attended the *mehfil* at the Ayn al-Shifa mosque which Philip had attended just before he was arrested. The marks on his face suggested that violence had been inflicted on him.

The merchant was asked to swear on al-Quran that he would speak the truth. He spoke in a very low, broken voice, not daring to face Philip. But he did not mention the meeting. He testified that on a single occasion he had prayed together with Philip at the mosque. The evidence was enough to condemn him. As he was leaving he looked up at Philip with tearful eyes and in a voice that was heard throughout the hall he said: 'Forgive me. They threatened to rape my ten-year-old daughter.'

At this point Philip, greatly angered by the sight of an old friend who had been humiliated and tortured, demanded to speak. The Sultan nodded. 'Burn me, if you will, but do not inflict suffering on innocent people. Yes, it is true I was a secret Believer, but my sin lay not in my belief but in my cowardice. I should have told the Sultan and for this I beg your pardon and plead for your mercy. I was very young when I came to the Court and you were so kind to me that I wished to please you in every way. But when I accompanied the Amir George to Mahdia, memories of my childhood over-whelmed me and it was at that time that in my heart I became a Muslim once again. I do not regret my choice. I know you will burn me today for that is the custom of your faith. But before I am sentenced I wish to address the Sultan directly.'

Rujari looked at him and for the first time their eyes met. Rujari nodded and turned away quickly. 'I thank you, gracious Sultan. You more than anyone else present here – and I do not see our friend Master Idrisi in this gathering for which I thank him – understand full well that the reason you and your noble father were able to resist the commands of the Popes in Rome was because, even after the conquest of Siqilliya and the handing over of the most fertile estates to your Barons and the Lombard barbarians from the North, even after all that, my people are still a majority on this island. That is why your Barons speak and understand my language. And that is why you and you father could resist papal demands to send soldiers to fight in the Crusades. We were your strength, we gave you the courage to be independent, our learning, our language, our culture enabled you to boast that you were superior in every way to your poor cousins in England, which was only the truth.

'Living under an occupation is never easy, but your family made it less painful because you needed us for your own reasons. And we needed you to survive. If you destroy us – and forgive my boldness ... but we all know that the decision to burn me is a victory for those who would like to burn every Believer on this island, if you destroy us you destroy yourselves. One, perhaps two, Hautevilles might reign as kings. Then your fellow religionists will sweep southwards and take what they believe belongs to them by papal right. At that time there will be no force left here to defend your family. As for these unfortunate eunuchs you have imprisoned with me, they are completely innocent. Their only crime is that they worked with me, but then so did the Sultan for many years. To punish them is base and unworthy and I would plead for mercy on their behalf. Spare their lives. You have mine. Your monks and Bishops wish to consign me to Hell. But Allah alone will decide.'

As he stepped back and bowed half-ironically to the Sultan, the Amir of Catania could not contain himself. He rose from his bench. 'Allah will send you to heaven, Philip al-Mahdia. *Allah akbar.*'

Angered by this display of insubordination, Rujari rose from the throne and still refusing to look his old friend in the eye he addressed the court. 'Most distinguished sirs who sit in judgement today, my words are for you.

My soul is pierced by the greatest grief, and roused to passion by severe torments, because this minister of mine, whom I raised from boyhood so that, having been purged of his sins, the Saracen might become Christian, is yet a Saracen and, under the name of faith, has done deeds of faithlessness. Had he offended our majesty in other ways, had he carried off a greater part of our treasure, we would have forgiven him because he had done great service for us. But because he has offended God and has furnished others with the opportunity and the precedent of sinning, and because I should not forgive an injury to our faith and a crime against the Christian religion by my own son, nor should I acquit anyone else. In this act let the whole world learn that I love the Christian faith with absolute constancy and do not refrain from avenging any injury to it, even by my own ministers. For this reason are laws set up and for this reason our laws are armed with the sword of fairness; they wound the enemy of the faith with the sword of justice, and thus they set a terrible snare for the infidels. Most distinguished sirs, you who are here to judge this crime, do your duty.'

The Barons clanged their swords to show approval of their king. Rujari, exhausted, slumped on the throne. The Barons, justiciars and judges did not take too long in their deliberations.

'We decree that Philip, a traitor to the name of Christian, and an agent of the works of faithlessness under the disguise of faith, shall be consumed by the vengeful flames, so that he who would not have the warmth of love shall feel the fire that burns, and so that no trace shall remain of this worst of men, but that, having been turned to ashes by an earthly fire, he may proceed to perpetual torment in the eternal flames. His fellow-conspirators in evil are also sentenced to death but by normal methods.'

The Amirs and the Muslim notables did not stay to watch the Christians savour their triumph. As soon as the Sultan limped out of the chamber, they left the hall and the palace. A loud wailing could be heard in a section of the palace as they made their way into the streets. To their astonishment these were empty. The people of Palermo, even the Nazarenes, had no desire to witness the fallen Philip dragged through the streets in ignominy. Before they parted the Amir of Catania took them aside and said: 'They have declared war on us. And I, for one, will not willingly become a headless chicken. We will fight in Catania. We will not surrender and become their slaves or be killed without a struggle. All of you will make your own choices, but I hope you listened carefully to Rujari's words. It is the end of Siqilliya as we have known it. My friends from Qurlun, your choice is very clear. Either you fight with us or convert now to their faith and turn your mosques into churches. Do not wait for them to do it. In that way you might save your lives, if not your property. I do not know if we will meet again. Peace be upon you and may Allah protect you all.'

A noble from Qurlun restrained his departure. 'Before you leave, give me your advice. Is there any way we could save our property as well as our lives?'

'Perhaps by offering the Barons half of what you own tomorrow and your daughters the day after. But don't delay too long. And one more word of advice. You Qurlunis are so inbred that you think you're cleverer than everyone else and that your secrets remain safe within your community. You saw what happened to Philip. If you convert, do it properly and don't meet in secret to pray and fast or circumcise your boys. Learn to worship the bleeding man on the wooden cross and the mother who remained a virgin after his birth.'

The Amirs of Catania and Siracusa walked away together, both enraged by Rujari's speech and the verdict.

'I hope Rujari dies soon, freeing us from our oaths of loyalty. Our presence here is now under serious threat. Our culture is tottering and if we do not act it will fall.' It was the first time the Siracusan had spoken that day.

'I think his speech has freed us already. Idrisi's messenger told me that the Trusted One will instruct his followers to capture three monasteries the minute they receive the verdict on Philip. I think the lighthouses will be

busy today. My ship is ready to sail. Are you accompanying me or did you
bring your own vessel?'

'I did and will sail later today.'

The two men embraced and went their separate ways.

Inside the palace walls, Philip was handed to the justiciars, who removed
his chains and tied him to the hooves of wild horses. The horses had to be
restrained as they reached the gates. Every palace window was crowded
with people. They watched in horror and it was later reported that young
William, the only remaining legitimate son of Rujari, had tears in his eyes.
He had been exceptionally close to the condemned man. Philip had taught
him astronomy. The Barons and monks and their retainers stood behind the
horses to follow the victim to his death. Outside only a few monks and
Nazarenes watched, but less than a hundred in all, and this in a city of three
hundred thousand people. There were reports that the mosques and synagogues were overfull that day as special prayers were said to honour Philip.
The *qadi* was seen hurrying in the direction of Ayn al-Shifa to try and
contain the hotheads.

The palace gates were opened. The grotesque procession moved
forward. Philip's limbs were bleeding, but he held his face high even as he
was being violently dragged and some of those who had come to watch
turned away. A lime-kiln close to the palace had been prepared and a fire had
been blazing even before the trial had begun. The justiciars untied the man
who was covered in blood. They lifted him above their shoulders and hurled
him into the flames.

Then they all returned to the palace where a grand banquet had been
prepared in honour of those who had passed judgement on an enemy of
their faith. Rujari pleaded ill-health and was not present at the celebrations.
Nor was his son William.

After a private conference with his friend from Catania, the Amir of
Siracusa had instructed his men to make the ship ready to sail at short notice.

Walking slowly towards the house where his wife was lodged, he felt a hand on his shoulder. A shiver of fear ran through him, but it was only a grim-faced Idrisi and his retainers.

'Ibn Muhammad, what a relief it is you,' he said wiping the sweat from his face.

'It has been a catastrophe. The trial was as you suggested, even worse.'

'I have just returned from the mosque. It was a dignified farewell but our young men are angry and I fear there will be some violence in the city tonight. Were you walking to my house? Good. We shall arrive together.'

'Ibn Muhammad, could you ask your men to let us talk on our own?'

Idrisi signalled to Ibn Fityan who told his men to slow down. The Amir confided to him that they would now plan a full-scale rebellion in their regions and drive the Franks out.

'It will take us a few years yet, but the preparations must start now. I know I sometimes give people the impression of not being as steadfast as the Trusted One. But whatever doubts I may have had disappeared today. They declared war on us. That's why I have a favour to ask of you ...'

TWELVE

Idrisi's love for Balkis and its consequences.

Idrisi did not have long to wait for the three women outside the Chamberlain's room at the front of the palace. Relieved of their hurriedly packed clothes by his retainers, he walked back with them to his house. The sky was so starry and active and Idrisi so delighted that he almost forgot the weight of events to come.

'I thought that nights like this happen only when one is young,' he said.

'I am young,' replied Elinore. 'And I will never forget this night.'

'I'm not as old as you and I too will remember this night,' said Balkis.

'I am older than both of them, but why should enjoyment be left to the young?'

'How far is your house, Abi?'

Idrisi smiled before replying. 'None of you know the loneliness that has afflicted me for so many years. When Walid left home without telling us I thought everyone was forsaking me and I became despondent. Tonight I feel all that is over. And we are nearly home. Can you see those lit windows on the hill? Another few minutes and we'll be there.'

A palace messenger had already conveyed news of the Sultan's decision releasing Mayya to Ibn Fityan and so he was waiting with the rest of the household to welcome the new lady of the house and the master's daughter. Balkis was was welcomed equally warmly. The torches held high charmed the women as they walked up the steps.

'Have the rooms been prepared?'

'Yes, Ibn Muhammad,' replied the steward, 'but we were not expecting a third guest. It will not take long to prepare a guest chamber.'

'This is the Lady Balkis, who is my wife's sister and whose husband, the Amir of Siracusa, will probably join us here tomorrow.'

Ibn Fityan was impressed by this news. It answered all his questions.

'The *hammam* has also been prepared.'

The women had already bathed once that day and declined the offer. They asked for an infusion of fresh mint leaves and were escorted to the terrace. Mayya wondered whether she should accompany Muhammad and talk to him while he was bathed, but thought it might be too soon.

Idrisi's intention was to have a bath without being disturbed and meditate on the thorny problem that had been preoccupying him ever since they had left the palace: Balkis or Mayya? It might be his only chance to lie in Balkis's arms before her husband arrived and they departed for Siracusa. What if Mayya insisted, as was only natural, that they should spend the first night here together and make up for lost time? It would be inhuman to resist such a plea. Balkis, who loved her sister, would understand. He had made up his mind, but doubts persisted quite simply because his heart was pushing him in the wrong direction. Left to himself with no other considerations, he would have rushed to Balkis. He knew he might live to regret it and yet, if Allah was kind and gave him ten more years, it was futile to live them in a sea of unhappiness.

As he left the *hammam*, refreshed and ready to face his new life, he had decided in favour of Mayya. He would allow nothing to deter him from this path. Ibn Fityan had laid the table in the dining room that was rarely used. The rectangular table could easily seat twenty-five people, but he had prepared just one end of it for Idrisi and the ladies. As they walked in he looked admiringly at the different colours worn by Mayya and Elinore, but it was Balkis who took his breath away. She wore a high priestess off-white robe and had lifted her hair back with a silver clasp.

The welcoming feast was pronounced a success and the sweet home-made lemon liquor, which Idrisi insisted was a much more effective digestive than a similar concoction made from aniseed, was highly praised.

'Mayya told me you were a master of medicine as well,' Balkis said in a slightly indifferent tone, 'but I had no idea you prepared medicinal mixtures.'

'I do and I even have one which helps get rid of unwanted pregnancies, which is much in demand on Lombard estates. They rape our women who are too ashamed to tell their brothers, fathers or husbands. They go to the local medicine man and plead for the herb that will purge their system. It works. You will not find the prescription in al-Kindi's *Aqrabadhin*. When I was in Cairo I introduced it to the physicians at the al-Nasiri *maristan*. They were pressing me to write a book on compounded drugs and herbs that could help common ailments. If I have time I might yet write such a work.'

Balkis glared at him and Elinore, thinking her father was being somewhat insensitive to her aunt's lack of children, decided to change the subject.

'This lemon drink we all loved tonight. You distilled it yourself?'

'I used to, but the Sultan liked it so much that I was forced to part with the formula and from the palace it has spread to the monasteries and estates. My own supplies now come from the palace. I'm really surprised you have never tasted it before. I would have thought the eunuchs would have made sure the harem was regularly supplied.'

For some reason this made Balkis laugh. 'You speak as if this was the only drink available in the palace. And what if the eunuchs hated it?'

Mayya, aware of the slight tension between Balkis and Idrisi, wondered what, if anything, had taken place in Siracusa. She followed her daughter's lead in making sure he was confined to a safe subject.

'Muhammad, I was trying to remember that friend of yours who you talked about endlessly some years ago. The man who distilled what you said was the most beautiful elixir you had ever tasted. I could not recall his name or where he lived or even the name of the drink.'

Idrisi laughed. 'Muammar ibn Zafar! He died two years ago and his foolish son sold the fruit orchards to a merchant from Shakka. You would all have liked him. He was one of the most gifted cooks whose food I have had the pleasure to taste. But the elixir was something very special. He used to call it the Heavenly Nectar. Once when I was staying with him to ask his advice on cures for constipation, which was common amongst sailors, he devised a suppository with the most effective mixture. It was October and a great deal of fruit was lying on the ground. Oranges, lemons, peaches, apricots, tangerines and others I cannot recall. His men were ordered to collect these from the ground. The undamaged fruit was washed and placed in a large perpendicular earthenware pot, almost as tall as Balkis. No, a bit taller. To these fruits he added saffron, black pepper, crushed ginger, and peeled clusters of garlic. Then the pot was sealed with a flour paste and left outdoors till the following April. I was present one year when the seal was broken. The most delicious aroma greeted us. Muammar stood on a ladder and stirred the pot till it was properly mixed. I tasted it before and after it was distilled. Completely different each time but equally unforgettable. Al-kohl. Pure. Heaven. I would consider myself lucky if I tasted a drink like that again before I die.'

Elinore clapped her hands.'But surely we can try to make it ourselves. Can't we try? Just a small amount?'

'Certainly, child. You can try, but don't be disappointed if you fail. There are some things in this world that are best tasted once.'

'But I haven't tasted it, Abu.'

After the table was cleared, the retainers were dismissed for the night. The four of them looked at each other in the candlelight. Elinore and her mother exchanged glances before the young woman addressed her father.

'Abu?'

'Elinore bint Muhammad?'

'I know this is a difficult request, but as you know, the move to your house from the palace was sudden, perhaps too sudden and we were emotionally unprepared …'

'I cannot imagine your mother being emotionally unprepared for anything.'

'It's me more than her. I'm really happy to be here, but you must understand it will take some time for me to adjust to the change.'

'I understand that, child, and will do all I can to make it easy for you. Allah be thanked, I have finished my book. The Sultan has gifted me a small vessel and unless he revokes the order, which is unlikely as he is not a small-minded ruler, then we can travel together.'

The delight on Elinore's face was visible. But she now broached another matter.

'I would love to travel. I had never set foot outside Palermo till we visited Siracusa a few months ago. But Abi I want to ask … if I can sleep next to Ummi tonight? Just tonight because I'm feeling unsettled.'

That Idrisi managed to frown at this request was a tribute to his ingenuity – or so he told himself. 'Elinore, I grant your request – but do not repeat it too often. And now I wish to speak with your mother alone for a while, if that meets with your approval?'

She embraced her father before leaving the room, accompanied by Balkis who had barely spoken the whole evening and appeared engrossed in her own thoughts. She had avoided his gaze and restricting her talk to trivial questions about Palermo. Was she doing it simply to annoy him? It did not occur to him, that unlike her sister, she might not be feeling too happy.

Alone with Mayya in his chamber, they embraced warmly. Then she looked carefully around the room and at his bed.

'It was generous of you to let Elinore sleep in my bed tonight. She is uneasy, which is not surprising. Everything has happened far too quickly for her. I think she is torn about the move. A part of her wished to stay in the palace till Rujari's death. She is very fond of him, you know.'

'And he of her, but this Sultan is already dead as far as I'm concerned.'

'With Philip out of favour and Rujari dead, will the treasury continue to pay you?'

'The mother of my children lives on the estate in Noto, but I have another that I have not visited for many years. It came to me after my brother died without an heir. We could sell that to the Church or to a Baron. It is a large estate. Or I could leave it to you and Elinore. I have barely spent any money for the last ten years. This house and the retainers are paid for by the treasury and a few years ago the house was legally registered in my name for services to the state. Life will not be as luxurious as you are used to, but we will not starve.'

With that, he turned the conversation. 'I had a strange dream in Siracusa.'

She feigned ignorance as he told the story of the ageless high priestess who had left behind unmistakable scents.

'Surely you were mistaken. Your own body, as we know, leaves many a trace without the presence of anyone else.'

'Mayya, deceitful woman, how long are you going to maintain your story?'

She looked at him in astonishment. 'You found out?'

'How could one not? The drug was effective, but it did not obliterate my memory.'

'So what happened afterwards?'

'Has Balkis not told you?'

'Elinore did not give us a moment to ourselves, though I noticed a strange smile on my sister's face.'

He told her the rest. With a resigned expression on her face, Mayya asked, 'She really wants to live here, with us?'

'She had no idea any more than you and me that this would happen so soon. We were discussing the situation after Rujari's death and the inevitable changes in the palace.'

'But she would be happy to leave the Amir and live as your second wife?'

'Third.'

Mayya began to laugh. 'You lived on your own for twenty years. Now you want both of us?'

'I do.'

'Let it be her choice, not yours. Her husband is a kind and considerate man and she is more attached to him than you realise. If you have succeeded in impregnating her, I do not think the Amir will ask any questions. He will be delighted and thank Allah and there will be rejoicings in Siracusa. Why deny him that small pleasure?'

'I agree, it must be her choice. And she must think carefully.'

'You can discuss it with her tonight after you have finished pleasuring each other.'

'Mayya, I wanted to spend this night with you.'

'Yes, yes. I know, but since you can't, why remain alone when the high priestess awaits? I should leave you now. Elinore will be anxious.'

'And should I tell Balkis I have told you everything or do you wish to inform her yourself?'

'Of everything we have discussed today, that is the least important. It is a matter of no significance to me. Decide for yourself.'

'You are angry, my nightingale, but why did you help Balkis to set the trap in the first place? I know she insisted that only my seed was good enough for her, but you could have refused.'

'Complicity is better than deception. She was quite capable of doing all this without my help. And if she had succeeded, would either of you have told me?'

'I hope I would have told you.'

'Enjoy your night and sleep well.'

With these words Mayya left his room and returned to her daughter in the adjoining chamber. He remained seated, thinking of the turn his life had taken, how this latest phase had started and how it might end. But he did not stay alone for long. Tiptoeing out of his room, he made his way to the guest chamber.

They met just inside Balkis's door, each so choked with passion that words eluded them. He lifted her off the ground and placed her gently on the large canopied bed where they undressed. Then he whispered, *'Ishqan khumari, qum, atla.* Tonight, all five obligations in one. Are you ready?' She replied by putting her legs around his neck so that his beard covered her clean-shaven and scented mound. Whenever either of them wanted to talk, the other would take preventive action. Hours later he noticed the sky and realised that dawn was not far away.

Balkis, also awake, confessed her anxiety. 'I thought it would be difficult for you today, even after Elinore claimed her mother for the night.'

'I was undecided. I wanted to be with you because I know the Amir will take you away very soon. Yet I did not wish to hurt Mayya either. Elinore's request, I thought, was a useful one.'

She laughed. 'For whom? Every time I'm with you I can't bear the thought of going back to Siracusa. I know my husband is kind and considerate and all the other words Mayya uses to describe him. It's true I'm not unhappy, but neither am I satisfied.'

'I had noticed.'

She slapped his behind.

'Mayya told me tonight that if you became pregnant it would make your husband so happy that he would ask no questions.'

'Did she add that if it was a boy he would inherit large estates in Siracusa? That is what Aziz wants. What do you want, Muhammad?'

'*Habibi*, I want you.'

They made love for the fourth time that night. Then she repeated her question. 'I don't want loneliness in my life. Mayya and Elinore coming to live with me has solved that. But I will not be happy without you. Will you, could you be happy here?'

'Muhammad, have you ever thought how you would feel if I asked to live with you and another man at the same time?'

'Unthinkable. Why should I think about it? It is *haram*, not permitted by al-Quran.'

'Nor is adultery which you've committed four times already tonight and will again if you can manage to rise for the fifth time before the sun does. And al-Quran states that men who fornicate with each other should be immediately killed. Has that stopped anyone? And those who mask themselves in piety are often the worst offenders. So answer my question.'

'Balkis, Balkis. How can you ask that? The answer is no. I would not be able to tolerate you living with two men in the same house.'

'But you tolerate my husband.'

'He's only half a man.'

'That is unworthy of you.'

'I apologise.'

He hid his face between her legs. The taste of her juices revived him and he managed to rise just before the sun, thus completing the five obligatory fornications of the jihad suggested by Abu Nuwas. She held him tight and the sun rose and they fell asleep in each other's arms till a discreet knock on the door startled them both. A maidservant announced: 'Breakfast is waiting on the terrace, Lady Balkis.'

None of them left the house that morning. Idrisi half-regretted that he had not attended the trial. At least he could have said farewell in public to his friend. He paced up and down the terrace and the rooms, looking on the streets to see if a crowd was assembling. Ibn Fityan left for a few hours and returned to inform them that the justiciaries had ordered the fires to be lit even before the trial had begun.

Idrisi could stay indoors no longer. He announced that he was going to the mosque to offer prayers for Philip. Ibn Fityan and four retainers asked to go with him. Two of them were armed.

The women watched from the balcony in silence as the men walked down the winding path to the main road. Elinore, sensing that her mother and aunt wished to be left alone, went to unpack the belongings that had just been delivered by men belonging to the palace administration. Mayya had insisted that the men stay for a meal, but they had declined. The oldest amongst them, a gaunt man of sixty, with tears in his eyes had replied, 'I thank you for your offer, Lady Mayya, but our hearts are heavy today and we do not feel like eating. It's a sad day for us. Amir Philip looked after us and protected our interests. If they can burn him, how long do you think we'll survive?'

Mayya could do no more than thank them with genuine warmth. They saluted her and departed.

'It's a strange time,' she now said to Balkis. 'I have never known any like it in all my time at the palace. For days the eunuchs have whispered to each other, weeping copious tears and ignoring our calls. Philip inspired a loyalty which is astonishing.'

Balkis nodded but did not reply.

'The Amir of Siracusa will give us an account of what has happened. When do both of you leave?'

'My husband will want to return as soon as possible. Ibn Muhammad and I were lucky. The winds favoured us. But it can take two days to return and they're already burning monasteries in Noto.'

'Balkis, my dearest friend and sister, you seem agitated. Tell me what distracts you and speak the truth. Is it the tragedy of Philip that has upset you so much?'

'Please stop, Mayya. I can't bear it. You know perfectly well what ails me. I am sure I have his child inside me.'

'That should make you happy. It's what you wanted.'

'I know, but I don't know. I never thought this could upset me so much.'

'Ah, I understand. During the night, love's hand draped you in a garment of embraces, but cruel dawn ripped it wide open again. It happens to all of us. Listen to me now, Balkis. You must stop behaving like a lovelorn girl of sixteen. You're a married woman. Within a few hours your husband will return and demand you leave with him. What will you do? Think, child.'

'I will go with him,' replied Balkis meekly, 'but my heart will remain here.'

'I'll look after it, I promise you. It would be a terrible humiliation for your husband if you did not return. If you are pregnant, what if he became angry and accused you of adultery? You have to think of everything in these times.'

'Mayya, I will go with him, don't worry. What I don't understand is how you, who could share the Sultan's favours with fifty others, not counting his wife, are reluctant to share Muhammad with me?'

'I think in all my time in the palace, Rujari came to my bed twice. Do you hear? Twice! He knew I loved his friend and he averted his eyes and let the eunuchs bring Muhammad to see me whenever he was in Palermo. If I had to share Muhammad I would rather it was you than anyone else. But I prefer to keep him for myself. You barely know him. How can you love him without fully understanding him or what he writes?'

'Did you know all that when you first lay in his arms?'

'You have a husband, who is kind to you and ...'

'If you like him so much, why don't we exchange husbands? You go to Siracusa and I'll stay here.'

'You are a foolish woman.'

They fell silent just as Elinore walked into the room.

'What have you two been arguing about?'

Silence.

'Let me guess. My father.'

The sisters looked up in astonishment.

'It wasn't that difficult. My aunt was in a strange mood last night and so were you, Ummi. And the maids were giggling and whispering about how many times they would have to wash the sheets in the guest chamber. Are you bleeding, aunt?'

Balkis repressed a smile and shook her head.

'I thought not. So I realised that something of which I was not aware was going on between you two and him. Has everything been resolved? Clearly not. Are both of you pregnant?'

'Elinore, this is unacceptable.'

'I overheard the pair of you laughing and plotting when we were in Siracusa. I didn't hear everything, but enough to understand what was going on. I hoped my aunt would succeed and I would have a cousin-brother or a cousin-sister. Could one of you explain what went wrong with your plan?'

'She fell in love with your father and would prefer to stay here with us.'

'It's an interesting idea but, my lovely aunt, what about my kind uncle? He would feel terribly hurt. He's such a sweet man.'

Balkis left the room in tears.

'Elinore,' said her mother in the sternest voice she could muster, 'it's not for you to tell your aunt what she can or cannot do. It will be her choice.'

'You don't want to share Abi with her, or do you? Nothing that you sisters do could surprise me. Are you pregnant, Ummi?'

'I think so, I'm not sure yet.'

'I wonder which of you will be first?'

Their conversation was interrupted by the return of the men. Idrisi entered the room with the Amir, who was offered a bath and refreshments, but declined.

He wanted to speak with his wife. Ibn Fityan escorted him to the guest chamber.

'What is going on, Muhammad?' asked Mayya. 'And you should know that our daughter is aware of everything. She eavesdropped on me and Balkis in Siracusa ...'

'Overheard Ummi and Aunt Balkis in Siracusa,' Elinore cut in.

Moments later, the Amir and a strangely exultant Balkis joined them. The Amir hugged his niece and asked about life outside the palace. She replied it was still too early to judge.

Then he turned to Mayya. 'I am so grateful to my dear friend, Ibn Muhammad, for agreeing that Balkis should stay here for a few months. I will be travelling to various villages and towns in our region and she would be lonely in the palace on her own. She said she would accompany me on my journeys, but the situation is dangerous. Some monasteries have already been set on fire. With your permission, I will leave now. If Ibn Fityan would accompany me, I might reach my ship sooner. May Allah protect you all.'

The three women did not look at each other. Elinore, finding it difficult to contain her mirth, excused herself and left the room. Mayya and Balkis smiled vacantly.

Idrisi walked out with the Amir and bade him farewell. 'Do not worry about Balkis. She will be well looked after.'

'In these uncertain times,' replied her husband, 'it's the only thing of which I am sure.'

THIRTEEN

*The Trusted One frees a village and
gives battle to the Lombard barbarians.
The sweet scent of victory. Life and fate.*

At five o' clock in the morning the messenger sent by the Trusted One returned to the rough encampment. Autumn was nearing its end and the recent rains had veiled the countryside around Noto in green. The streams that wound their way from the small hills to the flat ground where the villages had been built were swollen once again. A slight chill in the air and the restless mules were an indication that thunder and more rain were on the way.

The messenger went to the rough shelter under which the Trusted One rested. 'Master, I delivered your message to our people. The men were frightened, but they will help as you requested. They say there are almost three hundred well-armed Lombard barbarians. Most of them live in the castle on the estate of Bishop John. They say these men steal our crops and harass our women each day because they have nothing else to do.'

'Did you tell them that the children and women should leave the village before sunrise and find shelter elsewhere today?'

The messenger nodded.

'They will. They were fearful that hostages might be taken and spoke of a village a day's ride from here where some years ago the children had been taken and killed, and their heads put on pikes and left to rot. It was a fearful story.'

'You have done well. Go and eat something. In a few hours we will surprise the barbarians.'

The news of Philip's death had reached the Trusted One over two weeks ago. He had decided against immediate reprisals for the simple reason that he assumed the enemy might be prepared. This turned out to be true. When the Bishop returned from the trial and burning he had alerted his mercenaries and they were prepared, but when they saw that there was no reaction, not even after the Bishop had announced Philip's death as a warning to all those who attempted to deceive the Church and God, they had relaxed their guard once again.

The Trusted One rose and covered his shoulders with a blanket. The men were eating stale bread, dipping it in warmed olive oil flavoured with wild thyme and garlic. He went for a short walk on his own till he found a spot, close to a stream. He lifted his tunic and squatted on the ground. Allah be thanked, he could allow his bowels to move without fear of disturbance. After he had washed himself in the stream, he climbed the small hill and saw the village they were about to attack. To his men he appeared to speak with great authority, but this was the first time he had led people to fight and he knew that some of them would die. Yesterday, before the evening prayer, he had spoken to them for almost three hours to explain why they had to do what they were going to do.

His own religious beliefs were undogmatic and contradictory, a result of the numerous theological discussions and fierce debates from his years in the seminary in Cairo. Excited by the texts emanating from al-Andalus, he had abandoned his family and left for Qurtuba and then Siqilliya.

That had been twenty years ago. Soon after his arrival he had met a young woman in Noto, the daughter of a wealthy merchant, and they had loved each other, but since he had no worldly possessions the merchant had forbidden the marriage. And so she had killed herself. He had become a mystic, wandering from village to village. The merchant, mortified by what he had done, died soon afterwards of a broken heart and since the dead girl had been his only child he had left his property to the Trusted One, if only he could be found. When news reached him of this he had returned to Noto, sold the house and the merchandise and distributed the money to the poor. Then he returned to his wanderings.

Now he – without any experience of military encounters – was on the verge of a battle. He had instructed his followers to hide their weapons underneath their clothes and adopt the demeanour of crushed and broken peasants. The plan had been carefully elaborated. They left the encampment while it was still not fully light, a hundred and fifty of them, mostly riding mules, with only a dozen on horseback. The latter had special instructions. The Trusted One rode a mule at the head of the procession. Nothing could have appeared less threatening. As they reached the gates of the castle they were asked their business.

'We are poor pilgrims,' replied the Trusted One. 'We used to believe in the false Prophet Muhammad, but have seen the error of our ways and wish to convert to the true faith so we can worship in church. There was none in our village so we came to the Bishop to see if he could baptise us. We have offerings for the Bishop.'

Although it was still early and most of the guards were fast asleep, they were allowed into the compound. The Bishop, on learning that his treasury was about to be enhanced and souls saved, hurriedly put on his cassock, pushed the young man in his bed aside and hurried to greet the pilgrims.

'Which of you speaks for these men?' he inquired.

'Each speaks for himself,' replied the Trusted One.

As the Bishop approached, three men grabbed him, covered his mouth and dragged him away. Seeing this, the local peasants who had remained hidden, emerged from every side with piles of wood with which they surrounded the castle. Oil was poured on the wood and soon they drew back. The castle was on fire. As they felt the heat, the Lombard mercenaries rushed out, many of them naked, but with swords in their hands. It was too late. The Trusted One led the charge and his men followed. It was a one-sided battle and an unpleasant one. Not a single Lombard survived. When the castle was truly alight, the Bishop was dragged inside, and the villagers would later recall that the Trusted One stood on a wooden platform, raised his voice so all could hear and said: 'That is for Philip al-Mahdia.'

These were the lamentable consequences of an unspoken civil war inaugurated by the trial and death of Philip that would, in the years that followed, lead to revolts in every corner of the island.

By midday the castle had become a ruin. The whole village had gathered to watch the dying blaze. Some of the women walked up to the dead Lombards and spat on them. The Trusted One understood their anger, but discouraged such acts and ordered that all the dead be given a proper burial. He had lost only six men, who were lovingly bathed, enshrouded and buried near the site of the old mosque. The village offered prayers at the funeral of the martyrs.

The half-dozen Nazarenes whose families had lived in harmony with the Muslims for two hundred years were now asked to bury their dead. At first they refused. 'We are Siqilliyans and they are Lombards. Do not force us to bury these monsters.'

But the Trusted One said they should be buried in consecrated ground and, reluctantly, his instructions were carried out.

Beyond the hills on the low horizon, the sun was beginning to set. The villagers and the Trusted One's soldiers were bathed in its glow. At darkness the stars appeared. The villagers lit fires in the square and celebrations began with singing and dancing. When the Trusted One arrived a sudden silence fell as they looked at him in awe. He signalled they should continue with the festivities, but a collective shyness descended on them. Instead, the villagers settled around the dying fire. They, who till early that morning had been the vanquished, were now the victors. What would happen now? A sense of expectation lit their faces and they were waiting for him to speak. Just as he was about to rise from his place, the men he had left on guard arrived, dragging a monk with them. He had seen the burnt castle and realised a rebellion had taken place, but had not seen the guards. The villagers recognised him and said he was not an outsider but had been a monk before the Church stole the land and brought the Lombards to act as its custodians. He had gone to stay with his family in Noto over a month ago.

'What is your name, priest?'

'Yuhanna ibn Yusef.'

'You can see what has happened. If you are prepared to tend your flock then you should stay, but if you have thoughts of revenge, then there can be only one solution.'

'I never liked the Lombards, but I'm sorry you had to burn the Bishop.'

The monk sat down among the villagers and was given food and wine.

The Trusted One rose to address them. He spoke simply, but explaining the history of their faith, its victories and its defeats and how so often they had lost because they had fought each other. That is how we lost Siqilliya and why we might lose al-Andalus. Then something in him decided it was time to move beyond what was already known to many of them.

'What is never discussed openly is the greed of our Emirs and Sultans who come and take the land and enjoy its fruits without lifting a finger. Why should we work and they eat? Just a hundred years after the death of our Prophet the peasants in Persia rebelled against their landlords. There were similar uprisings in Khorasan and Azerbaijan. These were all Believers. The poor fought the rich because they argued that all were equal before Allah.

The rich replied that on Judgement Day before Allah we may all be equal, but on earth as al-Quran teaches us the rich have their rights as long as they pay a tax. Allah has willed it. How could it be otherwise? And they got a rude answer from Ali ibn Muhammad in the year 169 of our own calendar. The Zanj rose in arms against the Caliph in Baghdad. I see from your faces you're shocked. Do you know of what I speak? The Zanj were slaves from Ifriqiya who had become Believers in Allah and his Prophet. They were the poorest of the poor. Compared to them all of you are rich. They worked for the lords of the land in the watery marshlands between Baghdad and Basra. Three times the Caliphs sent armies to defeat them and three times the Zanj defeated those armies. Why? Because nothing could divide them and they had nothing to lose. For ten years they ruled themselves from the madina al-Mukhtara. Basra became their city, too. They were prepared to make peace any time provided the new system they had in place was not touched. And the rich trembled and the merchants were asked to donate more and more gold to raise an army that could destroy them. After a long siege they were defeated, but so was slavery in that form.

'Why do I tell you this? Because how you decide to live after your victory will determine how long you will survive. If one of you decides to become the lord of the land and the rest of you accept, then you will not last long. If you work together, share your food, look after each other, as many of our people did in the early days, then your community might survive. A way of life that protects the interests of all is a way of life people will die for. What is taught from the lips of those who use laws and customs to defend property that they have stolen in the first place or have inherited from those who stole it is worthless. Be bold. Forget them. What you have accomplished today is worth more than all our customs. I am not one of those who believe that Allah decides all our actions on earth. If that were so, he would be a monster. What then would be the point of a Day of Judgement? I see the children are already asleep. It has been a long hard day. We all need some rest. We can speak more tomorrow. I will spend some weeks with you.'

That night, wrapped in his blanket, the Trusted One made his bed on the floor of the newly built church that, despite its proximity to the burnt building, had not suffered any damage. He lay awake brooding on the day's events. This was his first real triumph since he had left Cairo. In the past he had dreamed of writing a philosophical treatise that would demolish the foundations of al-Ghazali's system of thought and defend the work of Ibn Rushd. It would provoke a theological earthquake and he would be its cause. His notes had been nearly finished when his lover had taken her own life. He had abandoned everything and became an ascetic, but what had happened today was more important than his philosophy. Of course, without the scepticism he had imbibed he would not have had the courage to do what was required.

What had shaken him tonight was catching sight of a young woman, listening to him speak, who was the replica of his long-dead Bulbula. Did she have a sister? It had taken him many years to recover from her loss, and now this coincidence was unsettling. He needed to know if she was a relation. He would ask at daybreak.

But when dawn came, the thought fled as he went to see his men. He sat with them and broke bread while they remembered their fallen friends. Then he asked if any of them would settle in this village to give the villagers a sense of security. If twelve of them could stay, he would be able to move on with the others in the hope of repeating their victory near Siracusa. After a brief discussion twelve volunteers stepped forward, but they all insisted on the same condition: the Trusted One would send for them if ever he needed more men. He agreed and embraced each in turn. Raising their voices, they shouted in unison: 'Long life to the Amir al-Jihad!' He informed them in a quiet voice that he would rather be the Trusted One than an Amir of any description. His men never used the title again.

For the rest of the day the peasants showed him the extent of the estate attached to the castle. Thousands of acres extending on each side of the village, long uninhabited and uncultivated. Ibn Hamza's family had settled here two hundred years ago and the peasants told him their families had been here for almost as long. Five generations had lived in peace until the Nazarenes arrived twenty years ago.

'How many of them came? Why didn't you resist?'

The older men began to shift uneasily, pretending they hadn't understood him. It was one of the younger peasants who replied. 'Hamza ibn Omar, the lord of the land, was undecided whether to convert or not. He left it a bit too late and only converted to their faith a week before the Lombards arrived. They roared with laughter when they were told. The Bishop offered to let him go if he would tell them where the gold was hidden. He wept and fell on his knees and swore repeatedly there was no gold. They slew him and his family before our eyes. I was ten years old and the memory still tortures me. Several young children were decapitated. After that few could think of anything but how best to survive. Each for himself and his family.'

The Trusted One put his arm around the peasant's shoulders. 'Can you read and write?'

He nodded. 'My mother was a cook and worked for Ibn Omar's family. So I used to play with the children and learnt to read and write with them.'

'And afterwards?'

'Nothing. The Lombards, most of them could not read, threw out all the books from the library and lit them, but Allah decided it would rain that day. We children saved the books and they are hidden in different homes. I never stopped reading even when I couldn't understand more than three sentences on a page. My wife has named me Ibn al-Kitab.'

The others laughed, but the Trusted One hid his delight at discovering such an erudite peasant. Open praise would have excited the envy of the others.

'Ibn al-Kitab is a good name. I need you to question everyone and compile a register. I want to know which peasant worked on which field, how many hours were worked before and after the Nazarenes came. Then I want you to compile another register dividing the land equally between all the peasant families. This register must be backdated thirty years. I will sign the deeds on behalf of Hamza ibn Omar. This is to safeguard all of you against any authority. You had nothing to do with burning the Bishop or killing the Lombards. Blame the men who came from outside. In any case, why should you wish to kill anyone when your lord gifted the land to you thirty years ago? One more request to all of you. You must consult everyone before you reach your decision. Twelve of my men wish to settle here. They will work alongside you and, if it ever becomes necessary, defend you. But they must have an equal share in the land.'

The twenty or so peasants accompanying him nodded gratefully, assuring him that there would be no problem about his men. But he insisted that the village should decide this collectively. Ibn al-Kitab asked, 'When you say the land should be divided equally, does that include Yuhanna, the monk?'

'Does his family live here?'

'Yes.'

'Then he must be included. We can afford to be generous. There is a great deal of land, as we have just seen, and best to share it with everyone.'

As they were walking back, Ibn al-Kitab whispered, 'I would be honoured if you would join us for the evening meal.'

'I would like that and then you can show me some of the books you saved from the fire.'

Later that afternoon, after the peasants had returned from work a large *mehfil* was convened in the square. Ibn al-Kitab spoke of the plan that had been suggested by the Trusted One. It was greeted with shouts of joy. Then a semi-spontaneous chant erupted, during which the Trusted One's men remained silent: 'Long life to the Amir al-Jihad.'

The Trusted One rose. He told them it was their own strength that would now take them forward. He could do no more for them. Within a week they would have the deeds to their land and the register must be kept hidden in a safe place known only to ten families. It was only to be shown to the Emir of Siracusa or his agents, never to the Lombard who would immediately destroy it. That they were involved in a deception was undeniable, but he felt sure that Allah and God and the Prophets Muhammad and Isa would forgive them because they were correcting a grievous injustice that had been done. All that was necessary was that they tell the same story to anyone from outside who asked questions regarding the land. And he made one last appeal. The land now belonged to them, but he would urge them to make sure each family was fed, had milk and water and fruit before they sold the produce in the market. And they should make sure to rebuild their mosque. As he walked away from the throng, people of all ages touched him in silent appreciation. Ibn al-Kitab took his arm. 'Trusted One, if you could achieve the same in other places on this island we could raise an army that would take Palermo.'

'It will not be so easy elsewhere.'

It began to rain and both men were drenched by the time they reached Ibn al-Kitab's house. The Trusted One was shivering and his new friend insisted he change his tunic. A clean shirt and loose trousers were placed on the bed in an adjoining room where he could undress and dry himself. The Trusted One began to weep from a well of tears deep inside him. When he had recovered he changed into the dry clothes. They hung loose on him. He could not remember the last time he had worn a clean shirt or trousers. Beneath the uncouth bearded figure in a tunic that had never been washed was revealed the noble profile of an Amir.

In the front room, she was smiling with two young boys and a proud husband at her side. He kissed each boy on the head. Even her voice reminded him of Bulbula.

'We are honoured by your presence, Trusted One. News of you had reached us many months ago, but we wondered whether you were real or an apparition. I'm glad you're real. Please be seated. The children are going to bed and your meal is almost ready.'

The two men remained silent till Ibn al-Kitab showed him a book the sight of which made him stand up in excitement. It was Ibn Rushd's *The Incoherence of the Incoherents*, a spirited defence of Reason as something separate from Divine Truth.

'This was in the library?'

'Yes. This is the one I cannot understand, however hard I try.'

'It is difficult, but it is the most courageous text produced by our philosophers. I myself have only read extracts. May I borrow it to read while I am here?'

'I was going to give it to you.'

Tears came to The Trusted One's eyes. 'It should belong to everyone. When the mosque has been rebuilt it will contain a small library for books other than al-Quran, which as Allah knows, we have read so often that we can remember each verse.'

Then she re-entered the room and he could no longer contain himself.

'May I ask your name?'

'Zainab.'

'Forgive my abruptness. You remind me of someone I knew a long time ago in another life. You resemble her so strongly that with your permission I would like to ask you another question.'

Zainab's face paled. 'You may ask me whatever you like.'

'You were born here?'

'Yes.'

'Your parents have lived here always?'

'Yes, except in bad times, when my mother obtained employment in Noto. Like my mother-in-law, she is an excellent cook.'

'Do you know where she worked?'

'Yes. It was only for a few years and before I was born, but she talked about it often enough. She worked for a merchant, a widower who had a very beautiful daughter. She died in sad circumstances.'

'Could I trouble you for a bowl of water, please.'

He was trembling and they thought he was cold and gave him a blanket.

'Is your mother still alive, Zainab?'

'Allah be praised, she will be here very soon with our meal. When we told her you were coming she insisted on cooking. My father died a few years ago.'

'Is her name Halima?'

Now it was Zainab's turn to be surprised. Before she could question him, the door opened and they rushed to help the old woman bring the food indoors. She saw the Trusted One and came and touched his head and blessed him. Then he spoke in a voice she knew.

'Halima, you did not recognise me?'

She almost dropped a pot and turned around. He hid his beard. Her voice became weak. 'Ibn Zubair, is it really you?'

She was the only person left in this world who knew his real name. He embraced her and they both began to weep. When they had recovered he swore them all to secrecy.

'The resemblance to Bulbula had alarmed me, but it was already dark when I first saw Zainab. I thought I might have been mistaken. I could not sleep properly last night. The wildest conjectures passed through my mind. Today when I saw her with her family, I was no longer confused. There was no room left for doubt. She looks exactly like her sister, except for the colour of her hair. Bulbula's mother was a Greek and she inherited her hair, the colour of gold it was ... remember?'

Halima nodded and kissed his hands.

'Her father, may Allah forgive him, never recovered from her death. It was guilt that created the bad humours inside him. That's what killed him.

He left me all his money. I distributed it to the poor. Did he know about Zainab?'

'No. Nobody knew till now.'

'You should have told him. He would have been as pleased as I was to see her. It might have kept him alive. You and Zainab would have inherited a beautiful house in Noto and a small fortune.'

'My husband would have killed me. Zainab was our only child – or so he thought – and he was so happy when she was born, even though he had prayed for a son. If only the merchant, who was not an unkind man, had allowed Bulbula to marry you, who knows what would have happened.'

'If she had lived I would not be the man you see before you. She would have kept me close to her. I would be sitting in a library most of the day, reading, thinking, writing, but nothing more. In the life I chose I feel I have achieved something. In this village we have created an example that could spread. For a people to prosper, they must take their destiny in their own hands.'

Zainab had been waiting patiently till the Trusted One had finished speaking.

'Umma, what happened?'

Her mother told her.

FOURTEEN

*A dual pregnancy and Idrisi discovers an
unusual cure for coughs and colds.*

Several weeks later, news of the events that had taken place in a
village so small that it did not yet have a name reached Palermo.
The merchants who carried the information described what had taken place
in great detail, as if their own eyes had witnessed the Bishop being thrown
into the flames and the Trusted One standing up to declare it as revenge for
Philip. Then they would talk of how the Lombards had been hung naked
from the trees, their legs and uncircumcised columns swaying in the wind
and how, once the skin had been eaten by large birds, their skeletons had
become bleached by the sun and polished by the rain. But they had been left
in place as a mute warning to all infidels.

When Idrisi inquired whether they had seen the dangling skeletons with
their own eyes, the merchant would admit it had been told him by a friend
who had been told by another and before long the genealogy of the story-
tellers was so firmly established as to overpower the facts.

It has always been thus in our world, thought Idrisi, wondering if
anything had taken place at all. Most legends contain a kernel of truth so it

was clear that something must have happened. The problem was that news of the Trusted One's exploits was feeding the delirium that had gripped the city since the public burning of Philip. One of the justiciaries who had thrown Philip's body into the pit of fire had disappeared without trace. Fifteen days ago, a judge at the trial had died a natural death, but it was claimed in the *qasr* that he had been poisoned. What was undeniably true was that when his coffin was being carried to the cemetery, it had been attacked by a swarm of bees that emerged from nowhere. When the pallbearers were stung, they dropped the coffin in the street and ran away screaming in search of water.

Even after the bees – may Allah bless them – had disappeared, the coffin had lain unattended for some time and young boys had dared each other to go and piss on it. They took it in turns to keep guard, with the result that over a hundred boys under ten years of age had drenched the wood with their rain. When the funeral procession was resumed the discomfort of the pallbearers was evident. Their wrinkled noses made the boys who were watching from their hiding places giggle with delight. In this febrile atmosphere the Trusted One and his military campaigns were discussed endlessly in the old city, each shop-keeper vying with his competitors to retell the most bloodcurdling stories.

⅏

Idrisi was preoccupied with more intimate problems – unsurprising since he lived with them each day. Mayya and Balkis were seven and six months pregnant, their distended stomachs competing for his attention. He spent more time with Balkis than with Mayya and for a simple reason: Balkis was locked inside him. When questioned by Elinore about the apparent discrepancy in his affections, he assumed the air of a physician. 'Your mother has had you and knows what is involved. For Balkis it is her first child and the circumstances are difficult. She needs more care.'

Elinore raised her eyes and glared at him, but no words were exchanged.

Balkis had written to her husband Aziz and informed him of her state. A special messenger had arrived within three days to deliver a letter in return. He was delighted and would leave Siracusa in a few weeks to fetch her. He pleaded with her not to exert herself too much or do anything that could threaten the child. The news came as a relief to Mayya, but cast a thick cloud of gloom around the guest chambers occupied by her sister. For most of the time the sisters displayed a stoicism that greatly impressed Idrisi. What he did not realise was that what usually brought them close to each other was his absences from the house. If he had decided on a long sea journey the sisters would have become inseparable. These days he would not leave the island.

A week or two in Shakka or Djirdjent was the farthest he travelled to meet old friends and also to continue his research on herbal cures for the medical formulary he was composing. Nor were the two women exempted from his experiments. He inspected them closely and noted how their bodies reacted to the presence of the unborn child. Mayya could no longer eat meat and her body rejected all sweet delicacies except pastries that contained only honey. Balkis became allergic to garlic and onions, but developed a huge appetite for a long, thin pastry filled with almond paste. Neither of them could bear to taste the Arabian coffee which had been a household favourite.

Once, when Idrisi had developed a cough which persisted, he tried his own cure of honey, ginger and wild thyme boiled in water and, despite the unpleasant taste, he took it thrice a day. It had always worked before, but this time the cough refused to go away. In order to avoid infecting the two women he had stayed away from them, concentrating on writing and playing chess with Elinore.

One afternoon Balkis, who missed his presence more than her sister, entered his chamber and cradled his head on her breasts. The cloth covering her was moist with her milk. He licked it and liked the taste, then lifted her

dress, eager for more. That same night his cough disappeared. It could have
been pure coincidence, but Idrisi linked it to the milk. Was this real or a
hallucination? He decided it was real. Was it the combination of honey,
herbs and human milk that had worked the cure, or the milk alone? And if
it was the milk alone, could he include the prescription in his formulary? He
dreaded the thought of cough-ridden Sultans, Emirs and Barons scouring
their palaces and estates for women in late pregnancy. It would add another
burden on the poor. On the other hand, if he did not record the cure he
would be in breach of the ancient oath. He arrived at a compromise with
himself. Both women were likely to be breast-feeding the infants for a year
or possibly two. It was just as likely that he would develop a cough over this
period. When there was a conjunction between the two events he would just
drink the milk. If the cough disappeared he would have to mention the fact
in the formulary, regardless of the consequences. If it did not work, then he
could regard what had happened with Balkis's milk as a chance occurrence.
But clearly Balkis had other concerns on her mind. From the look on her
face he knew this was to do with her husband. She stood there, arms on hips
and gave him one of her fierce looks.

'Balkis, you must go with him, at least till the child is born. Afterwards he
will not object if you return.'

'You don't care for me now that I am fat and ugly,' she screamed, hurling
herself against his body and weeping.

'I agree that your body is not at its best, but to suggest that the love I feel
for you is dependent on such things is an insult to our passion. If what you
say were true, how do you explain that we make love almost every day,
ignoring your stomach which seeks to obstruct us? Do you think I'm
pretending when we are at the height of our union?'

'Then why do you say I must go?'

'It's because you are married to him, Balkis. How often have we discussed
this possibility? Believe me, all he wants is to show his child to his people

and his family. I hope, for his sake, it is a boy. That will make him very happy. He won't mind your returning here to create another child.'

She laughed. 'In that case you should pray it's a girl. Then I will definitely be returned to the great physician. But you speak the truth. I know that and I will do as you ask. The one thing I cannot bear to think of is being touched by him and if he does ...'

'Most men stay away from women when they are breast-feeding an infant. The reason I would not is because as a physician it is my duty to observe and record the functions ...'

She kissed his lips and might have moved further had Ibn Fityan not knocked on the door to inform them that the Amir of Siracusa had left the palace and was reported to be riding in the direction of the house.

Refreshments, including the exquisite lemon elixir, were served on the terrace where they could enjoy the warmth of the winter sun. Aziz described his visit to the Sultan. He had been questioned in detail about the Trusted One, but denied that a Bishop had been burnt or Lombards fed to the animals.

'But I can tell you, dear friends and trusted wife, what really took place. It is quite remarkable, but disturbing. They did burn the Bishop and the Trusted One did shout it was for Philip, but they dug a grave for the prelate and the local monk swears on the bible that he died a natural death. After his death the Lombards fought each other for the Bishop's gold and probably his store of young men and, to the amazement of all, they destroyed first the castle in search of the gold and later themselves. The single survivor died of wounds. They were all buried in consecrated ground. This is, incidentally, true.'

'But how did the battle start?'

Aziz told them the entire story, except what he did not know, namely, the meeting between the Trusted One and Halima and the discovery of his real identity.

'We tended to believe that the Trusted One was a slightly unbalanced preacher, wandering through villages and infecting the credulous peasants with religious dreams, encouraging martyrdom and revealing the stigmata that marked his own uncultivated mind. This was certainly the impression he wanted to convey. But what he has done threatens us all.'

'How?' inquired Mayya, her curiosity aroused.

'Shame has disappeared in that village. The people look into your eyes when they speak. Pride and insolence have replaced respect for their betters. One peasant had the effrontery to ask if I had read Aristotle. The only way to make them respect us is to grind them hard and make sure their yoke is heavy. If what they have done spreads we are all finished. It is the Trusted One who has taught them how to ensure they never lose the land again.

'What I am about to tell you is based on my own assumptions. I have no proof and legality is on the other side. I had not visited that estate before, but was aware of what had happened after the Nazarenes wiped out the family of Ibn Hamza. When I visited the peasants a few weeks ago, the Trusted One had long departed, but he had left behind the happiest village community I have ever seen.'

'How does that threaten you?' asked Balkis.

'When I asked who owned the land, now the Bishop was dead and gone, they replied cheerfully that the land had been gifted to them by Hamza ibn Muhammad many years before the arrival of the Nazarenes. I saw the register with my own eyes. It was impeccable. I find it incredible that Hamza, who often came to my palace, could have gifted away his hereditary lands. In fact I don't believe a word of it. It was the Trusted One's idea and he convinced them all and provided them with a single narrative.'

'Did you question the monk in private?' asked Idrisi.

'Of course I did. He repeated the same rubbish. His family benefited from the Trusted One's land distribution. He confessed to me he had never met a man like the Trusted One and wanted to convert to our faith, but the

Trusted One had told him he was more helpful to the village as a monk. If he wanted to he could pray in the mosque, but when outsiders came he had to be a monk.'

Idrisi could not conceal his admiration. 'He is inspired by Allah and the Great Satan at the same time. Where is he?'

'Far from my estates, I hope. Here in Palermo you cannot imagine the effect this is having on the peasants. Many of them visit the village and return full of ideas.'

'Did the Trusted One leave behind a plan if we are all defeated?'

'Strange you should ask that, Ibn Muhammad. It did not occur to me, but one of the peasants, a well-read boy, volunteered the information. If our people are defeated, they will all swear that the Bishop had converted the entire village five years before he died. They have a church register to prove it and the monk and the handful of Nazarene families will attest to the truth of this assertion.'

'This is incredible,' said Elinore. 'It makes me want to visit this place.'

'Whenever you want,' replied her uncle. 'Perhaps after the child is born you should all come and spend some time in Siracusa. Elinore could come with us tonight?'

Nobody replied to the invitation and poor Aziz, slightly embarrassed, turned to his wife.

'My sister, who you dislike so much, is praying you produce a girl. That way her son will inherit my estates.'

'In that case,' replied Balkis, 'it will be a pleasure to disappoint her. And if we are leaving tonight I should go and make sure everything is packed.'

'We'll help,' said Mayya and all three women headed towards the guest chambers.

'The Sultan could die any day, Ibn Muhammad. He asked after you today.'

'The sooner he goes the better. There will be a settling of accounts. I used to have many fond memories of him, but the treatment of Philip has changed everything. It made me angry with myself for being such a poor judge of people. Let us speak of more pleasant subjects.'

'Let me raise an indelicate one.'

Idrisi smiled in anticipation.

'I thank you for letting Balkis return. It was important for me, but you know this already.'

'I do and if it embarrasses you we need discuss the subject no longer. I hope it is a boy for your sake. Have you considered taking another wife?'

'There is no reason to do so. I have a serving woman in the palace who satisfies all my needs. With her there is no pretence. If Balkis gives me a boy I am content. And you?'

'I will be content even if Balkis gives you a girl.'

FIFTEEN

The death of Rujari.
Idrisi is a father again and twice.
Dreaming of Siracusa.

On a cold February day in the year 1154 of the Christian calendar, the Sultan died in his palace in Palermo and Balkis gave birth to a son in Siracusa, though Idrisi and Mayya did not receive the message till the Amir of Siracusa arrived to attend the Sultan's funeral, for the lighthouses had been too busy conveying the news of the Sultan's death and the date fixed for the funeral to bother with other news. Receiving the information, notables of every variety and from all parts of the island began the journey to Palermo.

Idrisi walked to the palace and was received by William, attired in the costume of a Sultan with the royal cloak draped around his shoulders. He was a large, black-bearded man of frightening appearance. Having embraced Idrisi, he pleaded with him to become the Amir of Amirs and return to the palace. Idrisi thanked the ruler warmly, but declined the offer to replace Philip. He pleaded scholarly duties, explaining the need to complete the Formulary this year so as to help physicians save more lives. The new Sultan appeared to accept this and proceeded to inform him that the Barons were intent on disregarding Rujari's testament. 'They want to bury my father in the Cathedral in Palermo.'

'He built a church especially in Cefalu to be his burial place. He loved the town and the church.'

'And someone else too, Master Idrisi, as we both know.'

'Nonetheless, it was his last request to me.'

'And to me. And to my mother. But the Church and the Barons insist on Palermo. Philip was the only person on this island who could have buried him in Cefalu. So let them bury him in Palermo. There is another reason why he can't be buried in Cefalu: Bishop Boso backed the wrong Pope and now Rome won't consecrate his church. How can a King be buried in an unconsecrated church? I've promised Boso that once he makes friends with Rome he can have my father's body as well and we can have two funerals for your friend. Did you ever meet his concubine in Cefalu? Come on, tell me. What was she like? Is it true she was with child and ...'

William, swaying slightly, began to laugh. It was an unpleasant laugh and Idrisi, who had once attempted to teach this boy geography, astronomy and medicine, gave his former pupil a stern look. It was obvious he had been smoking too many pipes of *shahdanj al-barr*.

'Sultan William,' Idrisi began, but he could not continue. William had fallen off the chair and was seemingly asleep on the floor. His attendants lifted him from the ground. He recovered and dismissed the attendants, although Idrisi was only too well aware that they were being watched from secret spy-holes.

'Master Idrisi, we shall see you at my father's funeral.'

'Have I the Sultan's permission to use the library? There are manuals of medicine which are not available elsewhere on this island.'

'Of course, and you did not need my permission. You organised that library before I was born. Use it as much as you wish. One question for you, Master Idrisi, and I wish you to be completely honest as you were with my father.'

'I will try.'

'How would you assess my late father as a ruler? Just in a few words, I mean.'

'I would say that Sultan Rujari of Siqilliya was for most of his reign a wise and considerate ruler, who protected all his subjects regardless of creed. He governed his people with equity and impartiality, impressing all by the beauty of his actions, the depth of his insights and the sweetness of his character. I wrote some of this in the dedication of my book. We could add that he killed fewer people than his own father and uncle. When he was ruler and people reminded him of the massacre of Believers in this city, just before it surrendered to the Franks, he expressed remorse and regret. He was a skilled administrator and a statesman who could outflank the Pope and the Emperor. Above all, he defended the interest of his kingdom before all else and did not allow it to be weakened by adventures in the Holy Land. He was always friendly to scholars and helped me considerably to improve the quality of my own work. It was in his last days, racked by a disease that made it difficult for him to breathe and affected his heart, that he weakened in mind, body and spirit. He allowed the Barons and the Bishops to convince him that a blood sacrifice was necessary to strengthen his family's claim to this island. And in his last months he committed a crime by burning one of the most talented leaders of this kingdom, Philip al-Mahdia. Thus began the decline.'

'I cannot repeat all of that, but I thank you. Men like you are rare in this kingdom. I wish you would stay by my side.'

'There are others more skilled in the art of administration than I and they will serve you better. My advice is very simple: beware the Barons. Your grandmother had to flee the mainland to Palermo when your father was very young. She felt safer here because of my people. They were a counter-balance to the Barons. So be careful of them. They tend to strike when a king is young. And never see them in private without a hand on your sword and armed retainers at your side. May Allah protect you, Ibn Rujari.'

'Just one other matter. It is of no great significance, indeed it is only curiosity. During Philip's trial when a lot of lies were being told, there were two loud farts from the benches occupied by your people. I tried to join their choir, but failed. Was it the work of the Amir of Catania or Siracusa?'

'I have no idea.'

'It was a very good effort. If you find out, kindly congratulate the Amir on my behalf. I have decided to build a new palace in the style of your Sultans and with the largest harem in the world. Larger than Baghdad and Qurtuba and I will fill it as well. If you ever need a woman ...'

He began to laugh again.

Idrisi found talk of this nature wearisome. Without replying, he bowed and left the audience chamber. As he walked slowly through the palace, he knew he did not wish to return here again. The eunuchs gave him nervous smiles of recognition. None of them appeared to be greatly affected by Rujari's death. Philip had belonged to them and, in this very palace, the older eunuchs had watched him grow and prosper.

Idrisi entered the library. Perhaps William would prove his detractors wrong and better his father, but even as the thought passed through his mind he knew it was without substance. William might be stronger than they gave him credit for, but he was not an administrator or a statesman. He was too strongly addicted to pleasure. He would become too dependent on advisers who would kill each other to be near him.

Idrisi did not stay long in the library. He picked up the two books he needed to consult and decided to take them home, looking forward to getting back to his new son, now six weeks old and sturdy in voice and appetite.

As he climbed the path to his house he heard the strains of Ibn Thawdor's flute and saw his daughter sitting on a wall next to the boy and watching him with entranced eyes. He smiled inwardly and did not disturb them. He was pleased she had found a friend in the musician. Elinore had been more upset by Rujari's death than he had realised and had asked to accompany Idrisi to the funeral. Nor was he sure what she really felt about her new brother. He must remember to ask Mayya. The arrival of little Afdal had removed the last traces of the tension between them and he would often hear her singing lullabies he had never heard before. She had actually laughed one morning as she wondering if Balkis would have a boy and whether it would be identical to her own.

The Amir of Siracusa arrived a day before the funeral. He had come alone and was staying at the palace. Given the unsettled conditions on the island, it was useful for it to be known that he was a guest of the Sultan. The joyful look on his face was enough to convey the good news: Balkis, too, had given birth to a son and both were well. He handed Idrisi a small parcel, which was handed to a retainer and despatched to his room.

'Any news of the Trusted One?'

'He has been seen in a number of villages. He is very close to your family and they tell me he is on your son-in-law's estates at the moment. Our people are ready to fight. Catania, Noto and Siracusa will not be taken without a struggle.'

'I do not think that William has any intention of waging war on us.'

'One year ago, did his father have any intention of burning Philip outside his own palace?'

'All I am saying is that a premature rebellion could lead to defeat. Timing is always crucial.'

'Then we are in agreement.'

When Elinore entered the room to greet her uncle, Idrisi noticed her flushed cheeks and shining eyes. The flute-player is affecting this child, he thought, and it pleased him. Mayya arrived with Afdal in her arms and the Amir made all the right noises, but did his mind's eye compare the two infants? At the end of his visit, the proud possessor of a new son invited them all to visit him in Siracusa.

'It will be spring soon and the best time to visit us. Balkis is desperate to see you.'

'We will try,' said Mayya, 'but it's such a long journey and the mere thought tires me.'

Idrisi retreated to his library to find the parcel from Balkis. He undid the string and unwrapped the cloth. Inside lay a carefully folded tunic made of pure silk, the colour of burnt milk. On top of it was a letter. Elinore knocked on the door and entered without waiting for his reply. 'I need to ask you something, Abi.'

'Let me guess. You want to learn the flute.'

She coloured slightly. 'I would like to marry him.'

'Has he expressed interest?'

'No, because he is in awe of you and thinks he is too low-born for you to even consider such a match.'

'Have you spoken to your mother?'

'Yes and she is not happy.'

'Why?'

'She thinks he is low-born.'

'Are you sure you know him well enough to marry him?'

'Yes. You once told me that affairs of the heart are determined by instinct, not reason. My instinct tells me that I will be happy with him.'

'That is all that matters to me, child. I have no objection. I like the boy myself, but how will he earn a living? Musicians are not paid regularly.'

'He doesn't only play the flute. He makes them and can teach children to play. He wants us to move to Djirdjent where his mother's family will help him.'

'I will help him if he wants to stay here and your uncle in Siracusa is a generous soul if he wishes to move there. And you? Where would you like to live.'

'I'm not sure. There is a part of me which would like to leave this island for ever and move to Salerno.'

'Why?'

'Instinct. Something bad is going to happen here. Can't you feel it in the air?'

'Elinore, you are baptised and so is Simeon ibn Thawdor. You need not fear the Barons. No harm will come to you. But I am more worried about your two brothers. Will they survive? For how long? When some of my friends left Palermo and went to settle in al-Andalus, I mocked them for their foolishness. I was so sure I had made the right decision.'

He shrugged his shoulders in despair.

Elinore kissed him on his head. 'Even though we have not yet discussed Pythagoras and his numbers which you promised me, I love you.'

'The numbers were important for the merchants and sailors. But much more interesting was the way of life that he advocated. Perhaps you should go and live in Cariati, much closer to us than Salerno. The Pythagoreans fled here to Kroton, as they called it then, and their brotherhood flourished. Some of them came to Siracusa as well. The symbol of their brotherhood was the ox on the tongue. Each new recruit was pledged to secrecy and silence. In order to achieve their aims of creating a society in which each and every person had a moral responsibility, they had to be careful. And did you know they also believed that the only way to purify the soul from the infections of the body was through music? That is why Pythagoras and his followers were the first to explore the links between music and mathematics. And you will find books that can teach you even more than I know. He is not a philosopher I have studied closely. Is that your mother I hear shouting for you? Tell her I approve of Ibn Thawdor and she should not worry about your dowry.'

As she ran out of the room, Idrisi began to pace up and down, pausing to look at the map on the large table. It was his own map and he was thinking it was time to emigrate, but to which destination? Then he saw his unfinished manuscript and he knew that it had to be completed before he went anywhere. The philosophy of medicine he was advancing was based on providing simple and easily accessible cures for the diseases that afflicted the rich and the poor. He had read something in a book by Aflatun* that had displeased him and he had meant to tell Elinore. He found the book where he had marked the following passage:

'When a carpenter is ill,' said Sokrates, 'he asks the doctor for a quick remedy – an emetic, purge, cautery or the knife – that is all. If he is told to diet and wrap up his head and keep warm, he replies that he has no time to be ill, that there is no good going on living just to nurse his disease if he can't get on with his work. So he says goodbye to the doctor and returns to work, and either gets over it and lives and carries on with his livelihood, or else dies and is put out of his misery that way.'

'I understand,' said Glaukon 'and of course that is the proper use of medicine for a man in his walk of life.'

He smiled as he recalled how this had enraged him. The 'proper use of medicine' had meant the spread of infectious diseases that did not distinguish between carpenters and those who owned large estates and hundreds of slaves.

In the book he was preparing, Idrisi had written that a healthy diet was the best preventive medicine, but also that there should be no treatments that the poor could not afford. These should be available to all in special hospitals. Other considerations he had put aside for the moment, although, in private, he agreed with Hippokrates' injunction: in order to cure a man it was necessary to understand his origins and the causes of his evolution. This was a conviction forbidden to the People of the Book who were to believe that Jehovah, God, Allah created man – possibly a simplification of

* Plato

knowledge that had not helped the study of medicine. The Ancients, too, had their myths, but these contained the kernel of a truth. Prometheus, who gave man fire to save him from extinction, was clearly aware that man possessed the brain to make use of the fire and the makers of the myths themselves interpreted Prometheus as the symbol of human intelligence.

His thoughts were interrupted by Mayya, anxious to inspect the gift Balkis had sent him. She held the tunic against her own body, but it was too large.

'She was always good at making clothes, but let us see how it fits you.'

He rose and changed tunics. The silk clung to his body.

'It fits you perfectly. Balkis has not forgotten your body.'

Still he did not speak, but did not change back into his old clothes. He smiled vacantly at his wife.

'When will you go and see Walid in Venice?'

'After I have finished my Formulary.'

'And when will that be? When Afdal is five or ten?'

'It might be sooner if I was not interrupted so often.'

'I came to discuss our daughter. I can't believe you have agreed that she can marry Thawdor's son.'

'Because he is poor?'

'Well, not that, but …'

'What other reason could there be? Breeding, of course. Let me tell you that Thawdor's forebears included men who ruled this island hundreds of years ago. I would not compare his lineage with yours or mine, leave alone that of your brother-in-law.'

'If that is your opinion I will not object any further.'

'Mayya, I want our daughter to be happy. I will give them money to build a house wherever they wish.'

'I do not wish her to leave Palermo.'

'That, too, will be her choice and not ours.'

When she left the room, he looked at the shelves and sighed. If he did leave Palermo or Siqilliya these books would have to travel with him. He would never leave them behind. Realising it would be difficult to take them all, he began to make lists in his head of the books he would not miss. He might not be able to convince Mayya or Balkis to leave with him, but the books had no choice.

The silk tunic caressing his body made him think of Balkis, a mother for the first time. Her son would become the centre of her existence and she would settle down in the palace till she felt it was time to reproduce once again.

He took up her letter.

Muhammad,

I had thought of so many different names for you, but they sounded silly when written down and I wasted a lot of papyrus. They can only be spoken, so you will have to wait. I never thought the pain of separation could hurt so much till I left you three months ago. It did not only hurt me inside, but on the way back I developed a headache, a really bad one that had never ailed me before. What does the physician recommend? Don't suggest a cold infusion of almonds, milk and honey. It does not work.

I sit and write a few lines to you each day so that when the time comes I can add a line about our child. Sometimes I become tearful at the thought of it not knowing that you are his real father. Will we ever tell him? I can hear your voice: given your husband has been so kind and considerate why deny him the pleasure of pretending this is his child. And of course I agree, but .... And Mayya? How is she and how are you together? Has the child been born? Boy or girl?

It was an awful journey to Siracusa with a storm at sea near Messina, where we were forced to spend the night after leaving Palermo. I remembered our journey together. It must have taken the same time but it felt so quick. I suppose being heavy with your child doesn't improve one's humour. In Siracusa I thought of you a great deal and for some days could not eat any food. My kind and considerate husband was close to sending you a message asking you to join us, but however much I would have loved that, I thought of Mayya and her state and knew it was wrong. So I stopped him. He makes no demands of me and I know he has a woman in the palace who serves his needs. I think he told you about her. I'm pleased because it was not pleasant when he came to my bed. He is so fat and apart from the physical discomfort I also suffered a mental strain. Does the silk tunic fit you well?

There are so many things I wanted to discuss with you in Palermo, but we became so absorbed in each other that there was no time for lofty discussions. I wanted to ask what you thought of the poetry of Ibn Hamdis. I'm really angry with myself for never asking you. My husband – but you probably know this – belongs to the same family and we have all his poems in the library and some of them in very fine editions. You see, I'm even beginning to use your language! Some of them I find too sentimental. He was not 'banished from paradise'. He left. I mean, if he was going to miss Siqilliya so much, why did he go in the first place and then why not come back and re-live the pleasures of his youth? His brothers stayed. The family estate is intact. So his memories of Siqilliya do not excite me, though you try saying that to a Siracusan. Can you imagine my husband, who has calmly accepted that we are lovers and that you are the father of the son who will inherit his estates, who has never spoken a harsh word to me, became red with anger when I told him that Ibn Hamdis was not a very good poet compared to Ibn Quzman, Ibn Hazm and Abu Nuwas. He shouted, called me ignorant and left the room like a mountain on fire. Later he came and apologised. A few days after this occurred, I found a poem by Ibn Hamdis that really made me laugh. I wanted you to laugh with me, but you were not here. Read the words aloud to yourself and imagine both of us inside your silk tunic:

> *A cloistered nun unlocked her convent,*
> *and we were her night visitors.*
> *The fragrance of a liquor brought us to her,*
> *one that revealed to your nose her secrets ...*
> *I placed my silver on her scale,*
> *and from the jug she poured her gold.*
> *We offered betrothal to four of her daughters,*
> *so that pleasure might deflower their innocence.*

I want to know what you think about this and his Siqilliyan poems.

Muhammad, last night I was told an awful story and could not sleep. My husband came to see if I needed anything and with him was his awful sister who you and I spoke of once before. She is very tall with a large cucumber of a nose, breasts the size of water-melons and a loud, grating voice and I've always wanted to suggest to her that she join a band of wandering hermaphrodites and enjoy life. She came in, looked at my son on my breast and said, 'Praise be to Allah for this miracle.' It was on the edge of my tongue to say, 'Praise be to Muhammad' but I restrained myself. Then I began to feel a pain in my insides and I screamed at her to leave my chamber. The maid rushed in from next door, but it was nothing. My husband came back later to apologise for his sister. I said she was a serpent nourished by Satan. And then he sat down and told me this story, which horrified me:

'She is my half-sister, Balkis, and please understand she has had a hard life. My parents did not get on with each other and my mother must have been in a state of permanent sadness. When I was eight years old my father left Siracusa and went to live in Noto for six months. My mother was far from heartbroken, as you can imagine. She committed an indiscretion with a cousin and became pregnant. When my father returned he asked whose child it was but she did not speak. He never spoke to her again. That child was my sister who you hate so much. She was not treated well in our household. I don't think my father even

spoke her name. Not once. As a result, she became our mother's favourite. This annoyed the rest of us and we were all unpleasant to her. When many years later my father left for Palermo to conduct some business, my mother's cousin who had fathered my half-sister returned to the house. My half-sister was seventeen years old. One night in a drunken frenzy the cousin forced himself on his daughter. She became pregnant. My mother had her lover thrown out of the house. As I remember, he was actually stoned. My brothers and I lived in that large house but had no idea what had taken place till later. They tell me herbal concoctions were used to get rid of the child and they succeeded, but she never recovered. When I heard the story from a cousin, I confronted my mother. She wept and admitted it was true. She blamed my father's coldness and cruelty and I'm sure there is some truth in that, but I always recall my father as dark visaged, tall, dignified and simple in his tastes. In any event, after learning of this tragedy, I went out of my way to be nice to my half-sister. Like you, my brothers cannot bear the sight of her, which is unjust. She is our only sister. I don't expect you to like her, but try and understand. She's perfectly harmless.'

Muhammad, my dearest and closest, isn't that upsetting. The problem is that the woman is malicious and evil and I still hate her. I try and imagine what you would say in this situation.

It would probably start with my kind and considerate husband ....

Muhammad, your son was born on the day the Sultan died. We have named him Hamdis ibn Aziz. This should ensure he never writes poetry. My breasts are overflowing. If your throat aches again come to me.

Balkis

Reading her letter agitated him and he began to rub both hands on the silk tunic. That evening he declined both food and the *hammam*, but Mayya assumed he was deep in his work and did not wish to be disturbed. He retired early to his bedchamber and began to pace furiously. Till then he had thought that his passion for her would gently fade and they would see each other once, perhaps twice a year. Now it suddenly struck him that it was his heart that would not tolerate such long absences.

Perhaps he would return to Siracusa with the Amir after the Sultan's funeral. The more he thought about it, the better this idea seemed. Elinore, Mayya and Afdal could come as well. He would go and see his grandsons near Noto, perhaps visit the village where the Trusted One had performed miracles and, above all, Balkis would not be far away. The thought improved his spirits, but still he would not take off the tunic and when, late that night, there was an urgent knock on the door he was still dressed.

Ibn Fityan apologised for waking him up, but he wanted him to know that an incident had taken place in the gardens that evening. The young son of a Baron from Messina, barely twenty years old himself but accompanied by two or three older soldiers, had gone in search of young boys in the gardens. They were about to dishonour a boy when they found themselves surrounded by fifty men carrying short daggers and axes. The Franks fought fiercely and decapitated one opponent, but they were badly outnumbered and were overwhelmed. They were executed on the spot and the bodies were taken away and thrown into the sea.

'Why is this considered serious enough to wake me early in the morning?'

'When the son did not return, the Baron went in search of him. Naturally he didn't find him and he has demanded that unless the *qadi* produces his son, he will take hostages from the city back to Messina.'

'Intolerable and unacceptable.'

'They want you to tell William that if this were to happen the city would explode and delay his coronation indefinitely.'

'I will speak with him after the funeral. Ibn Fityan, was this ambush carefully prepared?'

'It would appear so.'

'Is there any possibility that someone might reveal the truth?'

'Nobody knows who organised and carried out this attack. It is a secret organisation and they are all sworn to secrecy.'

'Remarkable.'

'Would you like me to help you undress?'

Idrisi looked at himself and laughed.

'I think I can manage. Peace be upon you.'

Wide awake and alert, Idrisi undressed and made his ablutions. He began to compose a reply to Balkis in his head, but it was only half finished when he fell fast asleep. He was woken by Ibn Fityan to prepare himself for the funeral.

The cathedral was filled and a few people had gathered on the streets, but the spectre of the martyred Philip hung over the proceedings. The Archbishop of Palermo, who conducted the obsequies, appeared to be so delighted with his role that he almost forget that it was supposed to be a sad occasion. William paid his father a glowing tribute, with more than a few of the phrases he had heard the previous day from Idrisi. Later, the new ruler summoned his old tutor to the palace. A wake had been organised and the great hall that had witnessed the humiliation of Philip was now lavish with food and wine.

Idrisi was present for one reason alone: in detaching William from the clutches of fawning courtiers, he informed him of the situation in the old city. The young man was greatly angered at the thought of his coronation being subverted because of baronial excesses and summoned the Archbishop. The prelate, delighted at being singled out at such a distinguished gathering, nodded sagely and disappeared to do his ruler's bidding. 'Tell the *qadi* he need not worry any longer. And, Master Idrisi, I have discovered it was the Amir of Catania who farted on both occasions. Remarkable man.'

SIXTEEN

Spring in Siracusa. Good and bad poetry.
Fathers and sons.

There can be few delights in the world as pleasant as a Siracusan spring. The fragrance of the lemon, orange, apricot, almond and peach blossoms pervade the city, enriched by the moist, salty sea breezes. On the hills outside the city the age-old, laboriously cultivated plantations of olive trees are being carefully inspected for the damage caused by the winter storms and lightning. The sun radiates a welcome warmth and the air is fresh, not mournful and lazy, as in summer.

And all this is greatly enhanced when a person is in love. Since his arrival from Palermo a month ago, Idrisi and Balkis had revelled in each other's company. There was nothing furtive in their behaviour, but were it not for the fact that they went riding openly and were sometimes accompanied by the Amir himself, there would have been an incessant wagging of tongues. The palace eunuchs and a few loyal serving women were aware that Balkis often spent the night in Idrisi's room and, while they talked to each other, they ensured the secret remained confined to the palace.

One glorious fresh morning, before the sun had dried the earth, she insisted they discard their sandals and walk to bathe their feet in dew, on the leaves and grass. It was one of his cures for persistent headaches and he asked if she was feeling well.

'I read a bad poem by Ibn Hamdis this morning while you were still asleep and it gave me a headache.'

He smiled. 'Balkis, you are unfair to the poet. There are some unbearable poems, but he has also written some very fine verses. You must not punish him because Aziz belongs to the same family.'

'You cannot imagine the praise they reserve for him. It's as if no other poet had existed. Aziz is more restrained, but even he insisted on naming our son Hamdis. Why are you laughing?'

'I shouldn't encourage you, but I suddenly remember a quatrain written by Ibn Hamid, one of my childhood friends from Noto.'

'You never mentioned him before.'

'Too many painful memories. We quarrelled before he left. He accused me of being a creature of the Sultan. I miss him greatly now and ...'

'The quatrain?'

'Let me try and remember. A minor poet from Noto, well-known frequenter of bars and brothels, is visiting Siracusa to sample his favourite male prostitute. He runs into Ibn Hamdis. The great poet is agitated and his clothes are ruffled. The visitor from Noto inquires politely as to the cause and a brief exchange between the two is abruptly brought to an end:

> *"I have been robbed! The thieves have ruined me!"*
> *"I sympathise, I share your grief."*
> *"They stole a batch of my own poetry!"*
> *"I sympathise – with the poor thief."'*

She laughed unrestrainedly.

'My headache has gone. Your cure has worked.'

◖◖

Idrisi had come prepared for a long stay, accompanied by Elinore, Ibn Thawdor, and three hundred books considered necessary for his still uncompleted work. Mayya had promised to come later when Afdal was slightly older. Idrisi's day was carefully organised. He spent five hours in the palace library where he was surprised to find a few manuscripts by authors previously unknown to him. He was impatient with any book that contained superstitions and presented them as scientific knowledge. And there were many of these he had angrily thrust aside during the course of his work.

The rest of the day was spent in Balkis's company. They could talk and laugh together for hours. She accepted his balanced critique of Ibn Hamdis and phrased her own remarks more carefully, but her basic view of the poet remained unaltered, although they agreed never to discuss the matter with the poet's descendant.

Elinore had begged him to let her marry as soon as possible. He had observed the young couple on the boat journey and was convinced that they were destined for each other. He asked them both whether they were happy to be married in the absence of her mother and his parents and was told that both parties had recommended this course of action. The Amir took charge of the matter and on a beautiful Sunday morning, Elinore bint Muhammad and Ibn Thawdor were married by a Bishop at a quiet ceremony in the old Byzantine church. They were assigned a set of rooms in the palace and at the feast that evening, Ibn Thawdor played the flute to mark his own wedding.

Several weeks later a messenger arrived from Noto with a letter from Sakina, his oldest daughter, informing Idrisi that her mother had died peacefully a few days earlier. The rest of the family had gathered, with the exception of Walid, and she pleaded with Idrisi to return to the estate and decide what should be done. It was not a decision for her or anyone else.

'I will have to go,' he told Balkis. 'I was quite content to die without seeing my house again, but Allah has willed otherwise. It is strange, but I feel nothing for the departed woman. Nothing.'

'Take Elinore and Ibn Thawdor with you. You enjoy their company and she should see the house where her father was born. If I did not have to carry out the five obligatory breast-feedings for Hamdis, I would have accompanied you as well, just in case the dust on the journey gave you a sore throat.'

They left early one morning in a large covered cart drawn by two horses and with a retinue of four armed retainers. A new path had been opened to reduce the time it took to reach Noto. The reasons for this were military, but everyone benefited and the traders had been especially pleased. As they passed an ancient viaduct he insisted they break the journey. He had seen it from afar on previous visits and now he had an opportunity to observe its structure more closely.

'I agree to stop,' said Elinore, 'provided we are spared a lecture on ancient Rome.'

Idrisi smiled and ignored the remark, but to punish her he took Ibn Thawdor with him and improved the boy's understanding of the ancient world. As they resumed their journey a silence fell. They were all thinking of what lay ahead.

Idrisi had not seen his oldest son, Uthman, for almost twenty years and the thought of the boy pained him. As a physician, he could try and cure pain and stomach disorders and fevers and snake-bites, but he had no idea what caused mental suffering or why his oldest child had been born with a disordered mind. There was no blemish on his body. He had been as normal as any other child except that he was slow to speak. This had not worried him unduly till the boy was five and barely spoke. He did learn eventually, but it became obvious that he was different from the rest. He preferred to be alone. He would talk to the farm animals at length and could be seen laughing with them, but when a human approached he would rush and hide in a barn or behind a tree or crouch in the open and imagine that nobody could see him.

Not wishing Elinore to be taken by surprise, Idrisi told her the entire story. Her only response was to hold his hand tightly. She had been wondering how the family would receive her and Ibn Thawdor. Perhaps it had been a mistake to come with her father.

The sun was still up as they entered the estate on the outskirts of Noto. The large house stood at the top of the exposed hill. It was built on two levels around a courtyard bordered by a row of orange trees. Behind the house were peasant houses built on the slope and near them a tiny domed mosque.

Below the house, on either side of the path, were gently sloping terraces, first cultivated by his grandfather. Fruits of every variety were flanked by mulberry for the silkworms. Vegetables and wheat were grown in the flat fields nearby. The sight pleased him. Sakina's mother must have been a good administrator – something he could not quite believe – but there was nobody else who could have watched over everything, once he had left and made it clear he had no intention of returning.

He saw Khalid riding towards them, waving. Idrisi waved back. The boy has lost a mother and a grandmother in the space of a year. A growing boy needs a woman in the household. Umar should marry again.

'Jiddu, Jiddu,' the boy was shouting, as he got closer. He abandoned the horse he had been riding bare-backed and boarded the cart, embracing his grandfather and managing a broad smile as he was introduced to his new aunt and Ibn Thawdor. How he had grown over the last six months. A beard and moustache were sprouting on his face. Elinore hoped her father would not refer to them and embarrass Khalid, but was disappointed.

'I'm glad to see a beard on the way. Have you decided whether you want to grow it long or short?'

'I do not want to grow it at all, Jiddu. No beard. No moustache.'

'Unthinkable, boy. Unthinkable. Everyone in our family has grown one or the other. I shall speak with your father. We shall see what he has to say on this subject.'

'The Trusted One says that these things do not matter at all.'

'Then why does he grow a beard?'

'Because he's too lazy to shave it off. He's looking forward to seeing you again.'

'Is he here?'

'Yes, of course. He came with us. He and Abu have become very close friends.'

There goes my estate, thought Idrisi.

The rest of them, too, had sighted him and were waiting to receive him. Sakina kissed his hands and he hugged and kissed her head. Her husband was present as well with the twins. He embraced Abu Khalid with special warmth. They were all introduced to the newly wed couple. Sakina, having lost a sister, was anxious to please the new one. She took Elinore and Ibn Thawdor to their rooms. Idrisi looked around him.

'Where is Uthman?'

'I'll take you to him,' replied Khalid.

The sight of his first-born had always had a disquieting effect on him. He must be thirty-five this year. The woman who looked after Uthman saw them approach. At least she's still alive, Idrisi thought to himself. Her strong bony frame must have helped her survive the worst of a hard life. Then he saw Uthman hiding behind a tree and observing him.

'Peace be upon you, son. Will you not come and greet your old father?'

Idrisi was shocked as he watched Uthman emerge from hiding. He had aged beyond his years. His hair was white and he walked with the step of a frail old man. Yet, he spoke in a strong, self-assured voice. 'Peace upon you, Abu. It is good to see you after so many years. You know, of course, that my mother and sister were killed by Roman soldiers.'

'Uthman, it's nice to see you after all these years. Is there anything you need? Anything?'

'I need a wife, Abu. A wife.'

'Do you have anyone in mind?'

Uthman took his father by the arm and walked him to the sheep pen. He pointed to a sheep.

'Yes I can see Uthman. Sheep.'

'That one,' he said pointing again, 'I want to marry her. Don't tell me it isn't permitted Abu. Who doesn't permit? Who?'

Idrisi realised that a reference to al-Quran would not carry much weight with his poor son. He decided to try something else.

'The Roman Emperor has forbidden marriage between humans and animals.'

Uthman yelled, 'I know that, of course. It's to defy him that I will go through with this marriage. Let his soldiers come. We will trap and kill them. Have you got your shield and spear ready, young Khalid?'

'I have, uncle.'

'Go and bring them.'

As Khalid disappeared Uthman sat down on the chair beneath the tree and spoke again.

'It was the great Greek thinker Pythagoras who taught us that humans were reincarnated as animals, father. Did you know that? Please arrange my wedding.'

'I did know that, son, but where did you hear about it?'

'In your library. I often go and read. There are many books of interest. I enjoy that a great deal.'

Tears filled his father's eyes. What had gone wrong with his child? The ancients wrote of people losing their minds, but had no cure. There must be a cure. Why should a mental ailment be ignored or be dependent on remedies based on pure superstition?

'Will you not come into the house and break bread with us?'

'I can't, Abu, because you will sit down and eat my mother-in-law. I saw her being killed, unclothed, marinated, after which little spears of garlic pierced her body and then they covered her in wild thyme because even they were ashamed of her nakedness. You can see her now being roasted gently on the fire.'

'Tomorrow, I promise we will not consume any meat. Will you eat with us then?'

'With great pleasure, Abu. I am glad to see you again. And I was glad to hear from my nephew that your book was completed. Thank you for coming to see me.'

As Idrisi walked back to the house he reflected on the fact that the only member of his family who had shown any interest in his book was his mentally disturbed son. Later, Sakina told him that on most days, apart from his conversations with the animals, Uthman was completely normal. It was only when he imagined the soldiers were going to find and kill him that he left the house and hid outside for days. And he was frightened of visitors – he thought they were spies who would return and inform on him to the commander of the Roman Legion in Siracusa.

'Why has he aged so much?'

'It has happened slowly, but we do not know why. Ummi thought it must be related to the disease.'

'I'm not sure about that at all.'

Khalid, who had been listening to them, had another theory.

'I think it's sadness that has turned his hair white. Day after day, he sits in his chair and watches the animals being slaughtered. It really upsets him. You know something, Jiddu, I sit with him when he talks to the animals. He tries to teach them our history and about our Prophet and then the battles, but usually he talks to them about ancient Greece and its great philosophers. I have learnt a great deal from him. Why can't we let him marry who he wants?'

'Khalid!' warned his aunt.

'The boy could well be right on why he has aged prematurely. Is there no way of moving him away from the animals? What if we removed all the animals from the estate?'

The suggestion panicked Khalid. 'Don't ever do that, Jiddu. He would only think they had all been killed and would kill himself.'

'You seem to know him better than anyone else, my child. Surely, one thing that could be easily organised is to make sure the animals are slaughtered at night when he is asleep. If it causes him so much distress, why do it in front of him? What do you think?'

Khalid thought for a while. 'It is a good idea, but he knows them all and would still miss them, but it would still be a better way.'

That same evening Sakina instructed the butcher, and the lambs and goats were removed at night. Over the next week Uthman appeared much happier and one afternoon whispered to Khalid, 'My friends are learning how to escape. They know they're about to be slaughtered and run away each night. I told them to go and hide in the caves near the sea. I hope my fiancée doesn't run away.'

'But my dearest uncle, wouldn't you rather she ran away? What if they killed her?'

'You are a very clever boy. I'm proud of you. I suppose I'll have to marry someone else.'

That night the sheep that had caught Uthman's eye was taken from the pen and made ready for the kitchen the next morning. They ate her at the midday meal and Idrisi noticed Khalid picking nervously at the meat rather than eating it properly.

Perhaps there is no medicine for his disease, thought Idrisi, but if there is a cure, it must involve entering his head and Khalid has done so more than any adult in the household.

The Trusted One was of the same opinion. He had engaged in a number of conversations with Uthman in the library and was amazed that he knew where every single book was located and, of the books he himself had read, he could cite page numbers and references without any problems.

'Perhaps only a part of his mind has ceased to function. The rest is fine. This is the part of the human body of which we physicians know the least.'

One night after the evening meal, they gathered around a fire that had been lit outside, ate dried fruits and sipped wild mint tea underneath the stars. It reminded Idrisi of his youth. He took Elinore aside and pointed at the lights of a distant village.

'I used to ride there once a day just to catch a glimpse of your mother.'

'And my aunt?'

'No, you wretch. She was far too young to be taken seriously.'

Abu Khalid suggestively cleared his throat and Idrisi and Elinore returned to the family circle. Idrisi spoke of the deaths in the family and praised his late wife for the efficient way in which she had run the estate. An unexpected reflection interrupted him.

'I wish Walid were present to hear you say that, Abu. It would have made him happy.'

Idrisi smiled. 'I, too, wish he was here, Uthman. May Allah protect all my children.'

He described how it had been a hilly wasteland when his grandfather first arrived one summer. It had taken them six months alone to dig the stones from the soil for the first few terraces. Many of the stones had been used to build the house. When the winter rains came, the earth was transformed, the hills turning green and the streams overflowing. Only then were they certain they had made a good choice.

'And now we have hard decisions to take. Even if I remain on this island I will never live here again. Sakina lives with her family. Abu Khalid and Khalid are happy on their own estate. Uthman, of course, will live here with his friends, but he cannot manage the estate. The peasants who work these estates, like their forebears before them, will suffer greatly if we were to sell the estate. I was wondering how we should solve this problem when Khalid told me that he and his father had invited the Trusted One to join us. So I turn to him. Holy man, if that is what you are, explain to us how we will teach the peasants to bear false witness with brazen faces in order to defend themselves against the future. We have all heard of the village where miracles took place after your visit.'

The demeanour of the Trusted One had altered since he had met Bulbula's sister. He had cut his hair short and trimmed his beard. He bathed more regularly and wore clean clothes, all this partly in response to a heart-rending plea from Bulbula's sister. But he was also aware that descriptions of him were circulating all over the island and that the swinish Lombards would soon seek their revenge.

The scholar had posed questions that required a response. 'Learned Master Idrisi, I thank you and your family for the hospitality you have given me. As I see it, there are few problems with this estate. The peasants have not been mistreated and they are all Believers. The size of the estate is not excessive. I have been making some estimates. There are a hundred peasant families in addition to six retainers in the household.'

'In fact, Trusted One,' said Uthman, 'there are one hundred and three families and eight retainers. You forgot to count the butcher and the wood cutter who eat daily in our kitchen.'

'I thank you for correcting me, Uthman ibn Muhammad. There is enough land here to be divided among these families. That will still leave sufficient land to maintain the estate, not as before but certainly without creating a problem. Then there is the question of bearing false witness. This is unnecessary for Ibn Muhammad will himself sign the papers of transfer and these can be registered in Noto. The problem is the future. If we are defeated, the only way for the peasants to keep the land is to pretend they are Nazarenes. You have a small mosque here, but no church. I think we need one. Greek not Latin. It's simpler. If the peasants agree, I have seen a site where it could be constructed quite easily. Once that is done, we will need a monk and a register where he will testify he converted this village the day Rujari died to honour his memory.'

'Trusted One,' Uthman asked in a nervous voice, 'will my friends be forced to become Nazarenes?'

'What are they at the moment?'

'They are neither Believers nor Nazarenes. They still worship the old Greek god, Poseidon.'

'It will not be necessary for them to convert.'

'I won't either.'

'That will not be a problem.'

'Perhaps all this can be done,' said Idrisi, 'but our peasants are very religious and I am doubtful whether they will agree to change their religion to keep their land.'

'This is a strange island,' said the Trusted One. 'Its climate and its way of life have a way of affecting everyone. The choice is either to let the tyrant reap the seed they have sown and be driven off the land or to pretend they have been baptised. They can pray to Allah five times a day in the field or at home. But the choice is for them, not for you or me. That much I learnt from the other village. We had won, but the peasants were scared of reprisals. And to promise them that there would be no revenge killing because we were going to be victorious and re-take the island was unconvincing. I'm not sure whether that is possible, given our present state, so how could I convince anyone else? It was then that I thought of conversions planned by us as a counter to those forced on our people by a sword. Where's the harm? Allah be praised, if we win. If we lose, let us ensure the peasants and their families are secure even though we may not be. It is the least that can be done for them.'

'It is sensible advice, I grant you,' said Idrisi. 'But on this estate they have not had to struggle against adversity and that has given them a remarkable self-confidence. I will back your advice.'

Elinore and her husband discussed their future through the night. She wanted to leave Siqilliya, but he wanted to stay so that their children would be born here. He reminded her that his family had lived in Siracusa since the town was built. She argued that she could not bear her children being brought up in the midst of bloodshed and uncertainty. If Rujari, whom she had loved, could kill Philip whom she had admired, the bloodletting on this island would never stop. He leaned and whispered something in her ear which made her laugh. It was a deep, throaty laugh, uncalculating and straight from the heart.

'Does that mean we have reached a compromise, my lady?'

'Blow out the candle, Simeon, and let me sleep. You will know in the morning.'

The next morning, the sound of the flute woke her. By the early morning light at the window she saw him, his face leaned sideways, his eyes gazing sadly at the distant sea. She had never realised that music could have such an effect on her. Now she wished she had bowed to her mother's pressure and learnt how to play the lute when they still lived in the palace. She had made up her mind, but would tell Simeon later.

The Trusted One had woken early so he could speak with the peasant families. He had organised a *mehfil* for the late afternoon, an hour before they usually finished working in the fields. All they had been told was that Ibn Muhammad al-Idrisi had returned to the estate and wished to consult with them. Sakina was already in the kitchen supervising the food that had to be prepared to feed the assembly.

Idrisi had taken Uthman on a walk to breathe the air and inspect the fruit trees. Uthman proved himself knowledgeable here as well, looking closely at each tree and estimating the fruit it would bear later in the year. His constant urge to assert himself delighted his father, who wondered whether they had left him on his for too long and whether talking to him each day and treating him as a normal person might not have partially cured him.

Suddenly, from a distance, they heard the sound of people running towards them and hailing them. Uthman froze, his face filled with fear. Idrisi put his arms around his son's shoulders and told him not to worry, they were friends, not Roman soldiers.

'Are you sure, Abu? Neither of us are wearing swords.'

A shiny-eyed Elinore and Simeon, his golden locks ruffled by the breeze, both slightly out of breath, stopped running as they saw her father. Uthman smiled and relaxed once again. He liked Elinore and loved hearing Simeon play the flute. Idrisi looked at her and knew instantly that she had something to say but had not expected to find Uthman with him.

'What is on your mind, child? There are no secrets from your brother.'

'I will go and sit under the tree, if you like,' said Uthman.

'No!'

'Then speak.'

'Simeon ibn Thawdor and I have been thinking a great deal. We have come to a decision, but only if it meets with your approval, Abi. We would like to come and live here with Uthman and … if the Trusted One is right about the need to build a church, then Simeon could, when the need arose, don a monk's robe and hide his flute.'

Uthman clapped his hands in excitement and Idrisi laughed. He was surprised and delighted. What had been worrying him was the thought of Uthman, abandoned by his family and dependent exclusively on retainers. He felt guilty that he had abandoned this boy at a young age. Now his daughter had decided to do what he should have done years ago.

'A wonderful decision! As long as you are happy here, everyone else will be. But till you need to become a monk, Simeon, you should choose a piece of land and work it.'

'I will,' he replied, 'but first we must build a small church. A single dome, a cross and unadorned, rough wooden benches inside. The map is in my head. It could be used as a school. Elinore is determined to teach the children how to read and write Arabic and Greek.'

'When will you have the children?'

'Uthman!' she shrieked as she stood, legs apart and hands on hips. 'We've only just got married. Give us time. Simeon was talking about the village children.'

'I am very happy you and Simeon will live here with me. Very happy. We have much to discuss, but now if you will excuse me, I must go and inform my friends.'

When the villagers arrived for the *mehfil* they were dressed in their best clothes. Idrisi, who knew most of the families, sat with them while they ate and they talked of what the island had been before they had arrived. All that had been grown was wheat. Now they had cotton and silkworms and the sumac tree for tanning and dyeing and our weavers – here they were talking of Noto alone – were the best on the island, if not in the world. A voice added: 'Noto was the last to surrender and will be the first to rise against them.'

After they had eaten, Idrisi and the Trusted One spoke in turn and explained how they saw the future of the estate. The villagers were overjoyed when Idrisi told them the land would belong to them, but less pleased when the Trusted One gently explained that the path to long-term survival might necessitate a detour via the church.

'Trusted One,' a young peasant asked, 'it is normal to dream of victories and triumphs, but you speak only of defeat. Are you so sure we will be defeated? Our village has pledged fifty young men to fight in the jihad.'

'My friend,' replied the Trusted One, 'it is best to be prepared for everything. I do not know if we shall win or lose. What you do must be your own choice. If we are defeated I am telling you that, as night follows day, so the Lombards will arrive to kill all of you and steal your land. They have been known to kill Greeks as well so the church might not be sufficient protection, but at least it offers you a chance.'

Idrisi introduced Elinore and Simeon to them. He explained without embarrassment how both of them had been baptised and would live in the house with his son, Uthman. He spoke of Elinore's wish to teach their children to read and write. He advised them to follow the Trusted One's advice and then, perhaps because he was thinking of Balkis, he quoted a couplet from Ibn Hamdis.

'Our poet has written: *I exhausted the energies of war/I carried on my shoulders the burdens of peace.* These burdens remain and it is to lighten the load that the Trusted One suggests that, if it becomes necessary, you hide your true religion. Such periods are not unknown in the history of our people.'

After further discussion agreement was reached and in their presence Idrisi asked the Trusted One to prepare a set of registers, one for the land and the other for the church. And then, as if to confirm their new dreams, Simeon played a joyful strain on the flute and everyone began to clap in rhythm, till a few young bloods rose and began to dance. It was, as Idrisi later told Simeon, a traditional Berber dance that he had not seen performed for many years, memories of life in the distant past.

That night Idrisi took Khalid's father aside. 'Umar, you are like a son to me. May I speak frankly with you?'

'Of course, Abu Uthman. Please.'

'Khalid is growing fast. Before you know he will be arguing and pleading with you to leave the estate and find his own feet and fortune elsewhere. But I feel the boy lacks a woman's affection. Have you thought of getting married again?'

'I have, but I have not yet met or seen a woman who attracts me.'

'Noto and Siracusa are full of them, their skins the colour of apricot and their laughter like the ripple of a stream. You won't find anyone on your estate. Get out for a while. Give yourself a chance.'

'It is good advice and I will see if I can satisfy both you and myself.'

The next morning, Khalid and his father, accompanied by the Trusted One, left the estate and Sakina followed them a few weeks later. Her husband and children had returned the day after the funeral and she felt that it was time to return and tend to their needs.

The house was virtually empty and Uthman was missing his nephew and so Simeon and Elinore had decided not to return with Idrisi the following day to fetch their belongings. 'All our clothes are already in Siracusa and my aunt Balkis can have them bundled and sent over here. I don't want to leave Uthman. If we all left the shock might be too much for him.'

'Please convey my respects and love to my father when you return to Palermo. And tell him I am building a small church. It will please my mother.'

Idrisi embraced and kissed each of them in turn and was deeply affected to see the tears in Uthman's eyes.

'Abu, it was a real pleasure to see you after such a long time. Please come again and before twenty years, eight months and four days.'

Idrisi's eyes were moist as he climbed aboard the cart and it was Uthman who was most in his thoughts as he journeyed back to Siracusa. He recalled how all his love and his hopes had been concentrated on Walid, how it was Walid he took everywhere with him. It was Walid who met the Sultan and travelled to meet old family friends in Shakka and Marsa Ali. It was Walid in whom he had confided. He did not regret that, but was angered now by his failure to understand that Uthman had needed him much more.

Observing the change in Uthman had been a revelation. Perhaps he would write about it in his book to help others who had to deal with abnormal children. In many villages children like Uthman were left in the open to die. They had not done that, but had his care been any better? He had been left in the hands of a deaf woman who had made sure he was fed and clothed. So who could blame him for seeking solace in the animal kingdom? Idrisi found himself wondering whether he should return to the estate for a time. He could complete the Formulary in his own library. Mayya and Afdal could come here as well. It was the turn of the house in Palermo to be empty for a while. And Balkis could come here whenever she wished. The more he thought about this the more it appealed to him. His ship was moored in Siracusa; he would return to Palermo and bring them all to Noto. The harbour was not as large as Siracusa, but fine for his vessel. And perhaps he would take Uthman with him to Venice and surprise Walid. He had been away from Palermo for almost three months – surprising how little he missed the city.

Even a year ago the thought of living anywhere else would have been laughable. History had changed everything. Rujari and Philip. The two men he had felt closest to in the palace. Not just history. Mayya and Elinore and Balkis.

Who could have predicted what had happened? Not Allah. Then he wondered: if Philip were alive and Rujari dead would he have felt the same way about Palermo? He had said no to William, but if Philip had insisted that he could be of vital service to the state, would he have been able to decline so swiftly, if at all? Who would have won the tug of war for his services? Philip or Balkis? History could only be the result of a disordered imagination.

SEVENTEEN

Massacre in Palermo.
Idrisi decides never to visit the city again.
He leaves for Baghdad.

He knew something was wrong the minute he entered the palace in Siracusa. When the guard saw him at the gate, he had signalled the doorman and sad faces kept turning away from him as a gloomy-faced Chamberlain led him to the Amir's private chamber.

I hope nothing has happened to Balkis he thought to himself over and over again. He entered the Amir's chamber to find Balkis there, her eyes red from crying. It was the sight of Abu Fityan that astonished him. The man fell on his knees and rested his head on Idrisi's feet.

'Forgive me, Ibn Muhammad. Forgive me.'

'Will someone tell me what's happened. Mayya?'

Balkis nodded.

'Dead? Why?' He wept loudly.

'Afdal?'

'Is safe here with us and fast asleep.'

'Allah be praised. Ibn Fityan, stop weeping and tell me what happened.'

But tears continued to flow. After some time the story began to unfold, interrupted by weeping and questioning from those present. It emerged that what had taken place was a revenge killing.

The Baron from Messina wanted to know why the young Sultan had ordered him not to take any hostages from Palermo. The Sultan explained that this was unacceptable behaviour and that Master Idrisi had warned it could provoke an explosive response. The baron had bowed and left. This much was reported to Ibn Fityan by the palace eunuchs who overheard the exchange. The mood of the city was tense. There had been another brawl and both sides were hurling abuse at each other. Two days later, Mayya felt that Afdal, who was recovering from a fever, might benefit from the sea air. She asked Thawdor and Ibn Fityan to accompany the child and the maid to the shore.

'When I returned, Master, there was blood on the stairs and my heart began to race. I rushed in and saw the bodies of the servants littered on the floor. They had been disembowelled and their throats were slit. There was only one survivor. He was in your room and hid underneath the bed. The Lady Mayya had been dishonoured and killed.'

Idrisi and Balkis, ignoring Ibn Fityan's presence, comforted each other, wiping the tears from each other's cheeks.

'What has happened Balkis? Why? I should have insisted she come here. I should have forced her. My poor Mayya. Why her? Why not me? It was me they were after. How will I face Elinore? You must go and tell her, Balkis. Yes, yes, Ibn Fityan, finish your story. Don't weep, man. I'm glad you're alive. Otherwise they would have killed Afdal and Thawdor and you. How could you have saved them? You would have been killed like the rest. It was not your fault. There is no reason to feel guilty. '

Ibn Fityan wiped his tears and continued. 'The boy who survived told me the men were in their cups, shouting obscenities and destroying everything. Some of your books were thrown out of the window. The rest were on the floor where these animals defecated and urinated on them.'

Idrisi's sadness was mixed with rage.

'Is there no limit to these barbarians?'

'The whole city is stunned by the crime, Ibn Muhammad. The Sultan has ordered the arrest of the Baron from Messina. He wants the Baron and the Lombard hirelings to be publicly executed. The English Bishop is advising caution.'

Idrisi recalled the Englishman, middle-aged with light brown eyes and thinning hair, intelligent, ruthless and with a mocking, unpleasant, rasping voice, but also with an unlimited capacity to flatter those in power or close to it. Most courts have them, but this Bishop was unique. Rujari had never liked or trusted him, often remarking that the man was in the pay of the Vatican.

'He is an evil one. Monks never advise caution when it's a question of killing our people.'

Ibn Fityan shook his head sadly.

'The Sultan sends his condolences and wishes you to return to Palermo.'

'I will not return. I do not wish to see that house again.'

'A wise decision.'

'Where is Thawdor?'

'He is here. He wished to see his son and, like me, he cannot bear the sight of Palermo or the house. I brought the maid as well since Afdal ibn Muhammad is used to her presence.'

'You were wise to bring him here. Both of you can accompany me back to the estate. Perhaps Afdal ...'

'Leave him here,' said Balkis. 'There will be time later. Elinore needs you and there must be no distractions.'

'Ibn Fityan, it would be helpful if you and Thawdor remained on the estate. He can bring his wife as well.'

'I will do as you suggest, master.'

After Ibn Fityan had left the room, Balkis drew Idrisi to her, resting his head on her lap, and combed his hair with her fingers.

'It is unbearable, Balkis, that she should be punished in my stead. It's unbearable. And those animals raped and humiliated her. My son Uthman would reprimand me for referring to them as animals. He thinks humans are much worse.'

'Uthman? Your son? You never spoke of him before now.'

'Humans have this capacity to shield themselves from unpalatable truths. I am ashamed I never spoke of Uthman. He was so happy to see Elinore that he demanded I tell him all about Mayya.'

'I want to know all about Uthman.'

To distract them both from their grief, he described Uthman's history to her in detail, how he found it easier to relate to animals or young humans like Khalid than to the human race. Balkis determined to take his new brothers to see him. But now Idrisi knew he must leave again for his estate to give Elinore the terrible news of her mother's death. Before his departure he wanted to see Afdal. Balkis took him by the arm to the chamber where the boy slept.

He wept again as he saw his sleeping son, not yet six months old. Who could love him like his mother once did? She almost read his thoughts.

'I have enough milk for both of them,' she told him. 'I will bring him up like my own son.'

'Perhaps in a few months' time I should take him to the estate. Let me speak with Elinore.'

As they left the chamber, they saw the Amir who greeted Idrisi with a warm embrace.

'Allah have mercy on us, Ibn Muhammad.'

'Nobody else does,' replied the scholar.

Some hours after he had left, Balkis was feeding both children and noticed that Afdal kept pushing her nipple aside before groping for it again, while Hamdis stuck to it like an insect. Perhaps my milk tastes different and he has noticed. But Eudoxia, the maid who had survived the massacre, reassured Balkis. 'He's like that with every tit, my lady, if you'll pardon my speech.

Your sister – may the Lord bless her – was always struggling to feed him. He's a strong one, this lad, and will give women a lot of trouble, bless him.'

'Do you go to church every Sunday?'

'Yes, my lady.'

'Do you think those barbarians who killed my sister and the servants would have spared you if they'd seen the crucifix hanging from your neck?'

'Oh no, my lady. Two of the girls who were killed had the same cross around their necks. They were animals, my lady, only worse. Lombards! They weren't from this island. Our people ...'

'There is an old Greek church in Siracusa. They say there are two icons that shine and smile in the dark. I have never been inside it. Tell me what it's like.'

'I will, my lady, and thank you for your kindness.'

When Idrisi had been away for over four weeks, Balkis began to panic. She felt neglected and remembered something that Mayya had said to her when they were both pregnant. 'Love and jealousy are sisters, Balkis. I'm love and you're jealousy.'

At the time she'd laughed and greeted the remark with loud protestations, but she knew it contained more than a single grain of truth. As long as Mayya was alive, Balkis had reconciled herself to staying with Aziz and sharing Idrisi with her sister. Now she wanted him all the time. If he decided to live on the estate she could see him three or even four times a week. It took three hours to walk to Noto. She could ride over in under an hour. She began to plan. What she wanted now was another child. Then she could leave Hamdis with his father and she could live with her Muhammad.

Idrisi returned the next week and went first to his son, who was with Eudoxia in the gardens. He held the boy and kissed him many times before he went in search of Balkis. She held him close while he told her of all that had taken place.

'Nothing you couldn't imagine, my loved one. Elinore was inconsolable.

There was nothing I could say or do to comfort her. She stayed in her room and refused to eat. I think it was Simeon's flute that lured her out again. She talked endlessly to Ibn Fityan and Thawdor, but they spared her the worst details. Then she, too, said she never wanted to return to Palermo. Uthman took her out for long walks and she came back with some colour in her cheeks. She is keen for you to go with the boys. Simeon was shaken by the news as well. It was pure chance that his father had survived and he pleaded with the old man to send for his mother. Ibn Fityan will stay on the estate. So, my poor Mayya's death has brought us all back to the Val di Noto.'

'And you, *habibi*? Where will you stay?'

'I want to see the boys grow and Elinore return to happiness. I will finish my book on the estate. And before you remark on how long the book will take, let me inform you, Lady Balkis, another three months and it will be done. I will return tomorrow. When will you come?'

'With you, tomorrow.'

'And the children?'

'Yes. You see, Ibn Muhammad, my husband is a kind and …'

He put his hand on her mouth.

'Mayya's death has made things worse for us. Not seeing you each day is now much more difficult.'

She stroked his hand.

They left early to avoid the boys being subjected to the midday sun. Balkis and Idrisi rode while their sons, Eudoxia and another maid were transported by cart. The party from Siracusa was welcomed with genuine warmth. Elinore clung to her aunt as both women wept. Simeon showed the now completed church to them proudly, Eudoxia falling to her knees the minute she entered to offer a prayer. Simeon watched her dispassionately.

'If the events predicted by the Trusted One come to pass, this little building could be the saving of this estate.'

Elinore was now the accepted lady of the household and the estate. She had assigned rooms for them and Balkis was taken aback to discover that she was to share Idrisi's chamber.

'Is this wise?' she whispered to her niece. 'Might not Uthman find this distasteful?'

'He is a true pagan, aunt. He would find it odd if you had separate rooms since he knows that Hamdis is our brother.'

'Have you created a world without any secrets at all?'

'Nobody knows I'm pregnant.'

Balkis hugged and kissed her niece. 'I'm so pleased for you.'

'I hope it's a girl, aunt. I want to call her Mayya.'

'Sometimes what one hopes, one gets.'

'Not according to Abi. His medical knowledge teaches him otherwise.'

'How is his book?'

'Almost finished he says, but Uthman, who uses the library more than the rest of us, is not so convinced. He says there is another six months' work. And that's another secret. He would be reprimanded if it was discovered he was reading the manuscript whenever Abi went for a walk.'

Balkis expressed surprise at Uthman's capabilities.

'He's normal most of the time. He likes living in an enclosed world. Once I asked if he would visit Siracusa and he ran out of the room and went to his tree. I have discovered the things that upset him and if we avoid mention of them he behaves like anyone else. He says odd thing at times. Once he told me that if there had been no library in the house, he would have died. And he meant every word of it.'

'It seems he knows himself better than most of you know him?'

'That's too simple, aunt, but I can't explain why.'

Balkis felt already at ease. She had no household responsibilities apart from feeding the children and while Idrisi worked she persuaded Uthman to show her the estate, listening attentively as he described each tree and plant. Then she met the animals.

Later that night after she had fed the infants, she returned to her room to find Idrisi having a bad coughing fit. As she approached, he looked up at her with pleading eyes.

'In Allah's name woman, can't you see I need some milk.'

Then she realised. 'Both my breasts are empty. Your sons are as greedy as their father.'

'When will they fill up again?'

'In a few hours.'

She cradled him. 'I don't want to leave you, Muhammad, but I must return tomorrow. There is a feast in honour of Aziz.'

'Why is there never a feast in honour of me?'

'Because he is the Amir of Siracusa, and you, my loved one, are only the Amir of the Book. The rich men of the city enjoy honouring each other. Tomorrow's host is a Jewish merchant, which means that few Nazarenes will attend. Aziz has asked all our notables and, what is unusual, their wives to be present as well. Most of them are placid, pampered, spoiled creatures and will complain bitterly at being forced to.'

'Strange how for the last five hundred years the fate of the Jews has so often been tied to our own future. Where we suffer, they suffer. Where we prosper, they prosper. Where they are present and we are not, they fail to defend themselves and are slaughtered like sheep. It's the same story here, in al-Andalus and in al-Quds, Baghdad, Cairo and Damascus.'

'I'll repeat these wise words to my husband. Perhaps he will find use for them at the feast.'

'And if you permit me, I would like to find use for you tonight.'

And Balkis became pregnant for the second time.

Idrisi would look back on these eight months on the estate as the happiest of his life. Uthman surprised him each day. His bad moments became fewer and fewer and his health improved considerably. His limp vanished altogether and the marks of deprivation on his skin disappeared. Elinore confided to her father that although he still loved sheep, she felt he was ready for marriage with a woman and perhaps her aunt could help. Possibly, her father replied, Balkis can find someone who is intelligent but who also resembled a sheep.

Idrisi had realised that Uthman was secretly reading his book, but far from being angry he was thrilled. Once it was acknowledged, the two would discuss various sections and he would ask Uthman to compare al-Kindi with Hippokrates on a specific cure. Uthman knew every book in the library. Without the three hundred new additions, he had counted three thousand, four hundred and twenty-one volumes.

And there was Balkis, whose visits to the estate became more and more frequent, the larger she grew. He had never loved a woman like this before, not even Mayya. He would see Balkis and Elinore, both heavy with child, walking together and comparing their stomachs. It pleased him to see them like this and once Uthman had wondered aloud whether his nephew or his brother would be born first. What if it was a niece and a sister, his father asked him. He had shrugged his shoulders. It did not matter to him at all. While Hamdis was left behind at the palace in the care of a wet-nurse, Afdal was growing up on the estate. Even when Balkis had to return to Siracusa, she left him in the safe hands of Eudoxia. But the grown-up Afdal adored was his uncle Uthman who spent a great deal of time with him and spoke to him as he would to a peer. The result was that the first words spoken by Afdal were beautifully expressed: friend, sheep, book, butter, goat, flute and Simeon.

The book was finished two months before the new children were due and Idrisi became irritable. It was Balkis who suggested he and Uthman go and see Walid in Venice. The mere suggestion sent Uthman scurrying to his tree and he stayed there till Balkis and Elinore arrived to comfort him and apologise for the suggestion. 'Please don't get rid of me,' was all he said to them. Balkis was mortified.

Unlike his son, Idrisi was ready to travel again. He missed the sea, but he also knew that if he did not go to Walid now it might soon be too late. From there he would go to Alexandria and Cairo and renew long-forgotten friendships. He, who had been lost in his work for so long, now felt the need to be in a city where Believers ruled, but not any city. The barbarians are bad enough, he thought, but we have our own barbarians who burn books by our greatest philosophers and punish poets. If the real barbarians and ours ever got together, Allah alone would not be sufficient to help us.

His mind was made up. He asked Uthman to read the whole manuscript carefully and iron out the inconsistencies. When he came back he would prepare the final draft.

'When will that be, Abu?'

'A few months at most. Look after Afdal for me.'

This was the most painful farewell for they had become strongly attached to each other. After embracing his father, Uthman retreated to the tree once again. He did not like people leaving the estate.

Idrisi wished Elinore and Simeon well and asked if they had thought of a name in case it was a boy.

'Thawdor,' replied Elinore.

'Original,' replied her father.

Balkis had sworn to herself she would not weep and her eyes remained dry.

'If our child is a girl and Elinore has a boy, I will call our daughter Mayya. Agreed?'

'Agreed. And if it is a boy?'

'Nuwas! Agreed.'

'Agreed. And what if you both have girls?'

'I hadn't thought of that possibility.'

'Let there be two Mayyas.'

'I will. Muhammad I need to know the truth. Could you put a price on our love?'

'How could I? It's priceless.'

'Then make sure you return to me. I don't want to think of you as a beggar in a foreign land. This island is your home regardless of everything. And the elixir that cures your cough is not of the same quality elsewhere.'

He kissed her eyes and then her lips.

Two days sailing and Siracusa already seemed far away. Idrisi did not know it, but he had passed a merchant ship carrying Walid to Siqilliya. He wondered if they could ever take the island back from the Franks and get rid of the Lombards. But if we did succeed, what would we do this time that was different from the last? Would we be able to work together? Give the people something that they would die for without too much urging? The Trusted One had useful ideas, but the big problem was to break from tribal modes of thought and rise to the level of the culture we have created. But these are all golden dreams. How can one deal with hundreds of thousands of people who ignore their own interests and head proudly towards one disaster, then another?

Perhaps he would not visit Alexandria this time. He would go to the city of the caliphs and mingle with the poets and philosophers and search for new books in the House of Wisdom. He would go to Baghdad, the city that will always be ours. The city that will never fall. The city that will never fall.

LUCERA

1250–1300

Epilogue

Idrisi met Walid on his return to Siqilliya and lived on his estate till his death eleven years after that of Rujari. His Medical Formulary was published in Baghdad, but did not contain the remedy for coughs. Uthman and Walid never married. Balkis's son Nuwas became a wandering poet, leaving Siracusa when he was eighteen and moving from one city to another in al-Andalus. None of his poems have survived. Elinore's daughter, Mayya, and her three brothers and their children continued to live on the estate where a larger church had to be constructed to accommodate the new flock. The Trusted One, after teaching philosophy and history to Khalid and his children, died peacefully at the age of eighty-four. The village he helped to re-found still exists and venerates his memory – though he is now regarded as a Christian saint.

In the hundred years that elapsed after Idrisi's death, members of his family fought in every single rebellion. While the Franks were fighting each other for the throne in Palermo, armed bands under the command of Khalid ibn Umar and Afdal ibn Muhammad had liberated large parts of western

Siqilliya. The Franks sent expeditions to crush them, but were content to keep them confined to their strongholds. An uprising in Palermo had shaken Frankish self-confidence and severe restrictions had been imposed. The Friday *khutba* was forbidden and attendance of any *mehfil* was punished with death.

Khalid died at the age of sixty as church bells were ringing to mark twelve hundred years of the Nazarene religion. His son Muhammad joined Afdal and for many years they harassed and destroyed many legions despatched by Palermo to crush them.

It was Rujari's grandson, Frederick, who finally destroyed the last remaining strongholds of the rebellion in Siqilliya. His love of Arabic culture and his own palaces and harems had led some Believers to hope that the golden age might return. But they had forgotten that young Frederick was also the grandson of Barbarossa. The two strains in him often led to compromises. He did not wish to massacre the Muslims, but simply to remove them and thus purify the island. In the twelve hundred and twenty-fourth year of the Christian era, those who refused to convert were asked to pack their belongings and were taken to large enclosures in all the key ports of the island. For twelve months, over fifty thousand Siqilliyans who refused to surrender spiritually were transported in ships to the mainland. Among them were Idrisi's grandchildren, Muhammad ibn Afdal, Muhammad ibn Khalid and their families.

In the region of Apulia, near an ancient Roman town where once Caesar had battled Pompey, there was a tiny village, Lucera, virtually uninhabited. This is where they were transported. Within two years, Lucera had become one of the most prosperous towns of the south. The land surrounding the settlement was cultivated after years of lying fallow, workshops sprang up to produce arms and clothes and skilled craftsmen produced wooden inlays and ceramics that were no longer being made in Noto and Siracusa. Frederick built a castle for himself with its own harem. The settlers built a beautiful mosque with a large library, not far from the castle. The Pope excommunicated Frederick for permitting the construction of buildings where 'cursed Muhammad is adored'. It is said that when the excommunication was read to him in his palace at Lucera, he was in his cups, surrounded by concubines and listening to music. Extremely annoyed by what the Pope had done, he responded in the time-honoured tradition of the Siqilliyan side of his family. He farted.

Within the settlement, three young men began to organise secret *mehfils*. They would meet each Friday night and discuss the future of their people. Slowly more and more people, young and old, men and women, began to listen. Ibn Afdal would tell them that Lucera appeared peaceful and they were not persecuted, even though too many young men had been killed fighting Frederick's war against other Nazarenes.

'Having forced us to leave Siqilliya, he can be kind, but this same King who permitted us to build the Great Mosque here is destroying all our mosques in Palermo and the rest of the island. We have been discussing our future for many months now. I would suggest that we prepare to leave this place. It will not be safe after Frederick dies. I am not suggesting that we leave at once. They would kill us before we travelled too far. But each month one family should leave.'

'Where should we go, Ibn Afdal? Is there anywhere left for us?'

Fifteen men rose from the ground and stood on their feet in different parts of the *mehfil*.

'Yes. If you wish to go you will speak to one of these men. Look at them carefully. If you know them try and forget their names. Go and talk with them.'

Few wanted to leave and of these most wished to remain as close as possible to Siqilliya. One day, they thought, we will go back. We were born there. We built those cities. Why should we not return? They chose to go to Ifriqiya, to the cities of Mahdia and Bone which, Allah be praised, had been taken back by our people. If these towns could be won back, why not Palermo and Atrabanishi?

When Frederick died in 1250, panic spread in the city, but it was already late. The first massacre took place some months later. By that time Ibn Afdal was dead. And Lucera, too, was about to perish. Not long after Frederick's death, most of its people were massacred. A few thousand, mainly women, were forcibly converted. The mosque was burnt. Like the bright star that crosses the sky and is watched by all, but quickly disappears, the flourishing city vanished, the few traces buried beneath the ground. Frederick's castle was left untouched.

On the day that Frederick died, Ibn Afdal's son Uthman and his cousins Umar and Muhammad decided it was foolish to wait any longer. They had long prepared for this day and they took advantage of the confusion. Their horses were ready for the journey. Umar and Muhammad left Lucera in the afternoon. They were headed for the coast from where they boarded a merchant ship to Ifriqiya.

Uthman did not go with them. As a child his imagination had been fired by the stories his father had told him about the Trusted One and how they had organised different forms of resistance on the island, but the story he had liked the best was far from this world. He loved hearing of how the Franks had been defeated by Salah al-din and driven out of al-Quds and how the Great Mosque had been cleaned and made ready to thank Allah for the victory they had won. For many months Uthman had agonised over his destination. The more he thought, the more he realised he did not wish to die before his eyes had seen the dome on the mosque of al-Aqsa and kissed the earth where his people had triumphed over the barbarians. He took his family to Palestine.

Ragusa-Palermo-Byron Bay-San Felice dei Circe-Lahore
August 2001–August 2004